SAVANT

Bill McCambley

DEDICATION

In memory of my beloved Pat and the children we love:
Kate, Mary, Kevin, Gregg, Shane, Catherine, Carter, Gianna

"The moment you doubt whether you can fly, you cease forever to be able to do it."

- J.M. Barrie, "Peter Pan"

PART ONE

"You're mad, bonkers, completely off your head.
But I'll tell you a secret. All the best people are."
- Lewis Carroll – "Alice in Wonderland"

CHAPTER 1

When Chris Newman first drew breath and screamed, filling his infant lungs with air, Fixer awoke with a start four miles away. It was just after midnight. Fixer rose from his cot, pulled on his boots and jacket, and hurried to wake Miss Portice. Five minutes later they boarded a city bus for the twenty minute ride to the inner city hospital.

Chris' mother lay on the hospital bed and held her newborn son in her arms as the doctor, nurse, and anesthesiologist looked on. The nurse had cleaned the infant, swaddled him snugly in a white baby blanket, and presented him to his mother who now gazed upon her son and smiled weakly. "Hello, Christopher," she said. He no longer cried, but his tiny milky gray eyes looked upon his mother for the first time.

And the last.

Mary Newman is the name she had given upon admission, and therefore would be the mother's name on the birth certificate, but it was merely an alias. There was no father's name.

Her time grew short, yet she was happy. Her son would grow up where he belonged, on Earth. There was hope now.

And he would be safe. Fixer would see to that.

She communicated telepathically with her son, who understood all she said to him. He had understood her for some time now, even before his birth. He knew that she must leave him, and he was sad. He did not understand. There was much he did not understand, but that situation would change quickly. The lessons he most needed, the important lessons, could only be learned on Earth, Mary was saying to him now. Fixer was a very good man. *Listen to him, Little One. Listen to him.*

She kissed him, smiled her last as a tear fell from her eye, and the connection ended when her heart finally failed to pump blood to her brain. The nurse removed Chris to the nursery, then returned to the delivery room to assist the doctors who tried in vain to resuscitate their patient. Twenty-five minutes later, when the nurse returned to look in on the infant, she found an empty bassinette.

Chris Newman would have become a ward of the Commonwealth of Pennsylvania had he not been abducted unseen from the nursery by "Nurse" Fixer and "Doctor" Portice who, having discarded their hospital clothes in flight, now sat on a city bus for the return trip to their apartment, as police cars with red, white, amber, and blue lights spinning raced past in the opposite direction, to the hospital.

Fixer and Miss Portice looked out the bus window at the police cars speeding past on the avenue. They saw clearly, as only they could, a young detective driving one of the police cruisers glance fleeting_y at the bus as he zoomed past.

Miss Portice raised an eyebrow, speaking volumes to Fixer.

"'Burr in the saddle,' is the expression, I believe," Fixer said, dismissively.

That same astute detective, Joe Carter, focused on getting to the hospital quickly, subconsciously noted, as only he could, the transit bus headed in the other direction.

Miss Portice, cuddling the infant, folded the blanket back, as she smiled at their young charge. "Don't you worry, Dear," she whispered to the baby. "He's only of Earth."

****

Joe Carter was a police officer for just three years before he was promoted to detective, the youngest detective ever on the force. His superiors quickly saw that little escaped his notice, even the most obscure details. Combined with youthful enthusiasm for law enforcement, an innate high octane motor, taciturn disposition, and anticipation bordering on the mystical, Carter seemed custom-crafted for detective work. It was this last quality, an ability to see details and anticipate events beforehand, which led to the "Fey-Man" moniker conferred by his 6'10" 295-pound giant of a partner, Mike Mountain, who normally at this moment, after their shift, would be in the process of chowing down three cheeseburgers at the Red Robin Diner.

Carter typically would be driving home after dropping Mountain off at the diner. Not tonight, though. A newborn baby boy was abducted from Frankford Hospital, and Carter, whether on the clock or not, meant to find him. Minutes mattered in child abductions, Carter knew.

The hospital personnel had not been much help other than to confirm that a forty-something Caucasian male nurse and forty-something Asian female doctor were seen in the maternity ward not long before the infant was first reported missing. The security guards reviewed the tapes but nothing appeared amiss. The perpetrators somehow managed to avoid detection by the cameras, and by hospital employees and patients, upon entering and exiting the hospital. It was inexplicable. Carter snooped around the trashcans behind the hospital and found the discarded scrubs and name tags but nothing more. No cars were seen hurrying off. No people were seen running or carrying a bundle. There were no other telltale signs at all.

The mother's name was Mary Newman. "She called him Christopher," the attending nurse had said. A database search came up empty.

It was a complete mystery and Carter's analytic brain was firing on all cylinders as he stood on the sidewalk outside the hospital with Mike Mountain.

"Whatcha thinkin', Joe? Inside job? Has all the signs."

Carter, looking up and down the avenue, appeared to be deep in thought and didn't respond right away other than to absentmindedly parrot, "All the signs…"

Mountain had grown accustomed to the ways of his tight-lipped partner, enough to know the end of their shift thirty minutes ago meant absolutely nothing to him right now. Carter was hooked, again. It could make for a long night.

"The bus," Carter said suddenly.

"The bus?"

"There was a SEPTA bus going north as we arrived."

"You think they took the bus?"

"It's worth a call. Come on," Carter replied, walking briskly to their patrol car.

They were able to connect with the bus driver, via the precinct, and the driver confirmed that a couple with an infant did get on the bus near the hospital, had gotten off five minutes earlier at Rising Sun and Hellerman, and walked east on Hellerman Street. They had been seated in the rear of the bus and did not interact with the driver or the other two passengers.

Carter and Mountain called for support and raced up Rising Sun Avenue to Hellerman, arriving ten minutes later. Four other police officers were already there, canvassing along Hellerman Street with flashlights and two K-9s who seemed most intent upon pursuing further along Hellerman, proceeding slowly away from Rising Sun.

After another ten minutes, at a dead-end on Old Soldiers Road, several blocks from where they had started, the dogs lost whatever scent they had been pursuing. Carter and Mountain retreated to Rising Sun.

"Mind driving me to the diner?" Mountain said.

"I can't believe you're hungry at this hour."

"Joe…,"

"No, wait. Yes, I can," Carter smiled up at his partner. "You take the car. I can walk from here."

"You sure, Joe?"

"Yeah, you go ahead. I'll be home soon. I want to look around some."

"Got that crystal ball thing goin' again, Fey-Man?"

"I don't know. Maybe. Hope so, anyway. He's just a baby, Mike. How does anyone…"

"Lotta sick dudes, Joe. You know that."

A few minutes later Mountain sat in the patrol car and Carter tapped the top of the car. "Have a burger for me."

"You serious?"

"Something healthy. A veggie burger, seven grain bread, no cheese…"

"Yeah, right. Better odds of finding that kid…"

"Hope so. 'Night Mike."

"Go get 'em, Joe," Mountain signed off as he pulled away.

Looking in his rear view mirror at his partner, now inspecting the ground with his flashlight, Mountain knew Carter would be there for hours. He'd seen this eccentricity many times from his young partner. And he'd also seen the remarkable results. Carter was already considered a superstar detective among his colleagues, but none of that ever seemed to matter to him. Regardless of the accolades, the accomplishments, he was always on to the next challenge. And although Joe Carter attracted appreciative glances from women everywhere, he had never married. Mountain wasn't at all surprised. Carter was married to his work. Whatever demons haunted Joe Carter, Mountain hoped the insomnia they conferred wasn't contagious. *Dog with a bone,* he thought before allowing the words to escape his lips, "Spooky dude."

Mountain and the other officers and dogs were all gone now. Carter was alone in the dark on the avenue, sweeping the pavement with the beam of his flashlight looking for...what, he didn't know. Something though, he was certain. They had missed... something. Right here, or close by. He felt it. That feeling he could never describe, but could not fight. Not anymore. He used to try but had long ago learned to surrender when it appeared, whatever it was. In this otherworldly mode, Carter permitted himself to be led, to be directed. It was a feeling so strong, he felt its origins were psychic. For that reason, he had elected never to speak of it, never to credit it, for fear of recrimination, medication, or incarceration at a funny farm. People saw him as a great detective, and no doubt he was. But Joe Carter knew he could not claim all the credit because he had an unfair advantage, a rare gift - or curse. That extrasensory aura had him fully in its grip at that moment. So, he went with it as he often did, whenever it struck and long after everyone else had given up, as now. Yet again, Carter was alone.

A youth coach years ago had said that, in an effort to spur at-home practice and improvement, champions are made when no one is watching. How prescient those words had become, time and time again, for Detective Joe Carter. He hoped it would be the case again now. He could not get that baby out of his mind. Christopher Newman.

Standing on one corner of the intersection, Carter briefly considered crossing the avenue and heading west over Hellerman, even though the bus driver said they had headed east and the police K9s seemed to have picked up a trail leading east on Hellerman. He looked north and south up and down Rising Sun Avenue. Which way to go? It was very dark. The street lights on the avenue were too far apart to illuminate the area well. Carter walked to the middle of the intersection and looked briefly up at the stars, their light mostly obscured by the yellow sulfur bulbs of the street lamps.

"Which way did you go?"

He lowered his gaze to the line of windows above the retail storefronts on the east side of the avenue.

"There!" he said, as he began to walk quickly east on Hellerman, one-half block to the narrow alleyway behind the stores. Standing at the head of the alleyway, looking down the rear of two rows of brick buildings, he saw many vehicles parked in violation of the zoning code. This was typical behavior in a high population, inner-city neighborhood. He ignored the cars and trucks and focused on the buildings. "Which one?" he asked. "Which one is yours?"

It took him ten minutes to walk down and back along the alleyway, carefully inspecting the garage doors and rear entranceways for any sign of recent activity. He had searched twenty-eight properties in this way. Only two remained before he would be forced to admit defeat and hope that the Amber alert would turn up something.

Door number twenty-nine, however, was unlocked. This was the good news. He pushed the door inward. It squeaked loudly, ominously. The rear door was covered in dust and cobwebs, inside and out. It did not appear to have been moved in years.

Carter shouted inside, "Hello? Police. Anyone here?" He waited five seconds, and repeated his call. Receiving no reply, he entered the pitch black first floor of the store. The bad news was it was deserted, and had been for many years, he now recalled. There was a hardware store there for twenty or more years when he was growing up as a boy, but the owner moved to the suburbs, as many of the older merchants had when this section of the city began its decline. Drugs.

The back room in which he now stood was a mess. There were cardboard boxes stacked everywhere and cabinets covered in sheets along three walls. As a result, there was not much room to walk – just a narrow path through stacks of boxes leading toward the front of the store. The windows were covered in some kind of opaque plastic sheeting. Just then, something scurried across the floor in front of him.

The cardboard box corridor led him deeper

into the building. It was dark. Everything was covered with a thick coating of dust. Pieces of furniture had been knocked over, and trash was scattered everywhere. It was about as abandoned as it was possible to be. It appeared that no one had been there for a long, long time. The last of the boxes appeared just short of the front room.

"Hello," he called again. Nothing. He flicked a light switch, to no avail. The utilities were likely shut off years ago. He used his flashlight to guide his way up the stairway to the upper floor. The rooms there were also largely empty, the walls graffitied, as were the walls downstairs, and a few pieces of dust-covered furniture lay strewn about. No one other than squatters had been inside this building in a long time.

He could see nothing with his eyes but he knew, or his psychic sense seemed to indicate, they had been here. Very recently. So he searched in vain for another thirty minutes, in an effort that an outside observer might term worrisome, if not downright crazy. There was nothing there. No one had entered that building in years. It was obviously vacant.

Unwilling to concede defeat, Carter vowed to return. He walked the mile to his home and showered, once he arrived, deep in thought the whole time. What had he missed? He didn't know, but he was determined to find out. *They were in there. They were in that building. That baby was in that building.*

The demons were in control and it would be a long night. Mike Mountain was right about that.

Instead of going to bed, a possessed Joe Carter got into his car, drove back to the avenue, parked across the street from the storefront, under the penumbra of a yellow sulfur street lamp, and watched the upstairs window of the vacant building.

Because Detective Joe Carter knew that champions were made when no one was watching.

"I'll find you," Carter said out the window, as he gazed up at the apartment windows above the first floor retail stores across the avenue.

But even the gifted Joe Carter could not have known that, at that precise moment, someone was watching him.

"No, you won't," Fixer said.

"You could help him, you know," Miss Portice suggested. "He is rather extraordinary."

"He is neither our concern nor our mission," Fixer replied, resolute.

CHAPTER 2
(Three years later)

The main house of the St. Michael's Home for Children, an orphanage and safe house for children ages twelve and younger, was a palatial brownstone edifice which served as the administrative building. It was built as a family residence in the early nineteenth century by one of the several wealthy manufacturers who brought the industrial revolution to Philadelphia. His widow later donated the property to an order of Catholic nuns who had emigrated to the United States from Germany to care for orphaned and abused children. It was then purchased by a charitable foundation in the early 1980s when the religious order of sisters could no longer afford the upkeep. The Home was situated on twelve pristine, lightly-wooded acres of riverfront, an enisled oasis with an inner city neighborhood surrounding it on three sides. The rear of the property sloped down to the bank of the mighty Delaware River.

The estate was aglow in the early evening hour. A hundred or so cars were parked in a nearby vacant lot where an entire city block of blighted abandoned row houses had been razed a few years earlier. Scores of people, mostly married couples, approached through the black wrought iron gate at the foot of the circular red brick entrance drive, bordered by stunning verbena. The drive encircled a large, white marble fountain of St. Michael the Archangel, brandishing a sword on horseback, bathed in white light. A blue waterfall cascaded down the mountaintop-shaped plinth supporting the equestrian protector and his perpetually rearing steed.

The Home, always architecturally impressive, was magical tonight. Handsome men in crisp, glistening black tuxedos arrived with glamorous ladies bedecked in royal reds, turquoise, silver, gold, and bright whites. Most of them were benefactors, potential benefactors, board members, and their spouses, here for the important addresses by the governor, mayor, and headmistress. The annual ball and formal dinner was the primary fundraiser, widely covered by the local and regional press corps. Many guests had been residents at one time and returned with their loved ones every year, as reliably as Christmas morning, to wistfully recapture a little piece of their Halcyon childhoods. As Magic Kingdoms go, the St. Michael's Home for Children, now as never before surrounded beyond its locked gates by troubled lives and crime, was the city's sole representative.

Dinner was scheduled on the large, enclosed veranda overlooking the Delaware. A wind ensemble consisting of members of the Philadelphia Orchestra performed in the front room as guests arrived for the evening's festivities. Headmistress Maxine Brennan, and her retinue of volunteers and employees of the foundation which owned the Home, greeted each guest as they arrived, ushering them to the coat check booth and bar, then through the main ballroom and on to the veranda in the rear.

The headmistress and her staff were professionals, and they were clearly in their element. They loved the children they served and these patrons whose large, private pledges this evening would once again provide the primary financial support for the Home. Still, Maxine was nervous, though it was not obvious, Maxine was nervous. There were many details involved in having so many guests enjoy their evening and, although she could not have hoped for more highly-qualified help, the buck stopped with her. She was ultimately responsible. This had never bothered her before, but tonight she began to feel the weight of her fifty-nine years.

"Ah, Henry. It is so good to see you," Maxine beamed as she hugged a handsome young man upon his arrival. "And Mrs. Knorr, thank you so much for coming again."

"Headmistress Brennan, you know my husband and I wouldn't miss this evening for the world. It means so much to Henry. And the mansion looks as magnificent as ever," Mrs. Knorr said, glancing around.

"Seems smaller than I remember," Henry said, smiling.

Mrs. Knorr smiled, and rolled her eyes in

feign annoyance. "Henry, you're incorrigible. You say the same thing every year."

"That's good news!" Maxine said. "It means you are here every year."

Taking both her hands in his, Henry turned serious. "Thank you, Headmistress. Thank you for...well, for everything, really."

"Oh, tut-tut, now," Maxine said. "It is I who thank you. Wherever would we be without your generous support? Please, go enjoy yourselves. We have you seated with Ed, Randy, Pete, and their wives."

"Man, it'll be great to see the gang again. Come on, Dear..." Henry guided his wife away as she looked back, smiled at Maxine, and mouthed a silent, "Thank you."

"You look radiant tonight, Headmistress."

"Charlotte! Oh, my dear child. Is it really you?"

Charlotte Devine had grown, blossomed really, or metamorphosed might be more accurate, into a stunningly beautiful young woman. Orphaned as an infant, and a ten-year resident of St. Michael's as a young girl, Horatio Alger had nothing on her. If Horatio was the classic rags-to-riches example, well, at least he started with rags. Charlotte was one of those poor, delicate, perpetually picked-upon souls destined, it seemed, to forevermore attract bullies who repeatedly and forcefully took what little she ever had.

Until, one day, her abuse-O-meter timed out. From that day, she had vowed to take control of her life and circumstances. She refused to be bullied anymore. But, she never forgot what it felt like to be belittled, abused, and discarded.

She could not sing, and had no obvious talent or desire to perform, so she wrote songs, and millions were able to relate on a deeply personal level, to her soulful lyrics, even though few knew the author. Her ballads had become hits for many popular singers, including her husband, the country western superstar who held her hand now.

"Headmistress, permit me to introduce you to my husband, Clay Ballard."

"Welcome, Mr. Ballard. Welcome to St. Michael's. And thank you for bringing your beautiful music to the world. I'll have you know, it fills our halls here many a day."

"Why, thank you, Headmistress. That is very nice of you to say. But I owe it all to Charlotte and, from what she has told me, to you. So, this is where it all began," he said, removing his black cowboy hat as he stepped through the transom. He held Maxine's hands in his, bowed, and kissed them. Standing erect, he said, "The lives we touch."

"One of my favorites," Maxine said, smiling warmly.

"Perhaps," he began, looking now at Charlotte who held his arm and nodded for him to continue, "at some point this evening, you will permit me to sing it for your guests?"

The squeals of delight from several younger members of the staff answered before Maxine could. Turning, Maxine saw Alyson, Maria, and Demarra, huddled conspiratorially, now separate, heads bowed. "Sorry, Headmistress," they said. "It's just that he's Clay Ballard."

Maxine sighed. "Yes, I know who he is."

"Here at St. Michael's!" Alyson couldn't control herself, and looked up, beaming.

"So it would seem." Maxine nodded that they could make themselves useful elsewhere. She watched the girls depart before turning back to Charlotte. "Oh, to be seventeen again. You saw them, yes? Then you saw nothing less than… my fluttering heart." She turned to Clay, "I would be so honored." Squeals of delight emanated from inside the hall. "I suppose I get it right sometimes," Maxine smiled.

Charlotte laughed. "Come on, Clay," she said, leading him by the hand. "I'll show you where my river flows."

"Yes, please sing that also," Maxine called after them. "It is my absolute favorite."

"Mine, too." Frieda Kling nudged Maxine. "That boy is gorgeous. Charlotte is living the life, eh? Not that he's suffering any. Quite a catch, that Charlotte, as it turns out. Pity the poor fools who picked on her."

Maxine smiled. Her lifelong friend had an edge for sure, but she was a dependable steward of the mission. Few people Maxine knew had given more of themselves for the downtrodden, castoff, unwanted, or abused children of Philadelphia than Frieda Kling. Frieda had a heart of gold but for some convoluted reasoning, had always held people at arm's length. Other than Maxine, Frieda confided her true feelings to virtually no one. Sometimes, even after so many years, Maxine questioned how well she really knew her friend. Regardless, she knew better than anyone that there would be no St. Michael's Home for Children if not for the considerable gifts and efforts of Frieda Kling, warts and all.

"How you holding up, kiddo?"

"Pins and needles," Maxine replied.

"You hide it well. But you worry every year."

"It's an important evening."

"Everything will be fine. It always is."

"I worry about the governor and the mayor. Their support..."

"Discursive demogogues," Frieda said. "Don't worry about them. They'll get their camera time and will be out of here in an hour. Then you can relax, and have some fun."

"Fun? No. Not tonight. Tonight is showtime. But you? You go, work your magic."

"Right. No margin, no mission, huh? Oh, thank you, Ralph!" Frieda suddenly grabbed the arm, and hors d'oeuvre, from the hand of a passing elderly board member as she walked away with him. "Ta-ta, Maxine! Ralphie and I are on a mission."

Maxine smiled. "On a mission" was Frieda's code for pursuing the mission of St. Michael's, to serve the children and, by extension, to raise funds. Ralph Greenburg was the founder and controlling shareholder of a large food wholesaling corporation which served most of the restaurants in Philadelphia and the Delaware Valley and, at cost, St. Michael's. And while it was true that no margin would inevitably lead to there being no mission, the margins at St. Michael's were always razor-thin. Without Frieda, however, they'd be less than that. That woman certainly had a way with wealthy benefactors. She was also an absolute wizard of a placement consultant, finding wonderful homes for the children of St. Michael's. Thank God.

And the sharks! Some of them were here now. But they always were. Real estate developers circling, biding their time. Just waiting, waiting for the day when that razor-thin margin would evaporate and Maxine, or her eventual successor, would be forced to sell the extremely valuable land upon which St. Michael's sat. They would be only too happy to rid the city of this historic footprint and erect some modern steel and concrete monstrosity in its place: luxury condos, a hotel or, heaven forbid, a casino. But as long as her personal health was good, and the fiscal health of St. Michael's Home was manageable, that day was still a long way off, and the Home would survive to serve the children another year.

And, once again, as in so many years past, the evening was successful. Based upon pledges received, it would prove to be the most significant fundraiser ever. Frieda, the volunteers, and the last guests finally departed a little past midnight. Maxine bid them all farewell, thanking them repeatedly, profusely, and inviting them all to return as their busy schedules permitted. Frieda would return several times each week, because her work necessitated she be there. The staff and volunteers would be there daily, of course. The resident staff were already there, retired for the evening in their on-site apartments.

Maxine sighed as she watched the last of the guests walk down the brick drive, past the fountain of St. Michael, to their cars parked in the lot across the street. She closed the substantial oak front door, bolted it, turned and walked slowly through the large center hallway, past the two staircases which wound to meet at the second floor above, under the two large crystal chandeliers anchored in the ceiling three stories above, through the ballroom, and off to the left, into the kitchen.

She marveled at the Keurig machine which was brewing her tea in less than twenty seconds. *Will wonders never cease?* Once the machine stopped kvetching and quieted down, she assumed it was safe to approach, and tentatively retrieved the newly-filled, steaming olive green mug she had purchased from pottery artisans a few years earlier. Savoring the aroma and warming her hands on the mug, she left the kitchen, crossing the large marble floored center hallway, and continued slowly on into the study. Hours ago guests had danced in the formal great room while the wind ensemble had played, and Clay Ballard had sung. She sat in a burgundy leather easy chair in one corner, by the large floor-to-ceiling fireplace, and smiled to think of Clay and Charlotte and how in love they were. It seemed like just yesterday that a skinny little girl with a black eye, arms akimbo, stood crying right in front of where Maxine now sat. Maxine had taken that little girl in her arms, brushed her matted and muddy hair, and assured her that everything would be alright, that she would be alright.

"How…how do you know?" she sobbed in reply.

"Because I've seen it. Do you think you are the first little girl who has stood there, crying because she had been bullied?"

"I don't know."

"No, you're not. You're not even one of the first fifty."

"Really?"

"Oh, so now I'm a liar, am I?"

"N…no," Charlotte stammered, chastened.

"That's right. Headmistress Brennan does not lie, young lady."

"So, were…were they alright…too?"

"Of course."

"All fifty?"

"Well, almost all. Let's just put it this way. I like your chances."

Maxine smiled to recall that conversation now, one of so, so many similar assurances she had given over the years to troubled children. Charlotte, of course, did survive. As much as Maxine wanted to claim a bit of the credit, she wouldn't. Charlotte Devine became the successful, beautiful woman she had become through her own choices, her own efforts, and God's good graces. Maxine wondered how many more such wonderfully gifted children she would meet in this room. She finished her tea, put her cup and glasses on the small table beside her chair, pulled a blanket over her lap, and promptly fell asleep.

At 2:00 a.m. she awoke to the sound of the doorbell. Startled, she almost tripped over her blanket as she stood, reaching for her glasses. Who could be calling at this hour? She hurried as best she could to answer the door.

"Coming!" she called as she reached the door. Looking through the peephole, she saw no one. "Who is it?"

No answer. She unbolted the door, opened it, and was surprised to see no one there. She stepped outside and looked to the left of the entrance. No one. Turning to the right, her foot kicked something. She looked down and saw a white envelope. She stooped, retrieved it from the welcome mat, and stood back up. It was addressed to: Headmistress Maxine Brennan, St. Michael's Home for Children. There was no stamp and no return address. Looking around again, she called, "Hello! Is anyone there?" No answer.

"Strange," she said to herself. She turned, went back inside, and closed the door. Ernie, a handyman and resident beadle, was coming down the steps, yawning, trying to put his glasses on. "Who was it?" he asked.

"I don't know. No one was there. Go back to bed, Ernie. Thank you for coming down."

"No problem. Goodnight, Headmistress," he said, returning up the stairs. "It was a good night, wasn't it?"

"Yes. Yes it was," she said absentmindedly, as she turned the envelope over in her hands and returned to the study. She would sit and read the contents before going to bed. She began to open the envelope as she walked into the study. Looking up, she saw a very young boy sitting in her chair. Her experienced eye told her he was about three years old. He was well-dressed in a blue blazer, white shirt, blue tie, khaki pants, and white and brown saddle shoes which did not come close to reaching the floor. He sat, looking up at her with the most arresting milky gray eyes, hands folded in his lap. A suitcase sat on the floor with a small, black winter coat draped over it.

"Hello, Headmistress Brennan," he said calmly, with perfect enunciation.

Maxine, stunned, dropped the letter and reflexively raised her hands to her chest. "Hello," she said, recovering. "And who...who have I the pleasure of addressing long past his bedtime?"

"My name is Christopher Newman."

CHAPTER 3

Officer Mike Mountain drove the patrol car through the open main gate of the St. Michael's Home for Children. "Down here much, Joe?"

Detective Joe Carter was staring at the fountain of St. Michael as they approached. "Not really." Then, "Nice curb appeal."

Mountain noticed his partner's gaze. "That's what you need in front of your rowhouse, Joe. A huge fountain of an armed angel on horseback. We'll put it in the trunk when we leave; take it with us."

Carter leaned forward looking through the top of the windshield. "Yeah, right. That thing is massive. It's bigger than my whole front and back yards put together."

Mountain pulled the car to a stop where the driveway curved in front of the main door. "Come on. Let's get this over with." They both exited the car. "Think it's really him?"

Carter rang the doorbell. "Three years old. Orphaned. Milky gray eyes. Same city. Odds are good. Plus, the review board seems to think so."

After a few seconds, Ernie answered the door. "May I help you?"

"Yes, I'm Detective Mike Mountain of the

Philadelphia Police Department. This is Detective Joe Carter." Wearing plain clothes, they each presented their identification.

"Ah, Gentlemen! Do come in. Come in. You are here to see Headmistress Brennan, then?"

"Yes."

"She's been expecting you," he said, closing the door after them as they entered. Then, sweeping his arm toward the ballroom to the right, "Please, follow me. She's in the office, through the ballroom here."

On the far end of the ballroom, Ernie knocked lightly on one of the two French doors before opening one. Looking in, he announced, "The detectives are here, Headmistress."

"Thank you, Ernie. Please show them in."

Carter and Mountain then entered and were greeted by several people sitting around a large conference table. They all stood when the detectives entered. Frieda Kling was the first to greet them, of course.

"Gentlemen, welcome. Welcome. Do come in, won't you? Please allow me...My name is Frieda Kling. I am a volunteer here at St. Michael's. I assist with child placement."

"Good afternoon, ma'am."

"This is Headmistress Maxine Brennan."

"Ma'am."

"Thank you for coming, gentlemen," Maxine said, standing. I hope it is not too much of an imposition."

"Not at all, ma'am," Mountain said. "We've actually been looking forward to it since Captain Carroll called us this morning. I am Detective Mike Mountain. This is Detective Joe Carter."

"Welcome, gentlemen. It is our honor." They shook hands. "Your reputation precedes you."

"Yes, thank you, Ma'am," Mountain said, appreciating her politeness. Working with Joe Carter did have some benefits. Mountain had no reputation.

"And this is Mr. Emory Aldrich, counsel for St. Michael's."

"Gentlemen, a real honor," Mr. Aldrich said, shaking their hands.

"Thank you, Frieda," Maxine said. "Detectives, please sit anywhere. Make yourselves comfortable. Can we get you something to eat or drink?"

"No, ma'am, we're good, thank you," Mountain said, as he and Carter sat side by side at the conference table. Maxine Brennan sat at the head of the table. Mr. Aldrich and Frieda Kling sat on the other side, facing the two detectives.

"Detectives," Maxine began, "as I am sure your captain has told you, a few weeks ago, in the middle of the evening, and quite unannounced, we received a visitor here at St. Michael's, Christopher Newman. It was 2:00 a.m. I had fallen asleep in my chair. The front doorbell rang. I answered the door, but no one was there. Just this envelope," she said, indicating the envelope lying on the table in front of her. "I retrieved the envelope from the welcome mat, saw it was addressed to me, looked around outside, and saw no one. So I came back inside and locked the door. When I walked back to my study, young Christopher Newman was waiting for me. He was well-dressed, wide awake, and had a small packed travel bag. No adult accompanied him, and he did not appear to be in any distress at all."

"Extraordinary!" Mr. Aldrich exclaimed.

"Truly," Frieda Kling agreed.

"And you saw no car or lights, heard no footsteps?" Mountain said.

"No, nothing at all," Maxine said. "When outside, I called into the darkness but received no reply. I waited a moment, looked for movement, saw none and returned inside. I certainly hadn't anticipated that anyone could have walked right by me without me seeing them."

"Could he have entered some other way?

Perhaps through a window, a back door?"

"No. This is a safe facility. Unfortunately, it needs to be, given the neighborhood today. You won't believe what we spend on security. Given our palladium, I find the electronic security system an unnecessary extravagance..."

"Now, Maxine," it was Frieda Kling.

"Palladium?" Mountain said.

"Safeguard," Frieda said. "Maxine refers to the fountain of St. Michael the archangel out front."

"Exactly," Maxine said. "What more do we need? Who will protect us if St. Michael doesn't? Besides, I cannot tell you how many times I have locked myself out and someone has had to let me back in. Ridiculous. We are in lock down all the time."

"So, no broken windows, busted door jambs..."

"No. We looked. Believe me."

"Did you ask Newman?" It was the first time Carter had spoken.

"We did, yes. We asked him where his parents were, how he arrived, how he entered, and where his home was."

"And?" Carter said.

"And, at this point, I would like to turn this meeting over to our legal advisor, Mr. Aldrich. He will be better able to inform you from here, I believe." She slid the envelope across the table to Mr. Aldrich, who picked it up.

"The reason we are all here today," he began, "is because of this letter. It is extraordinary. Everything it claims would happen, so far, has come about."

"Like a crystal ball?" Mountain said. He and Carter shot glances at each other.

"Yes, just like a crystal ball. Incredible, really. May I?" he asked, indicating that he would read the letter out loud.

"We're all ears," Mountain said.

"Very well, then. It is undated and unsigned but, you will see, quite otherwise authentic, we believe. It has been thoroughly examined and vetted by police forensics. Remarkably, there are no fingerprints and there is no discernable residue, pieces of hair, dust, anything which would give away its source. It somehow arrived altogether pristine. It says,

Dear Headmistress Maxine Brennan,

My nephew, Christopher Newman, who now sits before you, in your chair, was born three years ago in Frankford Hospital. His mother, sadly, passed away giving birth. She was a truly remarkable woman. Christopher's father was a great man. A great man. But, he is no longer with us. Christopher is an orphan but, you will see, he is remarkable. My colleague, Miss Portice, and I travelled a great distance, as was Mrs. Newman's wish, to ensure Christopher would be raised in Philadelphia. Our understanding in this regard is incomplete, but Mary Newman's every wish was our joyful command, so great was she. We could no more deny her anything than refute our own existence. We are deeply saddened at her passing, but have made our peace with it and now our sole purpose is to ensure that her wishes for her son are fulfilled.

She wanted Christopher to be raised in Philadelphia by Miss Portice and me until his third birthday, to ensure the complete development of his intellect, sagacity. And so, he has lived with us, in Philadelphia, these past three years. You will ask him where. He will not know. You will ask him how he arrived in your study. He will not know.

Hypnotism is one of my gifts. I employed it with my nephew for his own safety. So, he will not recall his whereabouts. Nor will he recall us. But, he is a fine linguist, fluent in many languages, and has attained foundational capabilities necessary for excellence in all academic endeavors, including music. You will test him and see for yourselves. We have raised him well to this point, but he will not remember us. It is how it must be.

His mother has directed that, on his third birthday, he then live, and be raised by a good woman, in Philadelphia. We have delivered my nephew to you and trust you to fulfill Mary Newman's wish as we have stated it here.

We enlist your aid because Miss Portice and I are oftentimes much needed elsewhere and are quite unable, actually, to further forestall our own critical life missions. However, we are quite financially well able to provide for my nephew's welfare and, of course, are more than willing to do so. Enclosed herein you will find a cashier's check for $500,000 as downpayment toward Christopher's care.

"Holy crap!" Mike Mountain said. "A half-million bucks?" Then, looking around at the startled faces, "Um, sorry. Man, that's a lot of money." Joe Carter sat slumped, head down and arms crossed.

"There's more," Mr. Aldrich said.

Hereafter, you will receive an additional fifteen annual installments of $100,000 each, on the anniversary of this letter, until Christopher turns eighteen. We trust that the $2 million total funds delivered to you in this way will be more than sufficient to provide for Christopher's care and for his caregiver's compensation. Please accept any excess as our support of the overall mission of St. Michael's Home for Children.

"Man, two million bucks! You hearing this,

Joe?" Mountain said to his partner.

"Yeah, great," Carter mumbled, still looking down. He wasn't happy.

The annual installments will continue until Christopher's eighteenth birthday, or until you or his caregiver are no longer willing or able to provide for his welfare. We will know if this happens, and will take him immediately back into our care at that time, and the financial installments will then cease. How we will know is unimportant. But, just as he disappeared without a trace upon being born, he will once again be removed if you elect, or fail, to carry out his mother's wishes as we have stated them here.

"Creep," Joe Carter said, sitting up. "We'll catch him and his psychotic sidekick."

"A-hem," Mr. Aldrich cleared his throat, looking at Maxine Brennan, who now evidenced a ghastly pallor.

"What?" Carter said. "You think we won't catch him?"

Mr. Aldrich looked Joe Carter in the eyes, then continued reading.

And please assure Detectives Joe Carter and Mike Mountain that we are not evil or psychotic.

Mr. Aldrich looked up from the letter. Frieda Kling said, "Oh my!" Joe Carter slumped back in his chair, stunned. Mike Mountain said, "Impressive."

Detective Carter's sustained and continued diligence these three years has been laudable. We hope, with the safe reappearance of Christopher, that he will elect to rededicate himself anew to his community and to getting some long-overdue sleep...

"Jerk!" Joe Carter exploded, shoving his chair back forcefully, and rising from where he sat. "He's messing with the wrong guy."

Everyone looked stunned as they watched Carter pace. Everyone except Mike Mountain.

"Like I said," Mountain said softly. "Impressive."

"Et tu, Mike?" Carter growled through clenched teeth.

"Joe, c'mon. Calm down," Mountain said. Then, motioning toward Carter's chair, "Sit. Let's get through this."

"You buying this, Mike? Really?"

Mike Mountain elected to look straight ahead across the table, rather than make eye contact with his partner. He knew better than to challenge Carter at times like this which, lately, had been increasing in frequency. Staying up all hours, patrolling the avenue near Hellerman Street after his shifts, going into that empty building time and time again. It was crazy, just crazy. If anyone could use more sleep, it was Joe Carter. This fact alone made the letter Mr.

Aldrich was reading all the more remarkable.

Finally, Carter, as had happened so many times over the years, seemed to sense what his friend was thinking. He sat down. "Sorry," he said to everyone. "Trust me, we'll catch this creep."

Mr. Aldrich, having been interrupted, resumed.

We hope, with the safe reappearance of Christopher, that Detective Carter, in particular, will elect to rededicate himself anew to his community and get some long-overdue sleep. Please assure him, as we assure you and the leadership, judiciary, and bureaucrats of Philadelphia, that we will never be found. Devoting resources in any such attempt, as in the past, would be quite impolitic.

Carter closed his eyes. The silence in the room was exquisite.

If he and Mike Mountain will continue to make Philadelphia a safer place for my nephew, we hope that, one day, we may return the substantial favor. Please thank them for us.

We do thank you all and apologize for our secrecy. Nonetheless, it cannot be helped.

Take care of Christopher. He is a good boy.

Respectfully,

A. Fixer

Miss Portice

"Look," Carter said, "we can trace the cashier's check. Plus Forensics can dust it for prints. We'll find someone who talked to these child abductors…"

"Detective Carter," Mr. Aldrich interrupted, laying the letter on the table, "this matter has been adjudicated in the family court system, as I suspect Captain Carroll may have told you."

"So, it's a done deal?" Mountain asked.

"Yes, as far as the city and the District Attorney are concerned."

"So…so, we move on to other things and just forget about these perps?" Carter said, disgusted.

"I will leave the details to your captain but, for the most part, I would say that's what has been agreed to."

"I asked Frieda to find a good home for him, and we believe she has done so," Maxine said.

"Yes, Aliondra Covington, a wonderful, young, single mother of a five-year-old son has agreed. She will be perfect. She will provide a wonderful home for Christopher, right here in Philadelphia, just a few miles from here," Frieda said.

"Is she divorced?" Mountain asked.

"Widowed, sadly," Frieda Kling said. "Her husband was killed while serving in Iraq."

"Hmm," Carter grunted. "Well, I guess you all have it figured out."

"Christopher will be in good hands," Maxine said. "Thanks to Mrs. Kling."

"You have a lot of experience?" Mountain asked Frieda Kling.

"I do," Frieda said.

"Frieda has been a godsend to us, Detective Mountain. She has successfully placed many of our children in fine homes. Would you and Detective Carter like to meet Christopher and his new family?"

Mountain looked at Carter. "Joe?"

"I don't think so," Carter replied, standing. "I can see that our work here is finished. It's probably best that we get out of your way and let you get back to work. Thank you," he turned abruptly to leave. "C'mon, Mike. Let's go."

"Thank you, Mrs. Brennan, Mrs. Kling, Mr. Aldrich. Thanks for bringing us up to date. I guess we'll just let ourselves out. Take care."

He then followed after Carter, who now waited in the patrol car. Mountain hopped in the driver's seat. "You really don't want to see this kid after looking for him for three years?"

"The kid's fine. What do I care? He doesn't need our help, apparently. They have it all figured out. Kid gets abducted and the creeps get off Scott-free because they write some lying letter and pay some money."

"It was a pretty impressive letter, Joe. And a lot of money."

"They abducted a baby, Mike! And we're supposed to look the other way, for crying out loud!"

Mountain could see his partner had his mind made up. He sat for a minute, then turned the ignition key and began to slowly drive the car down the driveway.

"Sure you couldn't use that fountain, Joe?" Mountain knew his partner.

Carter smiled. "Nah. I already have one giant protector named Mike. We could get you fitted for some wings."

Mountain laughed. "Forget it. I like my wings with barbecue sauce. Plus the landlord won't allow a horse in the apartment."

"Time to move."

They both laughed and moved on. Mike Mountain put the matter of Christopher Newman behind him.

And Joe Carter? The meeting merely confirmed for him what he had already inferred, and had felt for several weeks now. They, whoever they were, had departed. They no longer inhabited the storefront. He still went back there several nights a week but, recently, he had the distinct impression that they were no longer there. The vacant store was truly vacant now. For this reason, he no longer spoke to them while sitting in his patrol car or as he walked through the empty building. It was just…just empty now. No one was there. Talking to someone who wasn't there would be crazy. And Joe Carter was a long way from crazy. Other people might think differently, but he knew what he knew. They were there. Now they weren't.

He knew, too, that they had beaten him. He had lost. They would not be brought to justice. So be it. But if they thought Christopher Newman was going to receive any special help from him, they had miscalculated badly. Joe Carter knew what he knew, and he knew this. The Newman kid had a rich uncle to rely on. Carter was done with him. There were plenty of other troubled people who needed his help.

And, he knew one more thing. "Take me home, Mike," he said.

"Home? Really?"

"Yeah, I need to catch up on some sleep."

PART TWO

"All the little boys and girls
With rosey cheeks and flaxen curls
And sparkling eyes and teeth like pearls
Tripping and skipping, ran merrily after
The wonderful music with shouting and laughter."
- Robert Browning, "The Pied Piper of Hamelin"

CHAPTER 4
(Nine Years later)

The clock radio on the nightstand went off at 5:30 Saturday morning. Chris Newman rolled over, heard the announcer say, "Phils won 2-0," and shut the radio off. "Yes!"

He put on jeans and a navy blue pullover, and wedged his feet into a pair of untied sneakers peeking out from under his bed. In the bathroom, he quickly brushed his teeth and splashed cold water on his face. As he toweled off, his slightly iridescent milky gray eyes stared at him in the mirror. "No, not normal," he said to his reflection, stuffing the towel onto the rack. His overnight dream of being a normal-looking twelve-year-old was still fresh in his mind.

He held up his right hand and spread his five fingers. Well, a thumb, three fingers, and another thumb where the pinky finger should have been. "Definitely not normal."

He pulled a pair of black leather gloves from his back pocket and slipped them on. Designed to conceal his extra thumbs, they made it appear as though each hand had one thumb and four normal fingers.

He walked downstairs, careful not to wake his mom and brother, ate breakfast, put on his red

Phillies cap, which his mother had left for him on the kitchen table the night before, filled the cat food bowl, and went outside on the back stoop, closing the door behind him.

"Hey, Mr. Mink." The black and brown feral cat immediately walked between Chris's feet, rubbing his arched back on one of Chris' legs. Mink had been born under the stoop and abandoned by his mother. Chris rescued and cared for him, a kindred orphan. He set the bowl on the stoop and scratched Mink behind one ear as he began to eat.

"Hey, no more presents, okay?" Chris picked up yet another headless mouse body by the tail. Mink considered this momentarily before returning to the bowl.

"Your little gifts scare the crap outta mom." Chris loped down the steps, placed the mouse body in the small metal garbage can, hopped on his bike, and rode down the alleyway.

It was one mile to the ball field. The lower-middle-class city neighborhood was almost entirely blanketed by concrete and asphalt. But the ball field, home to his older brother's sandlot team, was an oasis of sorts. Despite being crammed into a flood zone bordered on four sides by a factory, railroad tracks, an apartment complex, and subsidized housing, it still enjoyed the characteristic aura of inner-city baseball fields around the country: green diamonds in the rough.

Chris had been making this early-morning trek for the past three baseball seasons. Pre-game warm-ups would begin at eight o'clock sharp. As official scorekeeper and groundskeeper, he needed to arrive much earlier to line the field, set out the bases, open the snack stand, ensure the microphone worked, inspect and organize the umpire equipment and baseballs, raise the flags, and program the electronic scoreboard. Generally, he would need to transform an inhospitable flood zone vacant lot into the pride of the Lawndale A's and a home-field advantage. Hopefully, he thought, Billy-the-Trash-Picker had removed the debris.

Even though Chris loved baseball more than anything except astrophysics, and often daydreamed about playing in the big leagues, he rarely played. He was too slow, too clumsy. Four thumbs and four large toes will do that to you.

And only one specialty sporting-goods company made a batting helmet large enough for his head. That one helmet had set him back a cool one-hundred and twenty dollars. But he didn't really care about the money. He treasured his own red helmet with "Newman 1" stenciled on the back in white block letters.

He was rarely alone on these early-morning trips as he often encountered people he knew, even at this hour. Today was no exception. Halfway to the field he saw his bantam buddy, J.J., up ahead, outside of Stan's Corner Deli, preparing his newspapers for delivery. At eleven-years-old, "Flippin' J.J." was one of the more difficult placements at St. Michael's Home, Chris's home nine years earlier. J.J., though pint-sized, was quick with his fists. He had to be, to survive the 'hood. He was in that tenuous space between the Home and the inner city world largely outside its control; between "flippin" and the more salty language typically associated with a police record, gangs, drugs, and dead ends. Nobody wanted to adopt him, largely because he tended to punch out anyone who looked at him sideways. Some people have short fuses, but J.J. had no fuse. He bypassed the fuse altogether and defaulted immediately to spontaneous combustion. On the "JJ" scale from "Jesus and Joseph" at one extreme and juvenile jail at the other, Chris knew J.J. tended to skew closer to the slammer than to salvation.

Headmistress Brennan, who tended to see the good in everybody, surely would have disagreed with this assessment, Chris thought. He figured she was the reason J.J. was able to last at the orphanage this long, far past the normal adoption age. The staff at the Home loved him, and J.J. loved them. Orphanage jokes around J.J. tended to be suicidal.

J.J. was picking papers up off the ground as Chris approached. "Hey, if it ain't Doctor flippin' Einstein himself," J.J. said, looking up from where he knelt on the sidewalk. "I dropped the flippin' papers all over the place. Flippin' believe it?" Actually, Chris did, but he knew better than to say so. "Little help here, Doc?" Chris dismounted and stooped to help.

"Heard the Phils won," Chris said. "I fell asleep in the eighth."

"Yeah, flippin' Ruiz bunted to start the rally in the ninth. Flippin' unbelievable. Guy couldn't beat out a ballad with flippin' Beethoven, but he beat out a bunt." Chris recognized Headmistress Brennan's Beethoven reference. She was a huge baseball fan and similarly invoked Beethoven when talking about slow runners, sans adjective, of course.

"Well, it was a swinging bunt, and the ground was wet after the rain delay," Chris said.

If looks could kill. "No duh, genius. Man, for such a flippin' super sage you say some of the stupidest stuff on the flippin' planet."

"What?" Chris asked.

"What what? Like Ruiz could ever in a gazillion flippin' years beat out an intentional bunt, that's what. Help me get these flippin' papers in the bag."

It wasn't a question.

Chris got down on one knee now, and suddenly placed his palm down on the sidewalk.

J.J. looked at him. "Whatya doin'?"

"You feel that?" Chris asked.

"Feel what?"

"A tremor."

"What, like a flippin' earthquake or somethin'?"

Chris thought for a minute, then placed his other palm down on the sidewalk also. "There it is again. You feel it that time?"

"Don't feel nuthin'. Flippin' brainiacs..." J.J. said dismissively, shaking his head. Then, handing Chris three newspapers, he said, "Here, Mrs. K., Luigi, and old man Schwartz. They're on your way."

"Why me? I'm not scheduled for today," Chris asked.

"Builds flippin' character, that's why. Look, I know you're busy feeling up the ground and stuff. Just do it, okay? Might keep you from going all Norman Bates, ending up on the roof of a warehouse one day with a flippin' Uzi."

J.J. hopped on his bike and pedaled away. He shouted back, "Yo, Doc! Three o'clock."

Chris nodded and considered if J.J. had just set a new world record for the number of "flippin's" spoken before 6:00 a.m. Probably. If so, he knew that it wouldn't take him long to break his own record.

But J.J. had been right about a couple of things. Ruiz could never beat out an intentional bunt, and maybe sensing the tremor was "a flippin' genius thing" after all. Chris knew the tremor was something he perceived, a sense that something was different or off-kilter, more than it was an actual geological or physical tremor. Still, he'd never had such a sensation before. Whatever it was, however slight, he knew it was real. But what was it? Troubling, that's what it was.

"Change is coming," he said softly to himself, looking around.

Mr. Stanley Kaniewski, the deli owner, opened the front door of the store and turned on the lights inside.

"Dzień dobry, Chris!" he said, in Polish, as Chris entered the deli. *Good morning, Chris!*

"Dzień dobry, panie Kaniewski. Mam swoj papier," Chris responded, in Polish. *Good morning, Mr. Kaniewski. I have your paper.*

They each continued speaking in Polish. "Great, thanks. I will have your hoagies ready for you and your friends after the game. Big game today, isn't it?"

Chris handed the paper to Mr. Kaniewski. "Yes."

"Maybe today you will hit the big homerun."

"Maybe." Chris walked back out the front door of the store. "Do zobaczenia później, Pan K." *See you later, Mr. K.*

Mr. Kaniewski didn't understand, but Chris would not be hitting any homeruns today or any other day, more than likely, even though his eyesight was extremely keen. He could count the stitches on the baseball as it left the pitcher's hand, and could actually see the ball stop spinning when it hit the bat. But two large toes on each foot meant he couldn't beat out a ballad with Beethoven. Being a very slow runner, though, did not impede his ability to calculate and recall all the players' batting averages in his head as the game progressed, or his encyclopedic knowledge of baseball rules. Likely, he would never be a great athlete, but he was a world-class scorekeeper and fan. He figured that was the best he would ever do, baseball-wise.

"Buon Giorno, Chris." Pop sat at the table, playing chess with Luigi, as Chris entered Luigi's Bakery. Pop's hickory walking cane, sporting a bicycle horn and rear view mirror, leaned against the edge of the table. Pop's adult son, Ben, was baking pastries in the back room. The high school-aged part-time workers wouldn't arrive before 7:00 a.m.

"Buon Giorno, Pop. Hey, Mr. Luigi." Chris laid the paper on the counter. "Hey, Ben," he called into the back room. "Paper."

"Hi, Chris," Ben said, coming out front,

wiping his powdered hands on his apron. "Holy Cannoli?"

"I'm a little short." Same question, same response every time he entered Luigi's. At one-hundred dollars each, as posted on the menu board above the counter, Chris was pretty certain no one had ever purchased a Holy Cannoli. Regular cannolis were two dollars each, and they looked no different than the Holy Cannolis. Everyone attributed the pricing to Luigi's being eccentric. But Luigi truly believed his Holy Cannolis were each worth a hundred dollars.

"Hai visto la partita?" Pop asked Chris, in Italian. *See the game?*

"No. Mi sono addormentato in nel ottavo inning. Che vice cosa?" Chris always conversed with Pop in Pop's native Italian. *No, fell asleep in the eighth. What happened?*

Pop and Chris continued, as they often did, to speak to each other in Italian.

"Franco hit a two-run homerun in the bottom of the ninth inning after Ruiz got on," Pop responded without looking up. "Best young hitter in baseball if you ask me."

"Nice! Wish I'd seen it."

"Something to be said for stayin' awake," grumbled Luigi, in English, focused on the chess board. He always grumbled.

"Later. Mr. Luigi," Chris replied. exiting through the screen door which slammed behind him. Bam! Luigi jumped.

"What the…?" he screamed, looking up.

"Something to be said for stayin' awake!" Chris shouted back.

Now that the sun was beginning to rise, he put on his blue aviator sunglasses. He wore sunglasses to conceal his eyes. Blue aviators because they were cool. They also helped his eyesight, which weakened slightly in bright sunlight.

Turning left onto Rising Sun Avenue, he was startled by the figures sitting on the stoop of the F&H paint store: thirteen year-old Jack Helson and two of his conniving covey. Chris knew nothing good would come of this encounter.

"Move, Head, you're blocking the sunrise," Helson said, and his cronies snickered. "Yeah, keep moving, Head," one of them said. Chris ignored and detested them. He knew they wouldn't accost him on the avenue, where security cameras were everywhere.

Chris was sure that Jack Helson had one goal in life – to refer to him as "Head" every opportunity he had. Chris did have a slightly larger-than-normal head, but Helson's comedic creativity had crashed and freeze-framed on Chris's head. If Helson ever discovered the truth about his hands... well, Chris sheepishly preferred not to think about that.

"Go, Bobble Head!" Helson taunted again from behind, as Chris rode further away from him and his entourage. "Yo, where's Mrs. Potato Head?" Helson was standing with both hands cupped to his mouth, breaking the morning stillness with his loud taunts. Chris could hear them laughing back there. Why were they up so early and on the avenue? Couldn't be good.

He continued riding south on Rising Sun. Mr. Schwartz was entering his watch shop. "Guten Morgen, Mr. Schwartz."

"Guten Morgen, Chris."

"Hier ist das papier, sir." Chris handed a paper to Mr. Schwartz, who looked down. Chris quickly withdrew his hand and put both gloved hands behind his back.

Mr. Schwartz smiled. "I was looking at your wrist. It's an occupational hazard, I'm afraid. I always notice what kind of watches people wear," Mr. Schwartz said in German. Mr. Schwartz welcomed the opportunity to speak in his native language with Chris. "But you wear no watch."

Chris continued the conversation in German. "Yes, I don't need a watch, Mr. Schwartz."

"Ah, my boy, need has nothing to do with it. Desire," he continued, pointing upward to emphasize the point. "Desire will lead you to Schwartz's Jewelry Store someday for your first watch."

"Desire?"

"Yes, one day you will achieve something very wonderful, very great. On that day, you come to Schwartz's Jewelry Store and we will pick out the perfect watch to commemorate that occasion, okay?"

Chris smiled and nodded. "Ha ein guter tag, Herr Schwartz." *Have a good day.*

"Sie haben einen guten Tag auch," Mr. Schwartz responded. *You have a good day also.*

Mr. Schwartz watched him go. Then, as he turned to enter his jewelry shop, he looked up to the sky, pointed upward, and added a little prayer, "Halten sie die jungen sicher." *Keep the boy safe.*

The ballfield was located in an area zoned for light industrial use, at the dead end of a steep gravel path which bottomed out at field level. It was a forgotten several acres of eroded dirt without drainage, absolutely unfit for any purpose other than as a haven for mosquitoes, overgrown weeds, or a sandlot field. To Chris, it was heaven. He turned his Phillies cap backward on his head, and raced down the hill standing on the stilled pedals, cinders flying behind, yelling, "Warp factor ten, Mr. Scott!" At the bottom of the hill, his momentum carried him quickly along the path which bordered the fence running the length of the right field foul line to the aging cinderblock equipment shed outside the backstop behind home plate.

It took him about a half hour to nail the pitching rubber in exactly the correct spot on the mound and to secure the strings from home plate down each foul line to the outfield foul poles. These strings would act as straight-line guides when he lined the base paths and outfield foul lines.

Returning to the equipment shed, he was leaning forward pouring powdered white lime from a large bag into the liner when behind him, from the doorway came, "Yo, Head."

Chris froze, still bending at the waist. He turned to see a very large Jack Helson standing in the doorway.

"Answer me when I talk to you, Head," Helson demanded, picking up a baseball bat that was leaning against the door frame and smacking the palm of his left hand with the barrel of the bat. "How'd you manage to get your head through this door?"

Chris, straightening up said, "I have a field to line. Would you mind getting out of the way? I need to get through."

"You're not going anywhere, Head, until I say so," Helson responded pushing the liner backward into Chris with the bat. "So, tell me. What you always wearing them gloves for?"

Dude, spend less time cutting classes and more time learning how to speak English. "To protect my hands from the lime. It burns pretty good."

"You're lying," Helson said, continuing to smack the palm of his hand, more loudly now, with the bat. "You're hiding something. Take off them gloves. I wanna see."

Helson was becoming increasingly agitated and hostile. But, if he wanted a fight, he was going to get one. Chris, though frightened, had nowhere to run. He was trapped.

"I can't take them off. This lime stings. Come see for yourself, if you don't believe me. Don't get any in your eyes though. It could blind you."

"Are you threatening me, Head? Huh? Are you?"

"I'm impressed that you would consider attacking me with a baseball bat all by yourself. What happened to your buddies, Nimrod and Numbnuts? They get picked up for breaking parole?"

Helson raised the bat now. "I'd have to be pretty bad to miss hitting a head that big." Chris, though trapped and impotent against the much-larger

Helson, nonetheless had the presence of mind to grab a handful of lime, preparing to throw and duck at the same time. He was becoming, after all, a product of his environment. J.J. would have approved.

Suddenly, however, a hand grabbed the bat out of Helson's hands from behind, spinning him around. It was Chris's brother, James. Amazingly large and muscular for his age, James was the fastest and strongest fourteen-year-old athlete in all of Northeast Philadelphia and probably in all of Philadelphia, period.

"Whose head are we hitting today, Helson? Someone smaller and younger than you, no doubt," James said. Suddenly thwarted, Helson froze.

"Knowing how tough you are, it's probably someone defenseless. I know it wouldn't be my little brother you're threatening though, would it? Because you know what I would do to you if anything ever happened to my only little brother, don't you?"

"Y'all gonna yap in there all day, or are we gonna play some dad-gum baseball?" It was old Billy-The-Trash-Picker, drawling in his southern accent, standing outside the door behind James. Stoop-shouldered, he walked slowly, with a decided limp, burdened by the burlap trash bag slung over his shoulder and his ever-present trash poker.

James, momentarily distracted, turned to face Billy. Helson saw his chance, bolted past James, and ran for the railroad tracks.

James turned and saw Helson run away, but Chris's focus shifted to his big brother standing in the doorway. "Thanks, James," he said. "He was going to crush my skull with that bat. You saved my life."

James picked up the wooden batter's box template. "Quit exaggerating. Don't worry about him. He's a punk. Come on. Let's get this field lined."

James' team won the game, no surprise. They did not win every game, of course, but they had been consistently good the two years that James had been playing with them. Although a standout in basketball, his primary sport, James was a gifted athlete and tough to beat in any athletic competition.

Chris stayed behind after the game, as always, to close up the snack stand, shut down the scoreboard, fold and store the flags, and put the bases and umpire's equipment in the storage shed. "Nice game, Sam," he said as Samantha Banks, the center fielder, sat on the dugout bench and put her spikes into her equipment bag.

"Thanks, Doc. We stopping by Stan's?"

"Of course."

Sam Banks, twelve years old, "had wheels." She was the fastest runner anyone had ever seen. She and Chris had been best friends almost their whole lives. The older boys welcomed her as their center fielder because she caught just about any ball hit anywhere near center field, including the left-center and right-center alleyways. She struggled as a hitter against the older and stronger pitchers but, even though she was often overmatched, she was tough to throw out at first base if she made any contact at all.

More often than not, she would beat out infield grounders. If the infielders played in, she would either drag bunt or try to hit bloopers over their heads. Every once in a while, though, she would rip a line drive, so most defenders were very confused as to how to best position themselves. This, of course, played to Sam's advantage. If a fielder hesitated at all, Sam would beat him. The opponents knew this, and they put pressure on themselves to field the ball quickly.

The added pressure played right into Sam's hands. She may not get a lot of hits, or lead the league in batting average, but she didn't care if she got on base because she got a clean hit or because the fielder made an error from trying to rush. The important thing was she reached base, either by hit or error. She would settle for leading the league in on-base percentage, stolen bases, and runs scored. She loved baseball, and was a fierce competitor and a great leadoff hitter.

As they were leaving they stopped to talk to Billy-The-Trash-Picker, the only other person remaining at the ball field.

"Pretty good game, huh Billy?" Chris said.

"Yep. That brother o'yourn's a right fine hitter, ain't he?" Billy drawled (...*a rat fan itter ainey?*)

"Absolutely. Anyway, thanks for getting here so early and cleaning up. The field looked great today."

"Love the game, it'll love you back'n buckets," Billy said. "Your turn's comin' soon 'nuf, I reckon."

"My turn?"

"Yessir, t' get in th' game."

"Um, I don't think so. I'm not that good."

Billy chuckled and winked. "Ain't got no choice. All'n th' genes."

"Billy, James and I are adopted. He's not my biological brother. You have noticed that he's black and I'm white, right? We don't have the same parents."

Billy stopped picking up trash with his poker and turned to face Chris. One locked at the other, each wearing aviator glasses and leather gloves. There was an awkward silence as Billy seemed to think about how to respond. Chris was used to this sort of delayed reaction from Billy. Everybody knew Billy was "slow," which is why most of the players avoided him. He made them uncomfortable. Chris didn't mind, though. Finally, Billy turned away, resumed picking up trash with his poker, and repeated himself softly, but Chris and Sam heard him. "All'n th' genes."

Chris, exasperated, spread his hands in a questioning gesture, looked at Sam, who smiled, and then at Billy walking away from him. Talking to the old guy was difficult. "Whatever. Anyway, thanks again, Billy. And thanks for helping me with Helson. See you Thursday?"

"Sho 'nuf," Billy replied, not looking back. When Chris and Sam had gone, Billy-The-Trash-Picker stopped and focused on a stray chewing gum wrapper at his feet. He stuck the wrapper with his poker and said gruffly, "Helson."

Except, he had spoken clearly now, to himself, with no hint of a drawl, and had stabbed at the wrapper forcefully, his disapprobation palpable. There was no mistaking his meaning.

Hell's son.

CHAPTER 5

Ozzie was waiting on his bike at the end of the cinder trail leading up from the ball field. He had come through the broken gate of the dilapidated picket fence surrounding the back yard of his mom's corner row house, when he saw Chris and Sam. "Hey, Doc. Hey, Sam. Up for some halfball?"

"Definitely," Sam replied, as she and Chris topped the hill on their bikes. "Hoagie first, though. I'm starving. Gotta halfball?"

"Got the ingredients," Ozzie replied, pulling out a pimple ball and a switchblade.

"Whoa! A new pinkie." Chris said.

"Carried bags at the Ac-a-me. Made seven bucks in two hours."

"Nice. Shame to cut up a brand new pinkie, though. We should use it for handball or stickball first," Sam said.

"Yeah, I guess. There'll probably be some old half balls at Glenn's. If not, we'll use this. I'm guessin' you and James won?" Ozzie asked Sam.

"A lot to a little," Sam said.

"Mercy rule?"

"Yeah. Ump called the game after four

innings."

"Man, I hate the mercy rule. It ain't real life. Show no mercy, that's what I say."

"Nah, I like it. Some of the games can be pretty lopsided, boring," Chris said.

"Yeah, maybe it's better to put the poor slobs outta their misery," Ozzie said, thrusting his switchblade upward.

"Who we putting outta their misery this time, Oz?" It was Butchy, who had ridden across the street to join them. Butchy, at 5'6" and 180 pounds, was a human fireplug.

"Youth in Asia," Ozzie quipped.

"My old man will be happy to know you're going to Asia. That should drive up property values around here. Hi, Doc. You win, Sam?"

"Dipwad kinda question is that?" Ozzie interrupted. "Who's gonna beat her? You?"

"Guys, come on. Knock it off, will ya? Butch, you up for halfball?" Chris asked.

"Now?"

"What?" Ozzie said. "You gotta check your social calendar? Today Fat Tuesday or something?" Ozzie wasn't going to stop. Butchy hopped off his bike, as did Ozzie. They both squared off as Chris jumped off his bike and got between them. "Guys, guys…" he said.

Butchy threw a punch at Ozzie that hit Chris in the shoulder as he got between them.

"Crap! Thanks, Butch, you jerk."

"Sorry, Doc. Sorry, sorry. You okay?"

"You guys knock it off, will you, before someone gets killed?" Chris said, in obvious pain. Then, rubbing his shoulder, he said, "Yeah, I'll live. Come on let's pick up those hoagies." Everyone got back on their bikes.

After they rode another half block, Butchy said to Ozzie, "Inside fastballs."

"Definitely," Ozzie agreed as he fist-bumped Butchy. "No mercy." It took just five words for the two to conclude how to neutralize an injured Chris in halfball.

"Jerks." Chris said, continuing to rub his sore shoulder.

Having picked up their hoagies, sodas, and water at Stan's, they joined Glenn and Eric in the alleyway behind Glenn's house. Glenn was twelve. Eric was Glenn's younger brother, by one year. They preferred soccer to baseball and were considered "weird," for this reason, by the others. Their parents belonged to a German soccer club, so they were gone most weekends. They did other odd things, too, like play the accordion, the glockenspiel, speak German, eat strange stuff like bratwurst, pigs feet, and sauerkraut, build massive erector set Ferris wheels, model Messerschmitt planes, play ping pong, study engineering, and walk the family schnauzer, Fraulein. They had been Chris' friends for years. To Chris, engineering was not nearly as interesting as physics, just as soccer was not nearly as interesting as baseball, but he appreciated the discipline necessary to excel in any of those things. Only their love of sports had saved Glenn, Eric, and Chris from full-fledged Geekdom.

Glenn's driveway was where they played halfball. Glenn's garage door was the only one on the block that had the design necessary for a proper halfball vertical strike zone: a square on the garage door about two feet wide and two feet tall, beginning one foot off the ground. There were no base paths and no running in this parochial parody of the national past-time. Only pitching, hitting, and fielding. A double was any ball which hit the back of the house across the alleyway below the telephone wires running from house to house above the first story. A triple hit the house above the wire. A homerun landed on the roof and typically ended the game, because there was usually only one halfball. Thanks to Ozzie and his new pinky, though, they could afford to lose one halfball today.

James was dribbling a basketball down the back alleyway with the B-balls, his basketball groupies who, like James, were two years older than

Chris and his friends. "Mind if we play?" James asked, passing through. It was obvious James and the B-balls, long ago proscribed from playing with the younger kids, had no interest in halfball today. They were headed up to the "basketball court" in the rear of Chris' and James' house – the only house on the block with a basketball hoop. Not optimal, but good enough for individual practice or for choose-up in a pinch when the playground court was full. James practiced constantly. More than anybody. He knew basketball would be his ticket out of the slum.

"We have six," Glenn replied, meaning even teams and no need for more players, especially James.

"Oh, come on, one swing," James said, facetiously, as the B-balls chuckled. Everyone knew that James' one swing would most likely result in a homerun, and a lost halfball. Over the years, James had sent more halfballs to their final resting place on Mrs. Kling's rooftop than anyone else. Probably hundreds. The day Mrs. Kling were to have her roof tarred, if ever, would be the day halfballs would serendipitously rain down. Of course, that would be like winning the lottery. Unlikely. Mrs. Kling was a widow who lived alone, and her house obviously had more pressing needs than a roof covered with halfballs. At least it wasn't boarded up and abandoned, yet, as were several crack houses on the block.

Teams were chosen. It was always the same

teams: Chris, Eric, and Sam against Glenn, Ozzie, and Butchy. This spread the talent evenly and, over a long period of time, both teams had won about as many games as they lost. In the bottom of the 9th inning, the game was tied. Bases were loaded, one out, and Ozzie was batting against Eric. Chris and Sam both played shallow in the field to defend against a single which would win the game for Glenn's team. Eric pitched. Ozzie swung.

Chris was able to clearly see the halfball compress upon contact with the stick bat. It was a stunning capability that a long procession of pediatric and adult ophthalmologists had been unable to explain. In a split second, a screaming line drive raced at Chris, but out of his reach. As he turned to follow its flight, the halfball appeared, for a split second, to be stopped in mid-air, its flight momentarily suspended above and behind him, as he turned his head. Sam also appeared to be suspended in mid-air, both feet off the ground, as she leaped toward the top of a stone retaining wall. Immediately, however, the action continued.

Sam had raced back, leapt up on the stone retaining wall, and snatched the halfball out of the air as it was zooming over her head. Chris had never experienced anything like this before. He immediately became disoriented and nauseous, and dropped to one knee. Seeing that everyone was focused on Sam's spectacular catch, Chris quickly gathered himself, stood, ran back, and high-fived his teammate. Afterward, everyone agreed that it was the single best defensive play ever made in the history of halfball. Even James and the B-balls, watching from up the alleyway, clapped, shouted, and whistled an urban paean when they saw it. Amazingly, Ozzie trotted out and high-fived Sam who had just robbed him of a game-winning hit. "Awesome catch, man," he said.

"Thanks."

"Guess I'll have to hit it where you can't catch it," Glenn shouted to Sam as he picked up his stick bat. Apparently, none of them had noticed Chris go down on one knee.

Sam had likely merely succeeded in postponing the inevitable, because Glenn was now at bat. With the bases loaded, and two outs, there was no place to put him. Eric would have to pitch to his older brother who, everyone knew, was a very good hitter. Eric pitched carefully. After three straight balls which Glenn let go by without swinging, there remained no room for error. Eric was going to have to throw a strike. The fourth pitch was a sharp-breaking hard screwball which broke right and caught the lower outside corner of the strike box for strike one. Even Glenn could not have reached that pitch. The fifth pitch was a hard-diving sinker, thrown high, which just caught the top of the strike zone for strike two. So, the entire one-hour game came down to one final pitch.

"One more, little bro. One more," Glenn

taunted, waving the broom-less stick in a circular motion over his head. "Gimme your best shot," Glenn said the same line he had used in such standoffs many times. Chris and Sam tensed up in the outfield.

Eric smiled, confident. "Not today, bro. Not today," he said as he held the halfball behind his back and turned it open side up. Another drop. This time, however, he would throw it low and out of the strike zone, daring his older brother to swing at an unhittable ball four. All Glenn had to do to win the game was not swing, to be patient. Eric knew, however, that Glenn was not the patient type. He planned to use Glenn's aggressiveness against him, to fool his brother with a well-placed, hard pitch which would look like strike three and dive away from Glenn's swinging stickball bat at the last split second.

It was a good plan, expertly executed. Eric threw a perfect pitch. Hard, strike height, which dove down toward the ground at the last split second. As Eric predicted, his brother was unnecessarily aggressive. As Eric predicted, Glenn did swing at ball four. Unfortunately for Eric, however, Glenn was just a hair more talented, or more lucky, than even Eric knew. Glenn hit that pitch further than any of them had ever hit a halfball. It sailed clear over Mrs. Kling's house and into the street one block over. A grand slam. Game over. A stunning victory. Dejected, heads down, Chris, Eric, and Sam walked off the driveway as Glenn raced around the imaginary bases twice, hands held high into the congratulatory embrace of Ozzie and Butchy. Totally ridiculous. Totally adolescent. And totally as good as it gets for kids growing up in the 'hood. Even James and the older B-balls came down and shook Glenn's hand.

Way down at the end of the block, unseen by any of the boys, Billy-The-Trash-Picker saw the much, much more significant event in the game: Chris' stumble. Billy understood. "Change is coming," he said to no one.

CHAPTER 6

"Hi, mom."

"Hi, Chris." Chris's adoptive mom, Aliondra Covington, was standing at the kitchen counter, when he entered from the same back door he had exited that morning.

"Why are you dressed up?" Chris asked.

"I had to go to work today."

"On Saturday? You never go to work on Saturday."

"My boss, Mr. Lewis, called this morning and asked me to help on a project." She was sifting through the pile of mail in her hands, mostly bills. "Dinner will be on the table at five o'clock," she added, absently.

"What's for dinner?"

"I was thinking about making salad and baked ziti."

"I don't know, mom. You know what they say about Italian food."

"What's that?"

"In three or four days you'll be hungry again."

"Very funny," she smiled. "You and J.J. going over to the rec to watch a game?"

"Of course."

"Make sure you're here by five." Chris knew she meant for him and J.J. to be there for dinner. J.J. always joined them for Saturday dinner. Aliondra thought it important to treat the orphans to a home-cooked meal periodically.

"We'll be here. Thanks, Mom. Concert tomorrow, by the way. Wanna go?"

"I can't, Chris. This new project at work is going to tie me up for a while, I'm afraid."

"Even on Sundays?"

"Probably a few. Not every Sunday, but time will tell."

"That stinks."

"It can't be helped. I have to do what I have to do. The bills won't pay themselves. But don't you worry about it. I'll be fine. A little rough patch now and again makes me appreciate smooth sailing."

Chris had wanted to tell his mom how he experienced "stop action" during the halfball game, and how he sensed a change coming to the Earth, but he could see this wasn't the best time. She seemed to be facing struggles of her own. And, what could she really do? Send him to another long line of expensive doctors? No. Money was clearly an issue so, instead of focusing on himself, Chris offered yet again to help financially, though he knew it would be useless. "I could get a job."

"You have a job: to get an education. Your special gift is your intellect. My job is to see that you develop it, and I take my job very seriously, so I hope you do too. I need you to stay in school and apply yourself to your studies. Everything else will take care of itself. God will provide. Don't ever forget that. God will take care of His children."

Later, as Chris and J.J. walked to the PAL rec center, Chris related this conversation to his friend. J.J. asked, "Do you flippin' believe that stuff about God and guardian angels and all that religious stuff?"

Before he could respond, Chris and J.J. were jumped from behind by Helson and two of his hoolligans. Helson immediately felled Chris by sucker-punching him on the side of the head. He collapsed in a heap on the sidewalk while Helson stood over him, pointing and laughing. This so enraged J.J., a ticking human time bomb and no stranger to street fighting, that he punched one of the much larger assailants in the throat and finger-punched the other in the eyes. As both lay on the sidewalk in different stages of severe distress, Helson flicked open a 4-inch switchblade, "Yo, man. I have no problem with you," he said. As Chris watched from where he lay crumpled and hurt, J.J.

kicked the much-larger Helson hard, in the groin. Helson fell to the ground immediately and dropped the knife.

"You mess with my friend, puke face, you most definitely have a problem with me." Although Chris was in tremendous agony he noticed that, in the heat of battle, J.J. did not say one "flippin."

J.J. helped Chris to his feet, and propped him up as they hurried down the sidewalk, leaving Helson and his goons sprawled on the ground, incapacitated, and writhing in agony.

Ten minutes later, as they entered the PAL rec center, Chris had recovered sufficiently to be able to speak. "Yes," he said.

"Yes? What's that flippin' mean? J.J. asked.

"Yes, I do believe in guardian angels," Chris replied. "Thanks, J.J."

J.J. frowned. "Dude, you see any wings on me? I'm no flippin' angel. I'm just protectin' my meal ticket. C'mon, let's find some seats. The flippin' game's startin'."

Chris smiled to himself, but said nothing. He knew a 'flippin' angel' when he saw one.

One hour later, as Chris and J.J. watched from the stands, Captain Dan Carroll's three-point attempt hit nothing but air, before sailing out of bounds to stop the clock, with ten seconds left. His team trailed by three points and his ill-advised gaffe had just turned the basketball over to the opponents in the men's league. His 2nd precinct team now needed a miracle to win. Short on miracles, they did have the next best thing – Lieutenant Joe Carter, a fierce competitor who hated to lose.

As the ball sailed out of bounds, Captain Carroll called a timeout to organize the defense, much to the annoyance of Carter and every other player on the team. "Okay guys, we need a turnover here. Mountie, you defend against the in-bound. Everybody else, full-court press. We need to get that ball back," he said, stating the obvious. "Whoever gets it, call a timeout immediately," he said, stating the impossible. "Captain," Henderson said, "this is our last timeout. Ain't no timeouts left."

Carter flashed a sly smile at Mike Mountain. As they broke the huddle, Carter said to Mountain, "You cherry-pick. Lay it up. No threes. There'll be enough time. After you score, crash from the top of the key, bang-bang deflection on the in-bounds. Got it?"

Mountain smiled, "Got that crystal ball thing goin' again, Fey-Man?"

"Show time," Carter replied as he trotted to mid court, leaving his friend to guard against the in-bounds pass.

Mountain shook his head as he watched Carter run to mid court. He didn't know how Carter did it, but he knew better than to ever bet against him. Joe Carter was a born winner.

The other team, seeing the full-court press, successfully in-bounded the ball almost the length of the court and began to pass the ball around, to chew up the clock. Fortunately for the 2nd Precinct team, and as is so often the case among teams in recreational leagues, they hadn't cornered the market on the ill-advised three-point shot. With six seconds remaining, one of the guards from the opposing team attempted a three-pointer. The ball caromed off the back rim and all the way out to center court, where Joe Carter grabbed it and immediately passed it up the floor to Mike Mountain, who was all by himself under the opponents' basket. He banked the ball off the glass backboard and into the hoop with two seconds remaining in the game.

You cherry-pick. Lay it up. No threes. Mountain recalled Carter's premonition, which had just come true.

Up by a point, with two seconds remaining, the opponents once again had possession of the ball for an in-bounds pass. A successful in-bound would effectively win the game for them. "Top of the key!" Carter shouted at Mountain, who hustled back. Carter was now guarding against the in-bounds pass. Captain Carroll came running up, shouting at Mountain to guard against the in-bounds. Mountain shouted, "Joe's got it."

"Carter, get back!" yelled their fractious captain, running up to Carter as the ball was being inbounded over him. Carter leaped as high as he could and barely touched the ball being inbounded over his outstretched arms. The ball tipped off his fingertips and went up toward the basket as Mountain came crashing in full speed and leaped high to grab the ball and slam it through the hoop, in one motion, a split second before the buzzer sounded. The 2nd precinct team won the game by one point on Mountain's buzzer-beating dunk. Incredibly, the game had ended just as Carter said it would.

After you score, crash from the top of the key, bang-bang deflection on the in-bounds. Got it?

As his teammates high-fived one another all around, Mountain stood there, hands on his hips, looking at Joe Carter in disbelief. How did he do it?

They headed over to the bench to retrieve their towels and grab some water. Captain Carroll came up behind them. "All's well that ends well, I guess, but you two were seriously out of position. Good thing they're dumber than you are," he said while thumbing toward the other team. "Talk about dumb luck..." the pejorative trailed after him as he stormed past them and out the exit.

"Got that crystal ball thing goin' on!" Mountain shouted, as he low-fived Carter.

"Just dumb luck – you heard the captain,"

Carter replied.

"Ah, he's just sour grapes."

"Seriously sour," Carter agreed. "What's his problem anyway?"

"His air ball, I guess. Weren't no luck on that floor with that see-the-future predicting thing or whatever it is you got, that's all I'm saying," Mountain said. "How do you do it?"

"Dunno. Let's get outta here," Carter said, shrugging off the accolade and picking up his duffle bag. He was concerned about the captain's reaction. Winning in spite of his boss presented a dilemma. Annoying him could make for long days back at the precinct.

Joe Carter was the most decorated detective, not just in the 2nd precinct, but in the entire Philadelphia Police Department. He never sought the spotlight, he just loved his work. But the spotlight seemed to find him, especially recently, and Carter was getting the distinct impression that his status as somewhat of a local celebrity was not sitting too well with his captain.

Carter and Mountain left the PAL gymnasium and went outside to the parking lot where they hopped into Mountain's car. "Cookin' out today Joe, if you care to come over."

"What're you cooking?" Carter asked.

"Whatever you bring."

"I'll give you a call later," Carter laughed, as they drove out of the parking lot. "Got a lot of work to do on my garden though," Carter continued.

"Man, you're going to turn into a farmer, you keep that gardening stuff up, Joe."

"Hey, big man, somebody's got to feed you and that family of yours. I'm just thinking of your welfare, that's all."

"Who are you kidding? You ain't thinking about nobody's welfare. The only thing you ever think about is solving some crime or another. Man, when are you ever going to learn to give it a rest? You're making the rest of us look bad."

"Mike, every time we visit, you go through five pounds of food. You know my salary. You think I could afford to visit if I didn't tend to my garden? I would die of starvation within a week."

"Oh bull! Who you kidding? You love that stupid garden, and don't think I don't know it. You know what else I think? I think…"

"Pull over," Carter interrupted, as he reached into the glove compartment for his service revolver.

"What? Why?"

"Just pull over. Did you see those two guys go into the 7-11?" Carter asked looking back and out the passenger side window.

"Ain't no law against shopping, Joe."

"Yeah, but it's a little too warm for walking down the avenue in this sun wearing hoodies. Those two are up to no good. You pull around back. Better call for backup," Carter said, getting out of the car and running back toward the convenience store he saw the two men enter a minute before.

"Man's got some serious intuition," Mountain said to himself, as he watched Carter run toward the store. He then phoned dispatch and requested backup as he drove around to the back of the store.

Carter, evidencing his signature temerity, walked right up to the glass front door, opened it, and stepped inside, surprising the two armed gunman. One of the gunmen turned and shot at him. Carter turned sideways as the bullets missed him and shattered the glass door. He calmly returned the fire and hit the gunman in the thigh, as he had intended. The other gunman bolted toward the back door with a bag containing the cash register's contents. He ran full speed out the back door and into Mountain's waiting fist. The robber went down in a heap. He literally never saw what hit him. This little confrontation would cost him a fractured jaw, a broken nose, and a few minutes of consciousness.

As the police backups and ambulance arrived to take the robbers into custody, Mountain said to

Carter, "You got that crystal ball thing seriously goin' on today, Fey-Man."

"Just seriously lucky is all," Carter replied.

Within minutes a local television news crew arrived. "Uh-oh, you handle them," Carter said to Mountain as he turned to leave through the back.

"No way, Joe. Stay here and face the music. They don't want this mug on TV," he said pointing to his own face.

"Lieutenant Carter, Lieutenant Carter!" the newswoman shouted, pushing past Mountain, pulling the cameraman by his arm, and shoving a microphone at Joe Carter.

"We're rolling," the cameraman said.

"Lieutenant Carter – another busted burglary. That's the third this week. How do you do it?"

"No comment," Carter said.

"Some people say you have a nose for armed robberies, is that true?"

"No comment."

"You're the most decorated veteran on the force. A hero…"

Carter turned abruptly and headed for the rear exit. "I'm outta here."

"The Department will have a statement after it conducts its own investigation," Mountain said, stepping in front of the camera. "Captain Carroll will address the media at that time."

"Cut!" shouted the newswoman as she and the cameraman charged out the back door after Carter, but he was nowhere to be found. Apparently, he had vanished. "Wow," the newswoman said. "He's fast." She turned with the cameraman and they both headed back through the store and out the front door to the news van, passing Mountain on the way. "Carter is a serious hunk," she said to Mountain as she passed by.

As Mountain walked toward the back door, Joe Carter emerged from the restroom. "Mar, they're everywhere," he said, referring to the news crew.

"Maybe you'd better lay low for a while, Joe."

"Lotsa bad guys, Mike. We're in the game 'til time runs out."

CHAPTER 7

The following afternoon Aliondra Covington drove Chris and Sam to St. Michael's Home. Mrs. Frieda Kling would drive them home. This had been the routine every third Sunday of each month for the past two years.

In the back seat, Sam listened as Chris, sitting beside her and speaking softly so as not to worry his mom, related the events of the previous day, beginning with a headless mouse and proceeding through earth tremors, odd comments from Billy-The-Trash-Picker, getting punched by Ozzie, seeing the halfball stop in midair and feeling nauseous, getting mugged by Helson, rescued by J.J., and witnessing a remarkable come-from-behind win by the 2nd Precinct men's basketball team. "Well, if yesterday was the first day of the rest of your life, I guess you're in for one heckuva kick in the pants," she concluded when he had finished.

He squirmed in his seat, recalling Helson sprawled on the ground in obvious distress. "Poor choice of words."

Sam smiled. "One heck of an exciting ride?"

"Better."

"So tell me more about this seeing the ball stop in mid-air," Sam said softly.

"What are you two whispering about back there?" Mrs. Covington said.

"Suspended animation," Chris said.

"Uh-huh," Mrs. Covington said, rolling her eyes. "Since it's nothing important, then, I think I'll turn on the radio."

Chris smiled at her reflection in the rear view mirror. "Thanks, mom," he said.

She smiled back as she turned on the radio. R&B filled the car.

"There's not much to tell," Chris said to Sam, continuing to speak softly. It just happened and then, bam, it was over. A split second, that's all. But it was really weird. I mean, how would you feel if suddenly everything stopped, even for a split second?"

"I'd be freaked out, for sure. Does this condition have a name?"

"I Googled it and found nothing. Apparently no one else ever had symptoms like this."

"Symptoms? So, you think it's some kind of illness?"

"Who knows? I guess it could be just another odd thing in my life - thumbs, toes, eyes, head, brain, blah, blah, blah. I'm just different."

"Speaking of...are you still practicing

moving things with your mind?"

"My telekinesis exercises? No, not really. I guess I've given up on that for now. I really still think it's not such a crazy idea."

"Chris, come on, we've talked about this for years. No one can move things by thinking them into moving."

"Right. And no twelve-year-old can speak and understand two dozen languages, or play a dozen musical instruments, or solve a Rubik's Cube in seven seconds, or be a master chess champion, or create a fifth-level quadratic equation, or memorize poetry in one sitting, right? Except, guess what? I can."

"Chris, look..."

"I'm sorry, Sam. The point is. I really am different. I was born that way. To me, telekinesis really does seem to be something I ought to be able to do, even if no one else can. What's more crazy, moving things with my mind or living life in suspended animation? Maybe years of trying telekinesis led to freeze-frame action, I don't know."

"And you won't see a doctor about it?"

"No, I'm done being a lab rat. All the scientists want is to poke around inside my brain, wishing I were dead so they could slice and dice whatever's up here," he said, pointing to his head.

"They don't really care about me..."

"What about psychiatrists or psychologists?"

"Same church, different pew. No, I'm done with them. For better or worse, I'm going to have to figure things out on my own. Something tells me I'm the best one to do it anyway."

"Well, you'll always have me. Everyone needs friends."

"Thanks, Sam. You're the best friend I could ever have."

Sam smiled at Chris. "Teammates," she said.

"I'm counting on it," he said, taking her hand in his. "Wow, your hand is so soft."

She hoped she wasn't blushing. Her little genius could be so sweet and naïve at the same time. As smart as he was, in matters of the heart, he really had no clue.

"We're here already," he said, releasing her hand, as they pulled into the parking lot at St. Michael's Home. "Wow, look at that limo. Must be some big Mahoff here."

"Here comes your fan club," Sam replied, as a hundred or more young children ran to their car.

"They're your fans too." Chris said, looking at Sam.

"Uh, no. You are their hero, their pied piper. I'm just the sidekick," she replied matter-of-factly, as they got out of the car. Chris just could not see how people loved him for who he was and not for what he was able to do. She did not doubt that Chris believed the kids were only interested in him because of his magic tricks and music concerts. But, she knew better. Those kids looked at him with eyes of wonder, as if he were none other than Santa Claus himself.

The children, ages four to nine, swarmed around Sam and Chris, greeting "Mr. Chris" and "Miss Sam" enthusiastically. Headmistress Brennan trailed behind but eventually greeted Sam and Chris also. "No J.J.?" Chris asked her.

"That boy," Headmistress Brennan sighed. "We don't know where he gets to half the time. I'm sure he'll be along. He never misses your visits."

"Okay, are we all set up?" Chris asked her.

"In the auditorium," she replied. "The volunteers, staff, and a few others are waiting there also," she smiled.

Chris smiled, too, at her inside joke knowing, by the parking lot full of cars, what she meant by *a few others*. "Great, thank you, Headmistress." Then he addressed the children as he always did, with the question, "Who wants a parade?" They all cheered and shouted, "I do! I do!" whereupon Chris retrieved a piccolo seemingly from behind Sam's head, to "oohs" and "aahs" from the children, a roll of the eyes from Sam, and a proud smile from Headmistress Brennan. He began to play "Stars and Stripes Forever" as he marched around the parking lot, past the windows of the administrative offices, into the building and down the hallway to the auditorium, followed the entire time by Headmistress Brennan and Sam arm-in-arm, and the children. *Pied Piper*, Sam thought.

When they entered the auditorium, Chris saw it was filled to capacity. His visits drew two hundred children and adults from the surrounding neighborhood. Of meager means, they nonetheless paid admission to hear Chris perform, monies most welcomed by Headmistress Brennan to support the orphanage.

All the children ran for the seats reserved for them in the front, facing the stage. Chris climbed the steps and walked over to the grand piano at center stage. It was surrounded by stands holding a trumpet, a banjo, a violin, a clarinet, and a guitar, as well as a set of drums. All had been donated by a city high school whose music department had recently closed.

Over the course of the next ninety minutes, Chris played over two dozen requests from the audience. He would either play a requested instrument or choose the one which he felt was most appropriate for a particular song.

He played all styles of music: popular, rock

and roll, classical, hip hop, rap, country western, musicals, lullaby, and spirituals. He sang some of the songs and invited others to sing.

Sam now sat with Frieda Kling and the volunteers, as Maxine Brennan had been called away on urgent business. Sam loved Chris's concerts. She knew he felt his talent was a gift he needed to share with others. He felt it was an ability which he had been given, not something he had earned, even though he had practiced for thousands of hours in his young life.

It was at these times that Sam knew for certain why she liked him so much. He was not only talented and hard-working, but loving and upbeat in all that he did. He exuded a zest for life and a true love for others, especially the young orphans who had suffered the indignity of being deserted by their parents, as they both had. In this way, and quite unknowingly, he was the lodestar who had taught her how to overcome life's challenges. He was a diamond in the rough, and due in no small part to his influence, so was she.

Frieda Kling ushered three-year-old Joey onto the stage to sing his "special song" with Chris, the final act of the concert. Joey was adorable, sitting on a stool next to where Chris sat with his guitar. Frieda held the microphone as Joey sang, "Me and My Teddy Bear."

Chris saw J.J. enter at the rear of the

auditorium and take a seat in the back. When Joey was finished, there was not a dry eye in the house as everyone gave Joey and Chris a standing ovation. Frieda and the other volunteers joined a small group of parents newly interested in adopting, another benefit of Chris' concerts.

Chris and Sam walked to the rear of the auditorium and joined J.J. "Not bad. Not bad at all," J.J. said to Chris. "Let me know when you're ready to expand your act."

"Really? You want to join me?" Chris said.

"What? You think you're the only one around this flippin' place who can entertain?"

"No, that's not what I meant. I only meant..."

"Well, you're not," J.J. interrupted, clearly annoyed.

"I didn't know you played any instruments."

"I don't. Don't sing or dance either. I'm an actor."

"Oh, puh-lease," Sam said. J.J. seethed, but he would never threaten a girl. "All of a sudden you're an actor. When did you ever act?" she challenged.

"Just every flippin' day, for your information. In case you haven't noticed, people around the Home here actually like me. You like me too. You think that just flippin' happens?"

"He's got a point, actually," Sam said to Chris.

"Flippin' ay," J.J. said. "You think anybody could flippin' take me straight up, if I weren't turnin' on the flippin' charm all the time?"

Sam and Chris looked at J.J. They weren't sure how to respond without getting a knuckle sandwich for their effort. Finally, Sam said, "Well, it's good to know my friends are both thespians."

"Watch it," J.J. warned, clearly agitated. "I'm no flippin' thespian. Watch your mouth."

"Thespian means actor," Chris said, coming to Sam's defense.

"Yeah, I know that," J.J. lied. "See? I flippin' had you goin', didn't I? That's what good thespians do."

Sam and Chris stared at J.J. Sam sighed, "Yeah, I guess." Then to change the subject, she said, "That Joey sure is a cute little kid."

"Yeah, the cute ones are the lucky ones," J.J. said. "They get flippin' adopted."

"You think someone will adopt Joey?" Sam asked.

"You see the flippin' faucets in here? There wasn't a dry eye in the place. Yeah, he'll get adopted. But it better flippin' happen soon."

"Why?" Chris asked.

"Come here." J.J. signaled to them to sit close to him so he wouldn't be overheard.

J.J. began. "Look, while you two were goofin' off in here, I was flippin' working."

"Doing what?" Sam asked.

"Flippin' spying, that's what. The good stuff was going on in the living room. Headmistress Brennan was meeting with some big flippin' hotshots from New York."

"Meeting about what?"

"I'll tell you what, about flippin' selling this Home, that's what."

"What!" Chris and Sam exclaimed at the same time. "That'll never happen," Chris said. "Headmistress Brennan loves this place. She'll never sell, not for a million bucks."

"Yeah, well the flippin' New York guys were talking about twenty million bucks."

"Twenty million?" Chris and Sam exclaimed.

"Shh!" J.J. cautioned. "I'm not supposed to

flippin' know anything about this. I don't even think Frieda Kling knows."

"But why would they pay twenty million for an old orphanage in a poor neighborhood?" Sam asked.

"It's not the orphanage they want. It's the flippin' land. It's right on the river. That makes it valuable, I guess. This flippin' neighborhood may be a dump, but they were telling Headmistress Brennan that they could make it a great place if she would sell to them."

"How are they going to do that? By fixing up the orphanage?"

"No, not by flippin' fixing it up. By tearing it down."

"Okay, I'm lost," Sam said. "How would that improve the neighborhood?"

"Because they want to build a big flippin' casino and hotel here, that's why. They said a casino would create hundreds of jobs for people in the neighborhood. They said putting a big casino and hotel right next to the flippin' river would mean that millions of people would come here to gamble," J.J. said.

"To gamble," Chris said, almost to himself.

"Yeah, there's a lot of flippin' money in gambling," J.J. replied. "Maybe even I could get a flippin' job."

"But people lose money when they gamble," Chris said. "The only way the casino could make money is if people lose money to it."

"Hey, what do I flippin' care if some rich New Yorkers visit my neighborhood and blow some big bucks here? That should be good for us, right?"

"I'm not so sure," Chris said. "I don't know much about making money, but something isn't adding up."

"My mom tells me all the time," Sam said, "If it sounds too good to be true, it probably is."

"Yeah, well you two flippin' geniuses are living proof why some smart people aren't rich. You think too flippin' much. If you want to get rich, you have to grab the opportunity when it's hitting you upside the head. That's what those guys were telling Headmistress Brennan."

"And what did she say?" Sam asked.

"She said she wouldn't sell for any price. But those guys kept coming at her, telling her how she could use the money to help the children and to move this orphanage up the flippin' street or somewhere close by. They even offered to help her build a new flippin' orphanage."

Just then, they saw Headmistress Maxine Brennan through the French doors at the other end of the auditorium that led to the veranda which overlooked the river. "Maybe you should go talk to her," J.J. said. "Twenty million bucks and a brand new orphanage. Even Headmistress Brennan can't flippin' walk away from that."

"Alright, see you Saturday morning, J.J. Thanks," Chris said.

"Yep, bright and flippin' early. See ya," J.J. said, exiting the auditorium.

Chris and Sam walked out onto the screened-in veranda to visit with the headmistress.

"Sam! Chris!" Headmistress Brennan exclaimed, rising from her wooden patio chair, one in a row of similar chairs facing the river on the veranda. "I trust the concert went well today?"

"Yes, Headmistress, very well," Sam replied. "Chris was wonderful, as always,"

"Well, I would expect nothing less of a St. Michael's alum," Headmistress Brennan smiled. "Please sit, sit. Let's visit for a bit and enjoy the mighty Delaware."

"Thanks," Sam and Chris replied, sitting in chairs on either side of Headmistress Brennan. "Wow, great view," Chris added.

"Yes, I like it," Headmistress Brennan replied. "I come out here sometimes for private reflection, but it is nice to have some visitors. I am sorry I was not able to attend your concert today, Chris. I was tied up in a meeting with some visitors."

Sam stole a glance at Chris who nodded his head slightly. To Chris, Headmistress Brenann's words sounded like an invitation. Sam nodded back and proceeded. "We know. A little bird told us."

Headmistress Brennan looked quite surprised. "Now, Sam, we taught you better than to lie. I have it on good authority that birds cannot speak English."

Sam shot back without missing a beat. "That's right, but Chris translated for me."

"Ahh!" Headmistress Brennan replied. "I should have known. Yes, Chris, our resident linguist. And what, might I ask, did this little bird say to you, young man?"

"Well, my finch is a little rusty. It was something about either a cousin or a casino," Chris said, rubbing his chin as if deep in thought.

"Interesting," Headmistress Brennan said. "Well, one of the visitors did mention his cousin. Rocko, I believe. But, for the most part, yes, they were here to discuss the subject of building a casino on this property. However, I must ask you not to divulge this to anyone else. And, for heaven's sake, please caution J.J., um, your little bird, also. In all likelihood all this talk will come to very little, and we don't need to make people anxious unnecessarily. I plan to tell Mrs. Kling this evening, but I must insist that you tell no one else, am I clear?"

"Your secret is safe with us, Headmistress," Chris replied.

"Mum's the word," Sam agreed.

"And J.J.?" Headmistress Brennan asked.

"J.J. doesn't talk to too many people outside of the Home. You warn him and he'll be fine," Chris said.

"Good!" Headmistress Brennan said. "Thank you."

"What are you going to do?" Sam asked.

"Do? Do? I suppose I will do what I always do whenever I am faced with a big decision. I will consider the pros and cons, primarily the needs of the children."

"Do you really think there is a chance you would sell St. Michael's?" Chris said.

"I think there is almost no chance," she replied. "The whole idea that a major development in this location would somehow benefit the children strikes me as decidedly meretricious. This place, and the children who have come to us, are my life's work, my mission. This river, this view, this is my special place where I feel most at peace. If I moved away, I don't know what would happen. I am afraid of what might happen." Headmistress Brennan paused, and they listened to the river running below. "That's the music I fall asleep to every night," she continued. "And in the morning, the music of the river welcomes me and refreshes my soul for the day's challenges. It is almost as though here, in this place, we become refreshed, re-energized for the day, for the mission." After a few more minutes of silence, she concluded, "So, you see, given the choice, I think there is almost no chance I will sell."

They sat in silence and listened to the river for a few minutes more before she sighed, "But, I cannot lie. As much as I don't like to admit it, St. Michael's Home is a business and, as such, money is a factor. Therefore, I will pray that the choice remains mine to make."

CHAPTER 8

Mrs. Frieda Kling now drove Chris and Sam back home from St. Michael's. Chris and Sam lived on the same block; Mrs. Kling's house was one street over. She had placed both Chris and Sam with their adoptive parents years ago. She had a wonderful reputation for finding good homes for many of the children of St. Michael's over the years. Talk had turned to her enviable track record.

"You've been finding good homes for kids for years," Chris said to her. "What's your secret?"

"Secret? It's no secret. Like anything else, the path to success is paved with effort, determination, and a little luck. I get the word out about St. Michael's to just about anyone who will listen. Then I try to stay up to speed with the demand, with good couples and persons looking to adopt."

"But how do you know which kids to put with which adults?" Sam asked.

"Yes," Chris said. "You have a pretty high batting average."

"Pretty perfect!" Sam corrected. "The kids always know you will find the perfect home for them. You should bill yourself out as Yente the Matchmaker, like in Fiddler on the Roof."

"A perfect placement is fiction. There is no such thing," Frieda Kling said, shocking Chris. He had been looking out the window but turned now to look at her.

"What? What do you mean?"

"I mean what I said. There is no such thing as a perfect placement except, of course, by serendipity. I mean, of course wonderful placements happen every day. Your own placements are examples."

"Then why aren't they perfect?" Sam asked.

"Because the outcomes were not assured beforehand. Oh, maybe I am splitting hairs but, to me, a perfect placement not only resulted in a favorable outcome but did so without risk. That is, the desired outcome was a certainty or near-certainty. But, because there is risk in each and every placement, no matter how effectively we interview and vet the prospective new guardians and children, I maintain that no placement is perfect except, to varying degrees, by accident."

"Well forget placements, there are no perfect childbirths then, either," Chris said.

"Correct! Some of your friends don't get along with their natural parents and vice-versa. And there are a lot of broken homes in this country where parents have divorced, and one of the natural parents loses custody or visitation rights, or children have run away from their natural parents. Seems to me there's risk in pretty much all relationships so that none of them is perfect, really."

"Well, maybe they don't have to be perfect, just good enough, or wonderful enough," Sam said.

"I agree, Sam. The best we can do is the best we can do. No guarantees. Well, here we are," Mrs. Kling said as she parked the car in a spot in the street in front of her row house. As they were getting out of the car, her cellphone rang. "Oh, I need to return this call," she said. "Sam, would you and Chris be dears and walk my dogs, Abe and Gipper, for me, over to the playground? They've been cooped up in the house all day. It won't take very long."

"Sure, Mrs. Kling," Sam said, looking at Chris, who nodded. They each knew a walk to the playground and back with two dogs would take at least an hour. But, they would do anything for Mrs. Kling, who had already done so much for them.

"Okay, give me a minute and I'll put their leashes on them. Could you two wait out front here so they don't jump on you? I'm afraid they might get too excited in the house and have an accident on the carpet."

A few minutes later, Chris and Sam were walking Abe and Gipper, Frieda's two pit bulls, to a fenced-in city recreation center eight blocks away.

After having walked for a long while without saying anything, it appeared to Sam that Chris was deep in thought.

"What are you thinking, Chris?"

"That I prefer cats to dogs."

"Mr. Mink, your feral cat?"

"Yep. He's a lot less work."

"Um, okay, but that's not what you were thinking. We've been friends too long. You don't think about cats and dogs. Your mind was somewhere else."

"Yeah, I guess…"

"Well?"

"I was thinking about what Mrs. Kling was saying about no perfect placements. I never really thought about it before."

"What about it?"

"I think there ought to be a better way. Placements shouldn't be so risky, right? I mean, with the right data, we should be able to match the right kids to the right parents every time, with no risk."

"I don't know. You heard her, even natural parents and their kids aren't always good matches either."

"Yes, I know. That's true. But they don't get to pick and choose. Who knows what kind of personality or temperament a newborn will have? At least with older kids, orphans, we have some data. And, we have data on potential parents. Plus, adoptive parents are seeking children. They want children. Not all natural parents want children which, of course, is why there are so many orphans. I think there ought to be far less risk in matching orphans to the right parents."

"It sounds like you have something in mind."

"I do. I think I'll talk to Headmistress Brennan. Maybe I can build a computer program which will make better placements."

"That's a good idea. That might help her save some money and keep St. Michael's going so that she doesn't have to sell to the casino guys."

"I agree. That's what I'm thinking. Also, if I can really do it, maybe it will help Mrs. Kling not to worry so much about making mistakes placing children with the right parents."

"Then, once you're done with that, maybe you can invent something to keep dogs from peeing on carpets. That seems to worry her too."

Chris laughed. "Sam, come on, cut her a break. She has a nice house and wants to keep it that way. And she likes dogs. How bad can she be? Plus, that invention already exists."

"Really?"

"Yeah, tile floors."

PART THREE

"I had a good look at the first pitch I ever saw from Drysdale. If I had not ducked, it would have hit me right between the eyes."

- Whitey Ashburn, Hall of Fame Center Fielder with the Philadelphia Phillies

CHAPTER 9

Next Saturday morning, after helping J.J. with his paper deliveries again and preparing the field for the baseball game, Chris was back in the snack stand behind the backstop, watching James' Lawndale A's take pre-game warm-ups. He was programming the electronic scoreboard for the lineups he had just received from the home plate umpire when James ran up to the snack stand.

"Chris, we're going to need you to play second base for us today. Toby slammed his finger in the car door." James motioned at Toby who had his finger wrapped in a thick, gauze bandage. "Toby can announce the game. Come on, grab your gear and suit up. You can wear Toby's jersey. I'll hit you some grounders."

These were the times Chris loved, when he got to play. It happened only infrequently, maybe two or three games a season when Toby, the second baseman, couldn't play. Chris suffered no delusions of grandeur. He knew he was a serviceable sub, at best. The older guys were much better ballplayers, but he had proven himself to be better than nothing – admittedly a low bar. But, even the older guys enjoyed watching him bat, because it was obvious he could see the pitches so well. He rarely hit any, because his reactions were too slow, but he saw the pitches very, very well.

He would typically watch them all the way through his swing and into the catcher's mitt. It was actually pretty funny. James and Chris also knew that the other team would "tie themselves up in knots" trying to hit to Chris at second base and, because it was an unnatural thing for them to do, they would largely fail. Most of the time, the only balls hit at him would be weak pop-ups and slow grounders. He was rarely challenged to make a difficult defensive play in the field.

James had a secret, though. He did not tell Chris that the opposing pitcher was a serious fast ball pitcher. It wasn't a secret for long, however. As Chris sat in the dugout next to James on the bench, watching the opposing pitcher throw his pre-game warm-ups, it was obvious that hits would be few and far between today. "Um, did you forget to tell me something, James?" Chris asked.

"Would it have made a difference?"

"Probably not," Chris admitted. Still, he was glad that he was the ninth batter in the lineup. Since these games were only seven innings, he would have to face this pitcher, and no doubt embarrass himself, only twice. Chris didn't know that his older brother, in the interest of fairness and brotherhood, had already told the opposing pitcher to take it easy on his kid brother, "Our nine hitter's a late sub. The little white dude with the black gloves, red helmet and funky shades. Twelve years old. Can't run for nothin'."

When Chris entered the batter's box, in the bottom of the third inning, there were two outs and no baserunners. No hitter had yet reached base for either team. He could hear his brother rooting for him, and urging the rest of the team to cheer him on. But, as camaraderie went, the volume was a shade above a lonely cricket. The laughter, however, was clearly audible, from both dugouts. He tuned it out and focused on the pitcher and the baseball.

As the pitcher delivered the pitch, he could actually see the fingers on the ball. It was a 2-seam fastball. In an instant, however, the ball came right at his head. It was then that the freeze-frame phenomenon, which he first encountered Saturday in the half ball game, came back. The ball appeared stopped in mid-air, in front of his face. He leaned backward, turning his head to watch the ball race by his face and slam into the waiting catcher's mitt.

Both dugouts exploded in laughter and catcalls. They had not seen what he had seen. They only saw Chris, as calmly as you please, bend out of the way of, and then focus closely on, an intentional bean ball, without falling over or stumbling backward or otherwise reacting in the way any other human being on the planet would have done.

He also sensed something he could not rationalize. He felt certain that he could use this ability; take advantage of it. Something in his head felt warm. He took off his helmet and touched his head. He stepped back out of batter's box and looked down at the third base coach who was giving him the signal to hit away, as if he had a chance. But, he felt for the first time in his life that he did have a chance. Just then, in his line of sight beyond the third base coach, further down the third base foul line, he noticed Billy-The-Trash-Picker standing in the stands, leaning on his poker, and watching intently.

Chris replaced his helmet and called to the pitcher, "Yo, Shirley! You got a fastball in that spaghetti arm?"

James' team exploded in laughter. From behind his mask the catcher said to Chris, "Eat dirt, zipper head."

"Just what I was thinking," Chris replied, without looking back. He had an idea. If he was right, he would effectively win this game right now.

The pitcher, a typical hard-throwing, testosterone-flooded, teenage hothead, put everything he had into the next pitch, a fastball right down the heart of the plate. Chris saw the ball stop again in mid-flight right in front of the plate. He eyeballed a straight line from the ball to the pitcher's chin and swung the bat to send that ball right back at the pitcher. That's what happened. What everyone else saw was the fastest human swing in history drive that ball, at 100 miles per hour, right at the pitcher, a very good athlete, who caught the ball in his glove right in front of his face, before stumbling backward over the mound, twisting, and falling face-down in the dirt.

Chris stood in the batter's box. There were three outs and no baserunners. But, he had sent a clear signal to his teammates who would go on to win that game handily. He turned to the catcher and said, "Who's eating dirt now, zipper head?" and got a black eye for his trouble after his aviator shades were knocked off in the ensuing dugout-emptying brawl.

Later, when he retrieved his glove from the dugout, and went to his position at second base, James, the shortstop, looked over at him and smiled, proudly. "Mom's gonna kill me when she sees your shiner, little Bro." Then, after catching a practice ground ball and firing it over to first, James said, "But, you actually look better with a little black."

Chris smiled, then looked past James to the left field stands. Billy-The–Trash–Picker was no longer there. He had gone.

CHAPTER 10

The next morning was Sunday, which meant that the Philadelphia Inquirer was twice as large as normal. J.J. woke up sick and called Mrs. Covington to ask if Chris could deliver his papers.

Chris's mom was waiting for Chris in the kitchen as he came down the stairs. She had reluctantly agreed to let him substitute for J.J. This happened a half dozen times a year, usually when J.J. was either sick or recovering from a street brawl.

"Chris, here, I've made some hot shredded wheat for you. Sit. Eat." Aliondra stood at the counter with her mug of hot coffee while Chris ate. "J.J. said the driver would leave a customer list for you at Stan's Deli. The cat food's ready...on the counter here."

"Mom, James said I look better with a black eye. What do you think?" Chris asked, looking up at her as he spooned cereal into his mouth. Bad timing. Aliondra became near-apoplectic.

"I think he needs to have his head examined for letting you play with the bigger kids, that's what I think! I think I should get hazardous duty pay for putting up with you two conniving knuckleheads, that's what I think! I think you're lucky you didn't lose an eye. That's what I think! And I think I should have adopted girls, that's what I think!" she yelled.

Chris was stunned. The spoon hung from between his lips as he stared up at his mother with sleepy eyes. He rarely saw her so upset.

Aliondra's heart, try as she might to project disapprobation, went out to her son when she saw his badly bruised and swollen eye.

After an awkward moment of silence, she added more quietly, "Since you asked."

Chris chanced a smile at her and said, "My other eye is fine." It was an ill-advised gaffe.

"It might not be in a minute, young man!" She waved her finger in front of his face, vituperation resuming anew. "Don't you mess with me now. Sitting there smiling up at me like some gray-eyed twit You wear those glasses today. I don't need you advertising that eye like some badge of honor. You just finish up and get out of here so I can pray...pray that you don't get killed in another idiotic fight today. I don't need Child Services knocking on our door!"

Chris stood, placed the now-empty cereal bowl in the sink, and hugged his mom. "No worries, mom," he said, picking up the cat food bowl.

"Oh, I worry plenty, believe you me!" she said, as he opened the back door.

"Hey, Mister Mink," she heard him say as he stepped out onto the stoop. "Man, where do you find all these mice?" was the last thing Aliondra heard her son say before closing the door.

"God, please keep my son safe," was her prayer, as she began cleaning up. "My son that You sent to me, by the way," she looked up at the ceiling as she bent over to place the dishes in the dishwasher. She was not happy. Then, more gently, as she closed the dishwasher and stood back up, "Forgive me, Lord. If you could take care of him, and James it…and me, it would be a much-appreciated miracle. Please take care of my boys, Lord. I can only do so much. And, please forgive me for getting angry. Sometimes I…I think they need to see me angry. Amen."

Aliondra Covington then picked up her cup of coffee and sat down in one of the chairs at the kitchen table. She warmed her hands on her mug before placing it down on the table. Leaning forward, she placed her elbows on the table and held her head in her hands. "And please, if it is not too much to ask, please make Mr. Lewis stop."

It took Chris longer to finish the deliveries because the papers were so large, because he didn't know the paper route well and had to read the customer list as he rode his bike, and because Luigi, Ben, and Pop detained him when they saw his black eye. Everyone conversed in Italian, including Chris.

"You look like someone who could use your very first Luigi's Holy Cannoli, my friend," Luigi said, walking to the back of the bakery, returning with what looked like any of the other cannolis in the pastry display case.

"I don't have a hundred dollars, Luigi."

"Tut-tut, money. Please accept this as my gift to you. This is my way of helping you."

"Helping me?"

"Ah, yes," Ben said. "Luigi's Holy Cannolis are very, very lucky. If you eat it, today will be a lucky day for you." He continued to wipe down the tables.

"I guarantee it," Luigi stood tall and wiped his hands on his white apron.

Chris did not believe in luck, but with J.J. being sick, his mom angry, and himself tired, what could it hurt? It might help, and the cannoli did smell very good. "Thanks, Luigi," he said, taking the cannoli. He took a bite. "Hot dang, Luigi, that's really good! Thank you."

"Of course it is. Not to toot my own horn," Luigi replied.

Pop then sounded the bicycle horn on his walking stick loudly. HONK-HONK. "Don't mind if I do," Pop said. He and Luigi then high-fived each other half-heartedly, their hands not coming within two feet of each other, as they replayed their vaudeville routine for the several hundredth time.

Ben merely raised his arm halfway, never turning to face them, as he continued to wipe down the tables halfway across the store.

"Ora, che cosa volete?" Pop asked Chris. *Now, what do you wish?*

"Che cosa voglio?" Chris asked. *What do I wish?*

"Yes, you must make a wish," Luigi said, switching to English.

"Like at a birthday party?"

"Yes, something like that. Just make sure you don't tempt fate by wishing to live with two fools for the rest of your life like I must've wished once upon a drunken stupor," Luigi said, thumbing at Pop and Ben.

HONK-HONK. "Drunken stupors!" Pop, Ben, and Luigi shouted, in English, high-fiving one another in the same insincere way once again. Chris smiled. It never got old. These three old guys had been doing the same corny routine for years.

"What is it you want most?" Luigi asked again.

Chris knew what he hoped for. "I want to discover something important."

"Ah! You wish well. And so it shall be," Luigi assured him. "Now get out of here so I can take care of my paying customers," Luigi-the-grump had returned, apparently, and waved Chris away.

"Thanks, Luigi.See you, Ben. See you, Pop. Have a good day." Chris turned and ran out the door.

"And don't slam the door!" Luigi shouted after him, as the door slammed.

Chris honked his bicycle horn twice in salute as he rode off.

He finished delivering his papers around eight a.m. and rode over to the ball field. He hoped to experiment with the strange new attractive force he had sensed the day before. Sam had agreed to meet him there around 9:00, after she and her mom returned from church.

Chris wore his black leather gloves on each hand, as always, and his red Phillies cap. He raced on his bike down the steep cinder hill, standing on the pedals, shouting, "Warp factor ten, Mr. Scott!"

Dropping his bike at the gate behind first base, he pushed it open and stood there looking out over the field. It was a warm Spring morning. No one was around. The factory was closed on Sundays, and people in the apartments and houses were sleeping in. The crickets chirped and a few starlings dive bombed in the outfield. They chased one another up the steep slope beyond the outfield fence, above the oak trees at the top of the hill, up into the sky, and back.

"Cool," he murmured to himself, fascinated with the speed and coordinated grace of the tiny aviators. "Man, if I could run even half that fast…" He gazed in the direction of home plate as he replayed his favorite daydream.

He was in Citizens Bank Park, home of his beloved Philadelphia Phillies. It was a sellout crowd as he strolled from the on-deck circle to the batter's box, "Newman 1" emblazoned on the back of his Phillies team jersey. Whitey Ashburn and Harry Kalas were announcing the game, sitting in the broadcast booth on the third level of the stadium.

> Harry Kalas: Well, Whitey, it all comes down to Chris Newman. He's our last hope.

> Whitey Ashburn: Hate to admit it, Harry, but if there was ever a situation custom-made for a bunt, this is it.

> Harry Kalas: Only because of his world-class speed.

> Whitey Ashburn: Harry, did I ever tell you about the time Newman bunted a double?

> Harry Kalas: A hundred times. The kid has speed to burn, that's for sure.

> Crowd chanting: Newman! Newman! Newman!

Chris shook his head. He walked to home plate, looked up into the sky, and then down to the ground. He crouched like a catcher and picked up a handful of dirt, letting it sift through his fingers as the wind picked up slightly, carrying some of the dust away. Then, through his feet, he sensed the earth tremor again. He placed both palms down on the ground and felt the tremor again, briefly, then it was gone.

But, suddenly, he sensed something all around him, an aura encircling him. Looking around, he saw nothing, but he knew or sensed a presence, an omnipresent field or force or structure, infusing everything. "Weird," he said.

Then he stood and reached out his right arm. "What are you?" he asked softly. No answer. He closed his eyes and concentrated hard for many minutes, as if he were back in the clubroom practicing his telekinesis exercises. He stood there, at home plate all by himself for about ten minutes, eyes closed, both arms outstretched now, as dust devils wrapped around his feet. Why couldn't he feel what he knew must be there, everywhere, all around him? "Where are you?" he said softly.

"Here we are, stupid Head." Chris opened his eyes and spun around. It was Jack Helson and two members of his group. They had his bike. "Talking to yourself now, Head? It must get lonely for you, wandering around all by yourself inside that massive coconut, huh?" Helson's two buddies snickered derisively.

"That's my bike," Chris said, pointing at his bike.

"No, it's not. We found it over there on the ground, didn't we boys?" Helson asked.

"I need my bike," Chris said.

"This piece of crap?" Helson replied. "We were going to throw it on the train tracks and put it out of its misery."

Chris lunged for his bike but was pushed backward hard by one of Helson's friends. He lost his balance, tripped over his feet, and tumbled to the ground.

Helson and his friends laughed loudly. One of them walked over and grabbed Chris' Phillies cap off his head and put it on his own head. The brim of the cap came down over his eyes. He began to prance around with his arms outstretched, saying, "Where are you? Where are you?" The three creeps were laughing hysterically now. "Geez, Newman, it's like wearing a bag over my head. Anybody else wanna try?"

"Me, me," the other two shouted.

"Come on, hop in, there's plenty of room for everybody." More laughter.

Chris got up and dusted himself off.

"Alright, you toads," Helson shouted. "Calm down, calm down, we're not being very professional. Okay, Head, we have a proposal. A professional business deal. We'll give you the bike, but we need something back. That's the way deals work. You get something, we get something back."

Chris understood he was being taunted. "What?" he said.

"We'll give you the bike, but we want your gloves."

Chris, unflinching and knowing what was coming, said, "Okay, but I want my cap back too."

"Sure, sure," Helson replied. "It's not like we need that tent anyway. Go ahead, Zip," Helson addressed the one with the cap, "give it back." As Chris replaced the cap on his head with his gloved hands, Helson said, "Okay, Freak, let's have the gloves."

Chris held up his right hand and stretched out his fingers. He reached slowly with his left hand to take off the glove. "Come on, Head, move it. We don't have all day. Let's see what you're hiding..."

Helson never finished his sentence, as Sam jumped him from behind and clamped her arm tightly around his neck, dragging him down to the ground.

Sam maintained a firm hold with her arm

locked around Helson's neck as he struggled frantically to free himself. She knelt on the ground, and Helson sat on the ground in front of her, kicking at the dirt with his feet, trying to gain leverage. Chris moved to help her, but was pinioned from behind by the two larger bullies, one grabbing his right arm, the other his left, rendering him impotent. However, it was Helson who needed the help. His face was turning blue.

"Let him go!" Sam yelled at the two bullies holding Chris, "or I'll pop his head off."

The two bullies continued to restrain Chris and looked at each other quizzically. "Come on, Jack. Get up," one of them said. "It's a girl."

"You better tell 'em," Sam shouted into Helson's ear, her face pressed behind his head. "Tell 'em!"

"Let go," Helson gagged, barely audible. "Let...me...go!" he gasped, throwing a handful of dirt backward into Sam's face as he did so. Sam loosened her grip momentarily as dirt got into her eyes, nose, and mouth – enough for Helson to bite her forearm, hard. Sam screamed in pain, letting go of the much bigger Helson who jumped to his feet. He reached down, grabbed a fistful of her hair, and yanked her to her feet, so that her head was tilted backward.

"No!" Chris yelled, still struggling to free himself, as Sam screamed in pain yet again. The creeps tightened their hold on him.

"Calm down, Potato Head," Helson snarled at him, coughing and struggling to control Sam. "You ain't goin' nowhere."

"You bit me, you jerk," Sam cried. "I can't believe you bit me. I'm bleeding."

"Who'd o' thought Mrs. Potato Head would bleed, or would have real hair?" Helson laughed, yanking Sam's hair roughly.

"Knock it off, Helson," Chris screamed. "Leave her alone."

"Just defending myself, Head. Remember, she was going to pop my head off."

"Yeah, and you need these two idiots to help protect you from a twelve-year-old girl. Right, tough guy?" Chris mocked.

Helson approached him, Sam in tow, struggling like crazy, and raised his fist to Chris' face. "How'd you like a fat lip to go with your Mr. Potato Head-sized black eye?"

Chris knew that he and Sam were in a tough spot, being held against their will by three much larger teenagers, with no help in sight. He feared for Sam. He had to save her. What he needed now was a cool head and a strategy.

And, if they ever got out of this alive, he was

going to have a word or two for Luigi about his Holy Cannolis. Some luck they'd brought him – all of it was bad.

"Look, Helson, all you wanted was my gloves. I'll give you my gloves if you leave her alone."

"No, Chris, don't!" Sam shouted. "Ugh! Let me go, you creep," she shouted at Helson, continuing her struggle to get free.

Chris cringed, and wanted to tear Helson's head off, but knew he had to remain clear-headed now.

"Yeah, the gloves. I forgot about them," Helson said. "Hand them over."

"Let her go first and call off your friends here."

"How about we take your gloves, your bike, and a hunk of hair out of her head?"

Just then, Chris noticed a young couple jogging near the apartment buildings about three hundred feet away. Two small children pedaled their bikes along with them.

"I can see you're a feisty one, aren't you?" Helson said to Sam, who was now shoving at him. "Guess I'll have to knock it out of you," he said, raising his free hand.

"Not smart, Helson," Chris said. "There's a couple over there with their kids. The neighborhood is waking up. We're surrounded by houses and apartments here. There are probably a dozen people in those windows up there watching us right now. Witnesses." Seeing no one else around, Chris doubted his own words, yet he tried to sound convincing.

Apparently Helson wasn't buying it either. "Then I guess I'd better give 'em a good show," he said, slapping Sam hard in the face with his free hand. Chris saw Sam's head snap to the side, her eyes squeezed shut in anguish, tracks of tears running down her cheeks. Helson, laughing now, raised his arm to strike again, as Chris lost whatever bit of cool he had been able to muster.

Enraged, his eyes went wide, as a blinding, brilliant white light suddenly rushed at him, filling his vision. All sounds - Sam's screams, Helson's laughter, and his own scream - were drowned out by the deafening roar accompanying the light, as if a high speed train was coming directly at him. Terrified, Chris squeezed his eyes shut, sensing his own death.

The roar shot past him.

Then, no sound. Absolute silence.

When he opened his eyes, the world had stopped.

CHAPTER 11

Chris blinked his eyes, shifting his gaze rapidly from side to side and up and down, not daring to move his head. There had been no train. Nothing was destroyed. Nothing was changed. Everything was the same, and yet everything was different. Everything was where it should have been, but nothing was moving. It was as if he had somehow entered a 3-D photograph or painting. Helson's arm was still poised to strike Sam, but it wasn't moving, and Sam no longer struggled. Rather, she and Helson appeared to be statues frozen in place. Their eyes, fixed in position and wide open, didn't move or blink.

The joggers on the other side of the complex were frozen in mid-stride and their children were suspended upright on their two-wheeled bikes. Looking up, he saw the racing starlings frozen in flight, and the American flag no longer waved, although it remained extended out from the flagpole.

And the silence. The crickets no longer chirped. Traffic sounds, usually ever-present in a big city, had ceased. If he had entered a picture, it was a silent picture.

Looking at his sides, Chris saw that the two bullies who held him were also still, eyes open and unmoving, staring transfixed at Helson. Neither they, nor Helson, nor Sam appeared to be breathing.

Looking down, he noticed the dust devils around his feet were still there, but they no longer swirled. They were stationary, just above his sneakers.

"What the heck did you put in my cannoli, Luigi?" Chris asked, mesmerized.

Although he was somewhat fearful, he was more fascinated, similar to the feeling of riding a new roller coaster. He was clearly in uncharted territory: exactly where he had always wanted to be.

Not sure what's going on here, but I mean to find out. For the first time since he opened his eyes, he decided he should try to move something, so he slowly moved his head – first to the left, then to the right. Up, then down. When that didn't bring catastrophe, he was emboldened to move away from his captors. The one to the right had a grip on his upper right arm and shoulder. As Chris moved that shoulder, he noticed it slipped easily away from the attacker's hands. Looking over at his left shoulder, he achieved the same result as he pulled it away from the other thug. No longer restrained, he walked a few steps away from everybody before turning back and surveying the scene with cool detachment.

The two bullies who had been holding him remained still, bent at the waist, appearing suspended in the act of clutching at air and anchored against the efforts of a struggling captor no longer in their grasp. Chris had left the scene, but nothing else had changed. Realization dawning, he smiled and then started laughing. "Ha, ha, ha," he laughed out loud. "Hot dang! Hot double dang! I don't believe it. I don't *believe* it!" he screamed before spinning around on his heel, away from Sam and the others. He stretched his arms to the sky. "I did it! I did it! Didn't I? Is this what you are? Huh? Is...this... what...you...are?" he screamed.

"I did it. I found you! I discovered you! Dang right I did. Dang right!" he continued to shout. "I knew it. I knew you were here. I knew something was here. Right here. I knew it! Hot dang!" Then he spun and faced Sam, stooping low so his face was even with hers. "Wait 'til I tell you about this, Sam. Just you wait."

Suddenly, he took off running around the bases. "Who's slow now, huh? Who can't run now, huh? Speed to burn, baby! Speed to burn!" He threw both arms up above his head as he slid into home. "Safe!" he shouted. "Oh yeah, oh yeah. I was safe! Did you see me, Blue?" he shouted at a make-believe umpire. "No? Hah! Of course you didn't." Then, looking up to imaginary broadcasters Harry Kalas and Whitey Ashburn he called, "Tell 'em about that one, Harry! Tell 'em about the time you saw good ol' Chris Newman bunt a homerun, Whitey!"

He got up and resumed running down the first base line, circling the bases again and screaming, "Replay? You want a slow-motion instant replay, Blue? Forget it. It won't matter. Hah

hah!" Having rounded the bases a second time, he fell on his knees in front of Sam and hollered, "You hear me, Sam? I'm fast. I... am...*so fast!*" But Sam didn't respond, and Chris buried his face in his hands. "No, of course you don't." He looked up at Sam and said, "Well, we'll have to do something about that, won't we? Here, let me help you."

Chris went to pry Helson's fingers away from Sam, but pulled back. "Wait a minute, Newman. Don't mess this up. Think. Get it right," he said to himself. He wasn't sure what he should do, or what the results would be, but he was experiencing a powerful intuition. Something, some force, was helping him, guiding him. He didn't know if Sam could experience this, but he sure as heck did not want Helson to join in. If he had shortcomings, temerity wasn't one of them. He decided to avoid any contact with Helson. He would only contact Sam, to be on the safe side. "Please, Sam, please," he said. "Come with me. Please come with me." He reached out his hand and held Sam's chin in his hand. Immediately, her eyes blinked, and she looked at Chris.

And she let loose with a blood-curdling scream.

"Shhhhhh!" Chris covered her mouth with his hand. "Sam, calm down, calm down. It's okay. It's okay."

Sam stopped her scream but her eyes, wide

with terror, darted from Chris to the freeze-frame surroundings.

"Chris...what...what the heck is going on? What's happening?"

"I have an idea what's happening. Let me get you away from him first," Chris said, taking Sam by the elbow. As he did, Sam escaped Helson's grip as if he wasn't there.

Sam hugged Chris and started sobbing. "Oh, Chris thank you, thank you for saving me."

He hugged her back, awkwardly. He had never seen Sam cry, and never expected to be hugging her. Although she was his best friend, Sam had always been one of the guys. But, he figured, Sam might be holding *him* had he suffered the treatment she had received from Helson. "Sam, there's really no need to cry," he said, patting her on the back, trying to calm her. "Look," he said, taking her by the hand, trying to distract her. "Do you see what's going on?"

Sam's crying started to subside as she took a tentative step back from him, though she held tightly to his hand with both of hers. Raising her eyes, she began to look around slowly. "What's happening? Chris, what's happening to us? Are we de...dead?"

"Dead?" he laughed. "No, Sam. We are definitely not dead. In fact, we are about as alive as it is possible to be."

"Then…what's going on? Why is everything stopped? Why doesn't this feel like… like…life? Everything's…different."

"No, Sam, everything is the same. Only better. Look, Helson and his idiot friends are exactly where they were. The joggers up on the hill are still there, and their kids are still riding their bikes…"

"But they're not moving and not falling over," Sam interrupted, as she shifted her gaze to the starlings. "How can that be? How can birds be stopped in mid-air without falling down? And how does a waving flag not wave? And these morons," Sam said, pointing at Helson and the two thugs, "why are they frozen in place like that? How can you say everything's the same when nothing is the same? Oh Chris, nothing is moving. I'm so scared."

Chris, who had been looking around as Sam talked, now snapped his head around to face her. Her reaction touched him. No, not touched. More like stunned. Sudden realization hit him hard.

"Sam," he said. "I need to let go of you."

"No, Chris, don't let go, please," Sam pleaded. "Don't let go. Stay with me."

"I'm not going anywhere, Sam. I'll be right here with you. I promise. It's a little experiment, okay? Like in school. I'm going to let go for a second to see what happens."

"What do you think's gonna happen?" Sam asked.

"Look around," he smiled. "A whole lot of nothing's gonna happen, that's what. But, let's see, okay? Then I'll hold your hand again. I'll let go for one second, and then I'll hold your hand again."

"Promise?"

"Scouts honor."

"You were never a scout."

"You'll make a great lawyer someday."

Sam smiled feebly. "Okay, one second," she said. "But don't leave me here with these creeps, Chris."

Sam saw him smile, and she was reassured. And she would never forget what he said next.

"I will never leave you, Sam."

"Pinky swear?"

"Pinky swear," he smiled as he locked his two gloved outside thumbs with Sam's pinkies for only the thousandth time in their lives. He and Sam would be friends forever.

And in that regard, Sam knew Chris was right. Nothing had changed.

"Okay, on Kirk," he said.

"Bones, Spock, Kirk!" they shouted, and let go of each other's hands.

And Chris was not surprised. Sam was frozen again.

CHAPTER 12

Chris smiled and shook his head at Sam frozen in place in front of him. "Dude," he said softly.

Then he walked away from Sam and headed toward the pitcher's mound. He shouted back over his shoulder, "Don't worry, Sam. I know I promised to let go for just one second..." His voice trailed off as he approached the mound. He walked up and stood where he normally positioned the pitching rubber. Then he crouched low, picked up some dirt in one hand, and let it sift through his gloved fingers. "...and, unless I miss my guess," he said to himself now, "I won't take that long."

Sam's panic had switched a light bulb on in Chris' mind, because it was so unexpected. So different from what he had come to expect. Sam had never been afraid before, he was certain. She had always been the strong one, the fast one, the athlete, the competitor, the winner. In one regard, Chris had to admit that Sam had been right. Everything had changed. *For him.*

Back there, back in the world where he had spent his whole life, he was the odd one. Or, as some often said, the gifted one. He was different from everyone else, for sure. He certainly had both his physical challenges and his mental gifts. Back in that world, Sam and James were fast. They were the athletes. They were in charge. Back in that world, Chris, with his genius IQ, always received 'A' grades, would be in graduate school had his mom not insisted he stay at age level, and was a concert pianist and violinist by the age of 10. But, he could not do something as simple as think a piece of paper to move because, as James said, it wasn't allowed by the rules.

Here, however, things were different, like a freshly-lined quiescent ballfield awaiting its animated competitors. The only world he had ever known, the "normal" world, seemed somehow…inchoate, at least for him. In this new stilled world, however, he was no longer slow, no longer clumsy, no longer limited. He was super-fast. And, apparently, he called the shots. After all, no one could move as he did. But, he began to understand, it was really one world, the same world, not two separate worlds. He couldn't really run any faster. It's just that he was now connected, mentally, to some force which permitted him to move, apparently, at the speed of light. Everybody and everything else still moved but, relative to Chris, they moved so slowly that they seemed to be stopped.

"Get over yourself, Newman," he said. "Same world…same Newman… but… but… what?" he asked himself, searching the sky. "You go everywhere, don't you? Everywhere. I see that now. No, not see exactly. Sense. Yes, that's it. I can't see you. I…feel you, because I am…connected to you somehow, aren't I? Connected…mentally, right? Yes, that must be it. A big brain is the minimum requirement. That's why no one else can do it."

Satisfied with this line of thought, Chris left the mound and walked over to where he and Sam had left their bikes outside the fence. He wheeled Sam's bike over to where she was standing still, and stood it about fifteen feet behind her. Then he did the same with his bike. Now it was time. He walked back over and took Sam's hand. Immediately, she became animated.

"Whoa, what the heck just happened?" she said.

"What do you mean?"

"You just…I don't know, blipped or something."

"Blipped?" Chris asked.

"Yeah, like on TV when they use trick photography to make someone disappear and reappear and they don't reappear in exactly the same place or exactly the same pose. It's so noticeable. They blip."

"Is that what I did?" he asked. "Did I blip?"

"Uh, HUL-LO," Sam mocked. "Yes, you did. And how come you didn't let go on Kirk?" Sam asked, raising up her hand which he held.

Chris understood that Sam didn't realize he had let go of her hand at all - not for five minutes or even for one second. "I'll tell you later. Maybe we should get going," he said turning to face the bikes behind them.

Sam turned with him, then gasped and clung to him in shock, pointing at the bikes.

"Chris, the bikes. They, they.... moved!"

Chris started laughing. He couldn't help it. "Oh, I must've forgotten to tell you, before I reappeared I moved the bikes over here."

She backed away from him slowly, still holding his hand in one of hers, and then punched him playfully with her free hand. "What? What? Tell me what happened. What happened, Chris? You'd better tell me before I completely pop a gasket. What the heck just happened...with the bikes, the blipping...." She saw him smile. "OH MY GOD! You did blip. You blipped, didn't you? You... you... you blippin' blipper!"

"Sam, really. Such language. It's so unbecoming for a young lady of such high social standing."

"Yeah, well, I'm likely to become seriously unsociable, mister, if you don't tell me right now," she said, raising her index finger and pointing it at his nose.

Chris smiled and said, "Okay, I'll tell you about it, but let's get away from these guys first." He wanted them to be well out of the reach of the gang, and he didn't dare let go of Sam. Still holding hands, they struggled to walk their two bikes across the field and outside the gate.

As they propped up their bikes, Chris said, "Okay, here's what happened. I did let go of your hand. You became disconnected from this...this...force," he began, waving his free arm in the air. "As soon as you disconnected from the force, you stopped moving – or, at least to me you looked like you had stopped moving. But, it wasn't that you had stopped moving, it's just that I was moving at the speed of light, as we are now, and you couldn't see me moving."

"Chris, we are not moving at the speed of light," Sam objected.

"Yes, Sam, we are. Look, I know it doesn't seem like we are, to us, but we really are. Velocity is relative."

"What?"

"Velocity is relative. To you, I don't seem to be moving at the speed of light, but that's because you're moving at the speed of light too, right along with me. But to Helson and everyone else who's not moving at the speed of light, we're moving so fast they can't even see us."

"And to us they seem to be stopped?"

"Right, because they're moving at regular speed. But regular speed is so slow to you and me, everybody else appears to be stopped."

"How...?" Sam began.

"I am connected to the force."

"Connected? How?"

"Mentally. It's a mental connection. And as long as you hold my hand, you can stay connected to the force with me."

"Can you disconnect from it?

"Yes, anytime I want. And I can connect to it anytime I want. When I disconnect, we'll be moving at the same speed as everybody else, but everybody else will become 'unfrozen.'"

"So, when you 'blipped' to me, what was that all about?" Sam asked.

"Okay, on the count of 'Kirk' I did let go of your hand. Then I walked over to the pitcher's mound to think all this through. It took me about five minutes, but you never even saw me go because I was moving too fast. In fact, a few minutes ago I ran around the bases like a wild man but you didn't see me then either because I was moving at the speed of light."

"Then I left the pitcher's mound and got our bikes before holding your hand again. I guess I appeared to 'blip' to you because I wasn't in the exact same position when I came back as I was when I let go of your hand. You saw me in one place before we said 'Kirk' and in a slightly different position right after we said it. That's why I seemed to blip."

"Cool beans," Sam replied, eyes wide.

"Okay, watch now, Sam. Watch Helson and his buddies when I disconnect." Then he disconnected from the mental force. Immediately, all action resumed. The joggers continued to jog. Their children rode their bikes. And the birds resumed their flight. The flag waved in the breeze. The crickets chirped. And the traffic sounds resumed.

And, Helson swung at Sam, who was no longer in his grasp. Helson flung at nothing but air. His momentum caused him to twist around and fall down hard on his right shoulder, which separated from its socket, as the two other creeps, also no longer holding Chris, lost their balance and fell on top of him. Helson howled in pain.

Sam and Chris mounted their bikes. "Ooh, that looks really painful," Sam said, smiling, her schadenfreude evident. "Payback's a bear."

"So does that," Chris replied, pointing to the bite mark on Sam's arm. "We'd better get you back home and get that cleaned up before you get rabies or something. Plus, we have a lot of work to do. I'll tell you all about it on the way. But not a word to anyone. We have to figure out a lot of stuff. This is the hugest of the huge. Mega pinky swear. Mega, Sam! We have to keep this to ourselves for now."

Chris locked both of his gloved outside thumbs with Sam's two pinky fingers. As they mega pinky swore, he knew his secret was safe with Sam.

He also knew Luigi's $100 Holy Cannolis were way, way, way underpriced.

CHAPTER 13

"Go ahead, run!" Helson screamed at Chris and Sam as they rode their bikes away from the field up Hasbrook Avenue Hill. "You're dead, Head! Dead, next time I catch you. You and your little girlfriend!"

"Owwww!" Helson screamed again. His hand, which he had used to prop himself up from the ground, accidently slipped on the wet grass causing his dislocated shoulder to send bolts of pain like shards of glass through his chest and side. He immediately fell back down to the ground, stifling a scream through clenched teeth.

"What the heck happened?" Zip asked. "How did they get away? We just had them, and…and then we didn't. Poof! They're gone, just like that?"

"Shut up, Zip. Just shut up, will you? Help me up. Owwwww! Don't pull my arm you morons!" Helson screamed as his two accomplices grabbed his hands. "Grab me under my arms. And be careful. My shoulder's out."

Zip and Troll, the other member of the threesome, helped Helson to his feet. They walked Helson over to the first base dugout where they descended the steps and sat on the bench. "What do we do now?" Zip asked, once Helson was sitting.

"I don't know. Give me a minute to think,"

Helson said, grimacing. He slumped over, holding his shoulder, and rocked slightly. "How did they get away? There's something about that Newman kid. That's all I know. And I'm gonna find out what it is."

"Yeah, well, we'll help you, won't we Troll?" Zip said.

"Dunno," Troll replied. "Never saw anyone move that fast. It's like voodoo or something."

"Stupid Troll," Zip said. "Ain't no voodoo. Even a common, low-grade dunderhead like you gotta know that."

"Yeah, then what happened?" Troll challenged. "How'd they get from us holding them to, poof, sittin' as pretty as you please on their bikes just like that? Like we weren't holdin' 'em at all? Huh? If that ain't voodoo, tell me what is."

"Everything alright in here?" Billy-the-Trash Picker stood atop the steps leading down to the dugout. "You boys okay?"

"Yeah, everything's cool," Helson replied. "Go pick some trash or something. Leave us alone."

"Looks like there's plenty of trash in here," Billy replied, starting slowly down the steps.

"Hey, what's that supposed to mean, old man?" Zip asked.

Billy picked up a piece of paper from the floor of the dugout with his poker and held it up for Zip to see. "Just means I know where to find trash," Billy replied.

Zip and Troll both stood and advanced toward Billy, blocking his entrance. "Looks like you need an attitude adjustment," Troll said, smacking his fist into his hand.

"And we're just the ones who can help you with that," Zip joined in.

"Oh my attitude is fine," Billy responded. "In fact, it's exemplary." He raised his right hand as Zip swung at him with his fist. Zip's arm halted suddenly, inches before his fist reached Billy's face, although Billy hadn't touched him.

Billy leaned his poker against the dugout fence and raised his other hand, lifting Zip and Troll a few inches off the ground without touching them. He held them there for a second before transporting them further back down the dugout, still airborne. "I can see you boys don't learn very quickly, so let me see if I can help you," he said, lowering his arms suddenly, dropping Zip and Troll with a thud onto the bench next to Helson.

"What the..." Helson started.

"Not now," Billy interrupted. "You just sit there, shut your mouths, and listen. I assure you everything will be fine – much finer than you deserve. It's just that rules are rules, and I am the enforcer. Do I make myself quite clear?"

They glared at him sullenly saying nothing. Billy started waving the fingers on one hand up and down, and their heads started softly, but repeatedly hitting the cinderblock dugout wall behind them. "Let me know when I am clear," Billy said.

"Okay, okay, clear, clear," they all yelled.

Billy stopped moving his fingers and their heads stopped hitting the wall. "Very well then. We progress. Good. This won't take long at all."

"My real name is Fixer. My name is Fixer because I fix things, like separated shoulders and such," Fixer said, waving his arm at Helson, whose shoulder healed immediately.

"Oh, wow!" Helson said. "It's fixed. My shoulder is fixed! It doesn't hurt anymore!"

"You're welcome," Fixer said. "Now, please refrain from interrupting me again. My first name is Amnesius, because I help people forget things. And, although, you are only marginally and minimally human, my jurisdiction also extends to you."

"I think that was an insult," Troll said to Helson and Zip.

"Insulting or true?" Fixer asked him.

"Um...," Troll hesitated, looking to his

friends for help.

"Oh, come, come now, Mr. Troll. It's not a difficult question. Speak up. For once in your short, misguided, poor excuse for a life, take a stand, son. I ask you again, since I'm quite sure you have already forgotten the question, is it insulting or true to say you are all only marginally and minimally human?

"Um...," Troll hesitated again, as both Helson and Zip looked down. "Both?" he asked tentatively.

"Very good, Mr. Troll. There is hope for you after all."

Troll sat up straighter and smiled.

Fixer closed his eyes and shook his head ever so slightly before continuing.

"Yes, anyway, as I was saying, you three appear quite intent on harming Chris Newman. You have no idea how catastrophic that would be for the planet. For that reason, I cannot permit it. And you, Helson, you bit a twelve-year-old girl on her arm. That must never be repeated. In fact, I hereby ordain that you three will henceforth have absolutely nothing to do with Chris Newman and Samantha Banks. Do I make myself clear?"

"Um, what's ordain?" Troll asked.

"Yeah, what's henceforth?" Zip joined in.

"You idiots, he's saying we have to leave them alone," Helson said.

"Oh, and you will leave them alone," Fixer continued. "Make no mistake about that. Their demise will doom the world. Therefore, you will have no choice in the matter. In fact, when I leave here, you will remember nothing of what happened on this field or in here this morning, and you will never again take an interest, or have any interaction with, Chris Newman or Samantha Banks. Do I make myself clear?"

"Um, what's a demise again?" Zip asked.

"Oh, for crying out loud, will you shut up?" Helson shouted.

"Mr. Helson, why you have chosen to waste your life is beyond me, yet I see it time and again with so many young people, I am sad to report. I've seen so many young lives wasted. So unfortunate..." Fixer stared out over the ball field, remembering.

"This guy's Looney Tunes," Helson mumbled, and Fixer resumed.

"Looney Tunes you say? No, Mr. Helson. It's all too true, I'm afraid. No matter. I have wasted enough time on you and your acolytes. I must go. But before I leave I also ordain that you never again refer to Chris Newman's head. You, of all people, who have decided to misuse the minimal smattering of gray matter you have managed to cultivate, should never insult one whose abilities and efforts, even in a short span of twelve years, will outshine yours, should you live ten millennia. Therefore, if you recidivists ever again even think of referring to Chris Newman in a derogatory way, rest assured you will experience severe migraine-like pain which will only subside when you quit such thinking."

Fixer raised his fist. "So I ordain. So it shall be!" he commanded, as a large gust of wind suddenly blew through the dugout.

"This guy's Batso, but he does put on a good show," Helson said.

Fixer connected then. Helson, Zip, and Troll froze. Fixer touched each of them briefly on their heads and altered their memories. As he turned on his heel, he retrieved his poker and ascended the dugout steps, Fixer said, "Let's take it from the top boys. Let's see what you've forgotten, shall we? Try to get it right." Once outside the dugout he turned, stood atop the dugout steps, and disconnected.

"Everything alright in here? You boys okay?"

"Yeah, everything's cool," Helson replied. "Go pick some trash or something. Leave us alone."

"Looks like there's plenty of trash in here," Fixer replied, starting slowly down the steps.

"Hey, what's that supposed to mean, old

man?" Zip asked.

Fixer picked up a piece of paper from the floor of the dugout with his poker and held it up for Zip to see. "It means I know where to find trash," Fixer replied.

Zip and Troll both stood and advanced toward Fixer, blocking his entrance. "Looks like you need…uh…uh," Troll stuttered.

"What? What is it I need?" Fixer asked.

"Um, some help I guess," Troll responded, as he, Zip, and Helson got busy picking up trash all over the dugout and putting it into Fixer's bag.

"Thank you," Fixer said. "By the way, what are you boys doing here on a fine Sunday morning?"

The boys all looked at one another. "Um, that's actually a pretty good question. What are we doing here?" Helson asked.

"Um…um…dunno,   actually,"   Zip stammered.

"No clue," Troll chimed in.

"Well, thanks for the help and all, but maybe you boys oughta mosey on home, huh? What do you think?" Fixer asked.

"Yeah…yeah… I guess," Helson said, clearly confused. "Why are we here, anyway?' he asked again, as the three dazed boys walked up the dugout steps.

"Um, boys," Fixer called to them once they'd left the dugout. "I saw Chris Newman and Samantha Banks headed home on their bikes. Did you happen to run into them here this morning?"

"You mean Hea… oww!" Helson began, suddenly touching his head. "You mean Hea…oww!" he shouted again.

"I mean Christopher Newman and Samantha Banks," Fixer said.

"Nope, didn't see 'em," Zip replied. "You okay, Jack?" he asked as the three of them departed, leaving Fixer sitting in the dugout by himself.

"Nice job, Fixer," thought-transmitted Senior Senator Geemez from Maran, the distant planet Fixer called home. "They remember nothing of recent events at the field or their involvement with Christopher."

"Thanks," Fixer responded. "Easy assignment, though. Earthlings generally do not present much of a challenge, but these three were especially vacuous."

"Makes you question why we do what we do, doesn't it?" Geemez asked.

"No. Never," Fixer replied. "We must do what we can."

"Did you really need to knock their heads against the wall like that?" Geemez asked.

"You're such an old nit-picker," Fixer replied, cloaking his thought.

"Fixer, please stop cloaking your responses. You know I can't hear them."

Still cloaking, Fixer replied, "that's the idea." Then, so Geemez could hear him, he said, "I was very gentle. I didn't hurt them at all."

After a pause, Geemez added ominously, "The girl knows."

"Yes, she does," Fixer acknowledged.

"That situation must not persist," Geemez warned. "She cannot know."

"That's not exactly a news flash."

"Then you must relieve her of the knowledge."

"I will get to it."

"Do it soon," Geemez ordered. "Time grows short."

Standing outside the dugout now, with the sun shining on his face, Fixer said, "The Earth sun feels so wonderful, and the crickets...I'd forgotten how sweet they sound. The blue sky, and morning dew. Do you remember morning dew?"

"We remember everything," Geemez replied.

"I hope the boy survives this beautiful, dangerous place," Fixer said, looking at the puffy white clouds. "I surely do."

"He must, Fixer. God help them all if he doesn't."

CHAPTER 14

Chris's mom had returned home from working yet another Sunday morning. She was exhausted from a long week at work with her boss, Mr. Lewis. She was hoping to ask Chris to play the piano for her, as that had always been the anodyne for her tension. She called upstairs but Chris wasn't in the house. Retrieving a bottle of water from the refrigerator, she heard a basketball bouncing outside the open kitchen window. Looking outside, she saw James shooting hoops with three of the "B-balls."

"James, have you seen Chris lately?" she called out the window.

"Yeah, Mom. He and Sam came tearing in here on their bikes about five minutes ago. They ran up to the clubhouse. They were pretty excited."

"What was it all about, did they say?"

"No, but I'm guessing he made some major scientific breakthrough or something. He probably discovered he could think a dust ball across the floor when he opens a window and lets air into the clubhouse."

High-fives all around among James and his friends.

"Very funny," Aliondra said. "He's your only brother, James."

"Promise?"

Aliondra smiled as she turned from the window. James' dust ball comment was pretty funny, actually. She grabbed the mail one of her sons had put on the counter and her water bottle, and walked through the house to the living room. Plopping down on the sofa, she looked at the piano across from her. She would read the mail and her dog-eared thriller on the end table while she waited for Chris to come in. Aliondra Covington was a patient woman and Chris' music, she well knew, was worth the wait.

Sam and Chris had ridden their bikes from the ballfield to Sam's house to clean and bandage her arm. They were up in the clubhouse above the detached garage across the common driveway running behind the Covington house and the other houses on the block. The clubhouse had a space heater, an area rug, two old overstuffed chairs, a desk, an old wooden kitchen table and chairs, and a blackboard. Chris sat at the table while Sam stood, pacing and interrogating. She wanted to know all the details.

"So why did everything stop? Did you notice anything moving at all? How were you able to move the bikes so fast? You must've moved them in an instant. Did time stop, or you were in a different dimension? How did you 'get in'? Is there some kind of portal or something? How come…?"

"Whoa, slow down, girl," he had to stop her. "You're like a runaway train. Which question should I answer first?"

"How do you do it?"

"It is definitely a mental connection."

"Is it difficult?"

"The first time was. The second time was easier."

"Why?"

"Because I knew how to do it. What to concentrate on. It's like anything, I guess. Once you do something once, and learn how to do it, doing it again becomes easier."

"Can you only enter from the ball field?"

"No. I believe I can connect from anywhere. There is no door, no portal. There is nothing to enter. You don't enter, you connect, and since it appears to be everywhere, I should be able to connect from everywhere."

"If it is everywhere, why can't we see it?"

"It doesn't reflect light. Light passes through it, like it passes through air. That's why we can't see air."

"What is 'it' exactly? You keep saying 'it.' Is

it a thing?"

"Yes, it definitely exists and is inanimate. I believe it is a structured thing like a support or pathway or force field."

"So, could it be an alternate state, something outside our universe?

"It is definitely inside our universe, with us."

"If it's a natural phenomenon, part of our universe, part of the structure of our universe, then why are you the first one to discover it? Why have millions of years gone by for mankind, but you're the first one?"

"I'm not so sure I am the first."

"You think others have experienced it?"

"I don't know."

Sam continued. "If this thing, whatever it is, exists and is a structure or force field of some kind, though invisible and immovable, why don't we bump into it all over the place or somehow experience it? How do we pass right through it without sensing it at all? Can you explain that?"

"No, Sam, I can't. I also can't explain gravity to you, though everyone knows gravity exists. You certainly can't see it but, without using extremely powerful rockets, you can't get away from it either. Plus, if you think about gravity, it's an invisible field. After all, the earth spins on its axis at about one thousand miles per hour but nothing falls off the earth. Why? Because some invisible force we call gravity holds everything down."

"Since we can't see space," he continued. "maybe space is a fabric to which everything is connected, except the fabric is more like Swiss cheese with holes, or like an English muffin with nooks and crannies. Maybe I connected to the fabric of space or passed through a hole or tunnel in the fabric, or discovered a cosmic cranny."

Sam was quiet for a while, as she processed all this information. Finally, she continued. "Chris, all these questions about what it is, and why it is, are all very important and all, but we better figure out how to use it."

"What do you mean?"

"I mean, besides moving bikes around and scaring me, how do you plan to use your new ability?"

"Sam, look, I just discovered it. If I did connect to the fabric of space and this allows me to move quickly and undetected within our world, then it won't take too long for us to figure out a million ways to use it. And not just for us but for many people, maybe even for the good of the world."

"Can you teach me?"

"I don't know. There really isn't much to teach. It's a mental connection."

"Yeah, but you have a super brain. What's easy for you might be impossible for the rest of us. We should continue to connect together."

"Okay, well then, let's give it another shot. Here, hold my hand," Chris said.

They both stood and he held one of her hands in his. Then he concentrated and connected almost immediately. He turned to Sam. "Sam? You too?"

"Me too what?" Sam had connected too, but she didn't know it yet.

"We're connected, Sam. You too, with me."

"We are? Are you sure?"

"Yes I'm sure. Come on. The window." They walked to the window, still holding hands. Outside, everything had stopped.

Sam gasped. "Geez oh wiz. Chris, look! Nothing is moving, just like before! The laundry on the line. The cars in the street. Mrs. Glassman next door. James and the B-balls. The basketball in midair. Even the bird flying across the yard. Unbelievable."

"Sam, last time, when I let go of your hand, you disconnected, but I remained connected. Let's try it again now. I'll let go. If you disconnect, I'll disconnect after you do, okay?"

"Sounds like a plan to me. Later, gator," Sam said.

He let go of Sam's hand. She became disconnected immediately. Then Chris disconnected too.

"Okay, Sam, that's exactly what happened. When I let go of your hand, you disconnected. So, we'll have to figure out some way where we can connect together." No response. Sam wasn't moving. "Sam? Sam!" he shouted.

He was getting worried now and started moving around quickly, nervously. "Sam? Sam?" he shouted directly into her face, but she continued to stare straight ahead, stoic, lifeless. "Oh man, what the heck am I going to do now?" His mind was racing.

"Don't shout at me. I'm standing right here," Sam smiled.

"Sam, what the..." she was smiling broadly now, pointing at him as if to say "gotcha."

"Don't do that, Sam. You scared the heck out of me. I thought something was terribly wrong."

"You were scared?"

"Yes, I told you I was scared."

"Good. It serves you right for scaring me by moving the bikes. Now we're even," she said.

He glowered at her.

"Mr. Brainy meet Miss Kick Your Butt," she said, as she walked past him and down the garage steps.

"And since when have you ever settled for being even?" he asked.

She paused at the bottom of the steps with her hand on the doorknob, turned and said, "Don't forget to shut the light off." She went outside, and the door closed behind her.

"I shouldn't have moved the bikes," Chris said to himself, smiling, as he shut off the light and started down the steps.

As he exited the clubhouse to cross the rear alleyway to his house, James and the B-balls were already well into their choose-up basketball game.

"Hey, Einstein. Figure out when that asteroid's gonna hit yet?" James asked as he lined up his next foul shot.

"Yeah, next Tuesday, but it won't do any damage, so don't worry about it," Chris replied.

"No damage, huh? Where's it gonna land?"

"On your head. Like I said, no damage,"

Chris said as he strolled to the clubhouse.

Lots of laughter after that one. Even the B-balls appreciated a well-placed zinger.

"Very funny, wise guy," James said, as he now cradled the basketball in his arms.

"So what are you doing with all those equations all over the blackboard? I figured you must have discovered something by now," James taunted.

Chris stopped and turned around. "Actually, we had a big breakthrough yesterday. It's pretty exciting. We finally discovered telekinesis."

"Yeah, right."

"Really. All we had to do was open the windows in the clubhouse and we were able to think dust balls across the floor."

As Chris turned and walked away, James and the B-balls were stunned.

"Hey, James, did he really hear you say that?" asked B-ball #1.

"How could he? He was up in the clubhouse," said B-ball #2.

"No way he heard you, man. No way. What's he got, like super-sensitive hearing or something?" asked B-ball #3.

James watched his little brother as he stooped to pet Mink and then enter the house as the door closed behind him. "Sometimes I wonder," James said. "Sometimes I wonder."

PART FOUR

"Eliminate all other factors, and the one which remains must be the truth."
  Arthur Conan Doyle, "Sherlock Holmes"

CHAPTER 15

Chris had never before been inside the Headmistress' office. He had biked the four miles or so from home after school. Mrs. Brennan had invited him to come and take a look at the Home's placements records after he had broached the idea to her, by phone, a month earlier. He had suggested that he might be able to find some way to help her improve placements or to discover a less-risky way of matching orphans to the most appropriate guardians.

It was the idea that first came to him when he and Sam had walked Frieda Kling's dogs. He wasn't sure that he could succeed, because he had absolutely no business experience. But, he knew he was gifted in many ways and if he could find a way to help the Home, then he felt obligated to try.

His mother had agreed to approach Mrs. Brennan with the idea. Mrs. Brennan had politely declined, saying Mrs. Kling was excellent at placing the children, had been for many years, and she did not really see how there could conceivably be a better way. She thanked Chris and his mom for their concern and for thinking of the Home, but had nonetheless refused the offer of help. She had, however, offered up the possibility that things could change and that she might, someday, take them up on their offer.

That someday had arrived. Headmistress Brennan had called to invite him to take a look at her placement processes and procedures to see if something could be done to improve them. He sat before her now in her office, as she explained.

"Chris, first I want to thank you for taking the time to come here today and meet with me. I know I told you and your mother that our placements are fine. Well, I still believe that. Nothing has changed. But after a few weeks I thought maybe that's the problem. Maybe we could use some change around here. Not that I have any reason to be concerned with the quality of our placements. I'm not. I trust Mrs. Kling implicitly. In fact, if she knew what I was asking you to do I suspect she would be hurt, and quite upset. I don't think she would understand."

"Understand what?"

"The need for change, for inspection. The more I thought about it, the more I came to understand that I should not be turning away help, especially from someone like you who is gifted in so many ways. I guess I will have to run the risk of ruffling a few feathers. I love Mrs. Kling. And I have for many years. She is a great asset to St. Michael's and I do not want to upset her. Still, I have been asked to manage St. Michael's to the best of my abilities. Therefore, I think a periodic review of how we do things around here is prudent.

Just because we have been doing things the same way for a long time doesn't mean that there isn't a better way. Especially today, in the age of computers. So, I thought it would be best if you could take a look at things. I thought, as you suggested, maybe we should start with placements and see how that goes. If you can find a better way, perhaps I will let you look at other areas. Heaven knows, I could use the help. It seems if I cannot find a better way to operate, then St. Michael's may not be around for the long haul."

"So, there you have it. If you can help me, that would be great. I only ask that we keep this between ourselves, because I really don't want to offend Mrs. Kling. If we find a better way to place the children, then I will ask her to do so. I don't want to run the risk of offending her and losing her between now and then, okay?"

"Sure."

"So we can keep this between you and me for now?"

"No problem, except…"

"Except?"

"Except, if Mrs. Kling or J.J. see me here. They'll want to know what's going on."

"Perhaps you can ask J.J. to keep a confidence?"

"Yes. Yes, I will. He's cool. He'll be fine."

"Well, I hope so. As I say, I prefer Mrs. Kling not know of this, but if word gets back to her, I will deal with it at that time."

"Now, before we get started, I want you to understand that, by law, you must be paid as a consultant, and all the work you do must be held in strictest confidence. Your mother has signed the agreement as your guardian, and you should sign it also."

She slid the one-page contract across her desk to him. He read it and signed it.

"Good." Mrs. Brennan said. "So, let's get started. Have you ever worked with computers before?"

"Well, I have one at home. I'm pretty good, I guess."

"Good. Good. Have you ever worked with spreadsheets before? Do you know how to work Excel?"

"No, but from what I have heard, I think I could teach myself Excel pretty quickly."

"Hm-mm," Maxine said. "Well, maybe when you figure it out you can teach me. I've been working with it for years and I'm still not very good at it."

Chris did teach himself quickly, devoting two hours an afternoon, twice a week, to examining the placement procedures, files, and records. He never did bump into Frieda Kling while he worked in the office. Headmistress Brennan told him that Mrs. Kling usually came in the morning and left by lunch time to meet with supporters at their places of business. Other days, she escorted newly adopted children to their new parents, if they lived locally, or to the airport, if the adoptive parents were coming from a distance. New parents picking up their charges at the Home usually did so in the morning. Bumping into Frieda Kling in the afternoon was unlikely.

J.J. was another story.

"Doc!" J.J. called as Chris got off his bike and laid it by the front door one day. Chris turned to see J.J. walking toward him. "What you flippin' doing here, Doc?"

"Hi, J.J. I'm here to see Headmistress Brennan."

"Why?"

"She asked me to take a look at her computer system."

"What do you know about flippin' computers?"

"Good question."

"How much she paying you?"

"Not much. I'm supporting the mission."

"Flippin' mission. The heck with that. You need to get a flippin' paper route. I made ninety bucks last week."

"Nice."

"Flippin' ay it's nice. What's wrong with her flippin' computer?"

"Well, it's kind of old. I think it needs to be upgraded."

"I coulda flippin' told her that. I wouldn't o' charged her nuthin' either."

"I'll let her know."

"Don't do me no flippin' favors. Knock yourself out," he said, waving Chris off. "Gotta get my flippin' homework done. I'm workin' the flippin' kitchen tonight. Catch you Saturday."

"Hey, J.J.," Chris called, running after him.

"What?" J.J. turned to face him.

"Think you could forget that you saw me here today?"

"How come?"

"It's kind of a secret."

"From who?"

"From Mrs. Kling. From anybody. I'm asking you as a favor."

"What's it flippin' worth to ya?" J.J. asked, ever the businessman.

"Dinner Saturday."

"Nah. That's your mom. I'll flippin' get that anyway."

Chris stared at his friend. "Oh, come on, J.J. I don't ask you for much."

"Flippin' angels gotta eat too." J.J. smiled. He was reminding Chris how he saved him from Helson a few weeks back.

"Okay, okay...uh...a hoagie at Stan's. Saturday."

"Done. But that's some piss poor negotiatin' right there. I flippin' work and make money. You work and don't make money and now you're flippin' buying me lunch. Go figure."

"You're a peach, J.J. So you won't say anything to Mrs. Kling."

"Soda, too?"

"Whatever."

"Okay, mum's the word. You better flippin'

deliver though," J.J. said, turning and walking away.

"It's nice to know I can count on my friends," Chris said.

J.J. turned and faced Chris. "Just for the record, I woulda kept your flippin' secret anyway, even without the hoagie and soda."

"I know," Chris said.

"If you knew, then why did you let me weasel lunch outta you?

"Angels gotta eat."

"Flippin' ay!" J.J. said, walking away. "Later, Doc. Wait! You're not even here. I never saw you," he said waving his hand in the air as he walked away. "Now I'm flippin talkin' to myself."

Piece of work, Chris thought, looking after his friend. But he knew J.J. was as good as his word. He would not tell Frieda Kling.

Chris was stunned at the dozens of metal filing cabinets which held thousands of paper documents as well as hundreds of disks and thumb drives. It required just three weeks for him to further research readily-available off-the-shelf software solutions and make his report. He concluded that he should design and deliver a new digital online application, filing process, and cloud-based storage solution which would replace the in-place antiquated system. The new system would be secure, much more user-friendly, and would take up much less space than the current process.

"Christopher, this is quite extraordinary work, I must say," Headmistress Brennan said, as she finished reading his typed report. "I see no reason why we cannot implement your recommendations right away. I fully intend to do so."

"Thank you, Headmistress."

And although Headmistress Brennan was impressed by all this from a twelve-year-old, Chris was less than satisfied.

"Would you care to oversee the implementation?" she said.

"Sure," he said. "But, I would also like to try creating a custom placement algorithm to better match children and adults."

"Better than Frieda Kling does?"

"I don't know. I'd leave that to you to decide. If you give me the okay, I could begin working on it. It'll probably take a few months. The math is tough. When it's done you could beta test it against Mrs. Kling and see which works better."

"Well, let me think about that…no…no, that's the wrong answer. You have proven yourself here. If you want to do that then I concur. You like computer work?"

"Eh, it's okay. Computers can be helpful sometimes. I just like solutions, I guess, whether computer-based or not. I'm not sure I'll need a computer. But I'll definitely need a lot of blackboard time."

"Blackboard time?"

"I have a blackboard at home. It's where I do all of my mathematical modeling."

"Amazing," she said.

"I agree," Chris smiled. "Chalk is amazing."

"Well, okay then. Who am I to look a gift horse in the mouth? Truthfully, though, I was thinking of something else you might want to take a look at."

"Really? What?"

"As long as we are reinventing the wheel, we might as well look at cash receipts, right? Cash, it's the lifeblood of any business. It may be time for a transfusion."

"Don't you think you should consult with an attorney or an accountant, somebody like that? I don't have any experience…"

"I can and I do," Maxine Brennan cut him off. "But you…," she said pointing an index finger at his face, "I have a feeling you might find something important. After all, you're a St. Michael's alum!"

she said, proudly. "One of our shining stars!"

CHAPTER 16

On the day Chris discovered his ability to travel at the speed of light, Sam questioned how he planned to use it. The answer came a few months later, at a preseason high school football game.

Sam, Chris, and his mom had a tradition of going to the weekly Friday night games together to root for James. He wore number 84 and played tight end.

The lights from the football field spilled up into the night sky and onto the surrounding grounds and nearby park with a copse of woods. The score was tied 7-7 at halftime. The band took the field to begin the halftime show.

Aliondra gave Chris some money to buy hot dogs and sodas at the snack stand. Sam went with him so she could help carry the food back to their seats. While they were waiting in line, Chris noticed a small light gleaming from the woods about two hundred feet away. It didn't seem natural; more like reflected field lighting.

"Sam, you stay in line and get the snacks. I want to check something out. I'll be right back."

Curious, he trotted across the grass quadrangle toward the spot where the small light had shone through the trees. As he approached the woods and got further from the crowd, the field, and the snack stand, he noticed the crowd noise dimming. He also heard a voice screaming from inside the tree line. Someone was yelling for help, so he started to run.

He reached the trees and began to pick his way over the roots, ground cover, and twigs. The thick shrubs and brambles slowed his pace.

As he approached, he heard other voices. There were several people in there, and at least one was in trouble. Chris slowed to a stealthy walk, stepping gingerly over twigs and sticks, trying to approach without being heard.

Looking into a small clearing, he saw several older kids. The one crying for help was small. He sat on the ground, blood running down the side of his face from a cut in his cheek. Chris recognized him. Joey McManus, a freshman from the neighborhood.

Hovering over Joey was a much bigger kid, probably seventeen or so, brandishing a switchblade. Light glinted from the bloodied blade: the light that had first caught Chris' attention.

There were two other older boys standing behind the knife wielder. They laughed as Knife Wielder taunted the kid on the ground. "Go ahead, keep screaming, creep. No one's gonna hear you anyway. It's halftime. Hear that? Hear that? That's your competition. It's the killer band playing your funeral song while I mess you up, twerp."

His scurrilous accomplices, holding beer cans, laughed at this. "Yeah, Caz. Go ahead. Do it, man. Do it!"

Chris knew what he had to do. He stepped out into the clearing.

"Hi, Joey," he said. Startled, all three of the bullies turned to face him. "These goons giving you a hard time?"

All three turned and advanced toward Chris, momentarily forgetting about cutting Joey. Joey saw his chance and took off. Good. The other two now pulled knives from their jackets.

Knife Wielder said, "Hey punk, you made a bad mistake coming in here like this, shooting off your big mouth. This is frosh cutup night and since you cost us our honorary frosh, we're gonna have to cut you up." Chris slowly backed away from them as they advanced.

"Well, dirt bags, I'd like to oblige but I'm not a freshman. I'm in middle school. Think you big, bad, drunk bags of beetle dung can handle an eighth grader?"

Just then, he backed into a tree and stumbled. The two accomplices quickly advanced on either side, while Knife Wielder lunged straight at him with his knife.

In an instant, Chris connected, which is what

he had planned to do all along. The muggers froze, and he went to work quickly. First, with his own always-gloved hands, he removed the knives from their hands. He removed their wallets and their car keys from their pants pockets, and tossed them aside. Next, he turned and spotted Joey who had rounded up an adult covey, including Principal Bartle. They had been heading back to the scene of the crime. He walked to the other side of the clearing, hid behind some trees, and disconnected.

He saw Knife Wielder lunge with nothing in his hand and all three of the conspirators banging heads as they converged on themselves. When they saw the adults coming they quickly made their getaway on foot.

Chris waited and showed Principal Bartle, Joey, and the other men where the muggers had run. The men chased them across the gravel parking lot. When the muggers arrived at their cars, they could not find their keys, of course, so they continued running into the black night. Their pursuers returned to find the car keys, wallets, and fingerprint-laden beer cans and knives in the clearing.

Principal Bartle shook his head in disgust as he examined the driver licenses. "I could have guessed," he said. "Well, they can run, but they can't hide. These three should end up in jail before the game ends. Here come the police," he said as a patrol car and ambulance pulled up. Two police officers got out of the car, and two EMTs got out of the ambulance.

Joey identified Chris as having rescued him, but Chris did not want to call any more attention to himself, so he played down his involvement to the investigating officers, Lieutenant Joe Carter and Officer Mike Mountain. Chris told them he had noticed the light in the woods, that when he approached he saw the light was glinting off of a switchblade, that the three older bullies were drunken, knife-wielding fools who were seriously threatening to harm Joey, and all he had done was create a diversion. He had no idea why they would discard their wallets, knives, and keys unless, in their drunkenness, they had failed to retrieve them when they saw the adults approaching. It was all quite plausible.

Except to Lieutenant Carter. Carter dismissed the adults and released Joey McManus to the care of the EMTs, but detained Chris.

"Kid, look, we've been doing this sort of thing for a long time. I gotta tell you, things aren't adding up here."

"What do you mean?"

"I mean, I think you're not telling us everything. Maybe not on purpose, so can we ask you a few more questions?"

"Um, well, I really want to get back to the

game. My brother's playing."

"It'll just take a couple of minutes."

Chris looked at the two officers. They were both focused on him. Carter was closer; the bigger guy, Mountain, was next to Carter, though a step or two behind, perhaps less invested in more questioning.

Or so, in that instant, it seemed. Chris felt a warm spot deep within his head again. Something strange was happening, as if that part of his brain was somehow revving up, getting in gear. Not breaking eye contact with Carter, Chris touched his forehead, keeping his fingers there for a couple of seconds before lowering his hand. "Okay," he said, suddenly realizing that any other answer would not have been to his advantage.

"Good, good," Carter said. "See, we know these three guys," he started, looking at the driver's licenses. "Bad dudes. Really bad dudes. And big. They're what, Mike? Sixteen, seventeen, maybe a hundred seventy, a hundred eighty pounds each?"

"Yeah," Mountain agreed. "About."

"And no strangers to jail, right?"

"That's right."

"So what I don't understand," Carter said to

Chris, "is why three guys much bigger and older than you, each with police records, would give up their wallets and weapons and hightail it outta Dodge because you showed up. You're unarmed and much smaller. Three against one. These guys wouldn't see you as a threat."

Chris could almost feel his brain become active in ways it never had before. He had, in the past, experienced a similar, though much less intense, sensation when solving a Rubik's cube for the first time, or when first competing against adults at chess, also years ago, or when solving a fifth-level quadratic equation at the age of ten.

This interaction with Lieutenant Carter struck Chris as being a puzzle or competition, yet far more complicated because the puzzle was biological, human and therefore fluid, not fixed like a Rubik's Cube, a chessboard, or the laws of mathematics. And, although Chris knew no question had been asked of him, he somehow knew his best move was to respond. "I don't know. Maybe they saw Principal Bartle and the other adults coming."

"Maybe, maybe..." Carter said. "But the McManus kid said only one of them had a knife. You said all three of them came at you with knives..."

Chris' mind was racing way, way ahead of Carter's objection and future, yet-to-be-spoken arguments. As if he could see the next seven moves on the chessboard which suddenly struck him as interesting because, as opposed to chess competitions, he really had no experience in intense negotiations or criminal investigations. This tete-a-tete with Carter was proving to be quite an adrenaline rush. Chris enjoyed it. Very much.

"…yet they tossed them aside, and tossed their wallets aside…"

"No, I never said I saw them toss their things aside. I said they could have failed to pick them up."

"So you didn't see them throw their knives and wallets away?"

"Nope."

"Really?"

"Really."

"Well, okay," Carter snickered, looking first at his partner for confirmation and then back at Chris. "So as they came at you with their knives drawn, you somehow failed to notice them throw their knives aside. Seems unlikely, honestly, but okay. I'll give you that. But, why would three of them come at you with knives, then decide to just throw them aside?"

Chris could not lie. He had never lied and wasn't about to start. But he somehow knew that he must protect his secret ability at all costs. Sam knew of his ability, but he would have trusted her with his life. She would never tell anyone. Therefore, he began his parry. "What reason could they have?"

"I have no idea," Carter bit. "You were there. You tell me."

"I can't read minds," Chris said. "Maybe you should ask them."

"Look, punk!" Carter got in his face. Chris, stunned, stumbled backward, but did not fall. Mountain grabbed his partner from behind.

"Joe," he said, pulling Carter back. "Calm down."

Carter glared at Chris and exhaled loudly. "Okay. Okay. You're right. You're right." He looked down, ran his fingers through his hair and said, "You take it from here, Mike," before turning away from Chris and walking a few steps past Mountain, his head down and back turned, listening.

Chris' heart was pounding in his chest. Carter had scared him. It was obvious that Carter didn't care for him, but he knew no reason why Carter would have reacted the way he did. Yes, human beings were much more unpredictable than chessboards.

"You'll have to forgive my partner," Mountain said. "It's been a long day and we're going to have to track these guys down. That's no walk in the park, you understand?"

"Yes, sir," Chris said. "No problem."

"Good. Good."

"Look, Officer Mountain, Officer Carter, what difference does it make why they might throw away their knives and wallets?" Chris said.

"Because we have to write up an incident report, and it's got to be right so these guys don't get off on a technicality. We want them back in jail where they belong," Mountain said.

"But, you have a bloody knife. You have fingerprints. You have identifications. Joey McManus will testify that that Caz guy cut him, and so will I, and that the other two egged him on. The three creeps all have police records and they'll probably fail their breathalyzers. How else could their knives have gotten onto the ground? Do you think they'll claim I somehow disarmed them? Would you believe them if they did?" Chris couldn't believe he was talking this way. The words were spilling out of him as if he had any idea of what he was talking about. But, he very definitely did have an idea, which was weird because he had never before been involved in a police action. "Does it really matter how the knives and wallets got on the ground?"

Mountain was stunned. "Um…no, actually, I guess not…"

"Yeah, it matters," Carter said, moving into

the foreground once again to face Chris. "It matters to me."

"Why?" Chris said.

"Because I want to know, that's why. Because if they did throw their weapons and belongings on the ground, I want to know why they did. And, yes, I will ask them once we catch them, but I have a pretty good idea what I'm going to hear. I'm going to hear them say they did not throw the knives away. Know how I know? Because that's not the way thugs operate, that's how. What I don't know is how you operate. That's what I can't quite figure out. That's what I've never been..." he hesitated.

"What do you mean never?" Chris asked.

"Nothing, he doesn't mean nothing," Mountain said, pushing Carter back behind him. "Look, thanks for your time, kid And thanks for helping McManus. You did good. Real good. You should be proud of yourself. It's not that we're not grateful, it's that, like Lieutenant Carter said, we need to get the facts right as best we can. If after we catch these guys we need to ask you more questions, would that be okay?"

"Sure," Chris said. "Whatever I can do."

"Okay. good. Here, take this," he said, holding a business card out to Chris. "If you remember anything else, give me a call. Joe, give me one of your cards." Carter reached into his shirt pocket, pulled out a business card, and handed it to Mountain who held it out to Chris. "Here, take Lieutenant Carter's card too. Each of our cards has the phone number to the precinct and to our homes. You can call either of us at any time, okay?"

"Okay. Thanks, Officer Mountain."

"Alright, get back to your game, and we'll get back to tracking these guys down, okay?"

"Okay."

"Thanks, kid," Mountain said, as Chris walked away. Carter said nothing. Chris turned once to see the two officers watching him, except Carter was glaring more than merely watching. What's his problem?

As Chris climbed up into the stands and sat next to Sam and his mom, Sam said, "What happened to you?"

"I had to attend a meeting."

"A meeting?"

"Yeah, three losers were having a meeting of the minds."

"Huh?" Sam asked.

"I'll tell you later."

As Chris sat there, eating his hot dog and watching his brother's game, he knew he had learned a few things that evening. One, Lieutenant Carter had it in for him, for some unknown reason, and possibly had for some time now. Two, he himself seemed somehow very capable of responding well to stressful situations. It seemed to be an innate capability, certainly not something he had ever learned, because he had never been confronted like that by an adult before. Three, the perpetrators would definitely deny having thrown away their knives and wallets and would likely testify that they did not know how these belongings had ended up on the ground. Four, Lieutenant Carter was clearly a gifted, intuitive detective who, five, Chris would rather have as a friend than as an enemy.

On this last point, Chris knew, he had his work cut out for him. So, he pulled out his cell phone and saved Carter's phone number. It might come in handy someday.

"Who's that?" Sam asked, watching him.

"Lieutenant Joe Carter," Chris said. "I think he's a good man to know if I ever run into any trouble."

"Do you know him?"

"Not really. I ran into him back there and he gave me his card. He's a good basketball player, I can tell you that. J.J. and I watch him in the PAL games on Sundays. You want to put his number in your phone?" Chris asked, offering her the card.

"Sure. Thanks," Sam said, retrieving her phone.

"Here's Officer Mountain's card too. He's Carter's partner. He's huge."

Sam took Mike Mountain's card and entered his contact number in her phone. "I guess it doesn't hurt to be on the safe side," she said. "But I have you watching out for me, so these guys will have to come in off the bench." She smiled at Chris as she said this.

He smiled at her. "It's good to have a deep bench," he said.

Truer words were never spoken.

CHAPTER 17

Sunday was normally a full workday. J.J. rose at around 5:30 a.m. to begin his paper deliveries, which took twice as long as his daily route, because the Sunday papers were full of ads and much bulkier. Therefore, he couldn't carry as many papers in his newspaper bag and had to return more frequently to Stan's Deli to pick up more papers. Also, because each papers were so heavy, he couldn't throw them on the concrete sidewalks and stoops as he rode by on his bike. He either had to walk the paper to the front screen door and drop the paper between the screen door and the front door, or throw the plastic-wrapped papers on the lawns, when there were lawns. The grass cushioned the landing and helped to keep the plastic bags from ripping open and spilling their contents all over the place.

J.J. finished with his deliveries by around 8:00 a.m. He had worked up a decent sweat, so sitting on a stool in Stan's while Mr. K made his hoagie was a nice break, giving him a few minutes to relax and cool down.

Stan Kaniewski and J.J. never really spoke much to each other. Mr. K did appreciate him as a regular customer, but the boy couldn't speak Polish and what little he did say was usually said, it appeared to Mr. K, with a healthy dose of attitude. For some people, Mr. K. knew, surviving each day was a major challenge. J.J. seemed destined to be one of those people. The kid had developed a serious chip on his shoulder. But, he had to give the kid credit, he hustled. He was a worker with a tremendous amount of energy.

Mr. K had often thought about hiring him, but he didn't know if he could deal with all the baggage which would surely come with having J.J. as an employee. The boy was a major piece of work, for sure. Still, Mr. K had come to know that beneath that tough guy exterior was a good kid. A dependable kid. He wasn't Polish, but he could take care of himself. You had to respect that. He was no pushover.

Leaving Stan's, J.J. rode his bike the half mile or so to his next job at Mrs. Kling's house. The back of her house faced the back of Glenn and Eric's house, separated by the common alleyway which ran the length of the block.

J.J. dropped his bike at her back door, retrieved her key from his jeans pocket, and let himself into her house. Her car wasn't parked in the rear driveway. Normally, she was at St. Michael's Home early each Sunday morning. It was J.J.'s job to let himself in through the rear basement door so that he could feed and walk Abe and Gipper.

The dogs were in their crates in the basement. They didn't bark because they knew J.J., but their tails wagged excitedly. J.J. released them from their crates. They sniffed J.J.'s hoagie in its brown paper bag, and awaited their Purina breakfasts. J.J. went upstairs to put his hoagie in the refrigerator, and returned to the basement with two bowls of dog food.

After the dogs had eaten, J.J. put Gipper back in his crate while he got Abe ready for his walk. It would take him about an hour to walk Abe to the nearest fenced-in baseball field at the Belfield Rec Center. There, Abe would run around, and eventually find the perfect canine-suitable spot to make a deposit. J.J. would clean up after him, walk him back home, and put him back in his crate.

J.J. then repeated the entire process with Gipper. Except, by the time he returned, Mrs. Kling had returned from the Home and had parked her car, over the exact spot in the rear driveway where Chris had stumbled in the half ball game. So J.J. began to prepare for his next chore: washing Mrs. Kling's car inside and out.

As he hooked up the hose, retrieved the chamois, sponge, rags, and vacuum cleaner, and began to fill up a plastic bucket with water, J.J. looked up the alleyway to see that Chris and his brother had returned from another of James' Sunday morning Fall Ball baseball games. They were hugging their mother as she prepared to leave for work.

J.J. smiled at this. It was always a bittersweet scene for him. He knew he was jealous of Chris and his brother, of Sam, and of all of his buddies who lived in homes with parents. J.J. sighed and refocused on the hose filling the bucket at his feet. Someday, he too would find a real home. Someday, someone would find something to love about him.

And, if that day never came...he thought as he started to hose down Mrs. Kling's car...well, he would keep hustling, and putting money away, so that he could take care of himself and maybe, just maybe, when he was old enough, he'd adopt a whole flippin' family of his own.

A few minutes later, as J.J. stood on a small step stool soaping the top of Mrs. Kling's small SUV, Chris, Sam, Butchy, and Ozzie came down the alleyway on their bikes. Glenn and Eric came out of their garage on their bikes to join them.

"Hey, J.J., we're headed over to Belfield Pool. When you're done there, you wanna come over?" Glenn called.

"Maybe."

"Ah, J.J. hates the water, ain't that right, J.J.?" Butchy said.

"Come closer, numbnuts," J.J. said, stepping off the ladder and grabbing the hose. Let's see how much you flippin' like it," he shouted, starting to spray water at them.

"Ah, he can't even swim," Eric taunted.

"Hey, Glenn," J.J. called. "How'd you like to be an only child? Better get your flippin' bro' outta my face before I drop this hose and drop him."

"There's some trunks for you on the ping pong table in our basement, if you change your mind," Chris said, as they all continued down the driveway on their bikes, leaving J.J. to his chores.

"Yo, Doc!" J.J. called, and Chris rode back to him as the others waited at the end of the alleyway.

"How much you makin' at the Home for your flippin' computer work?"

"I told you before, not much. Plus, I'm not doing that anymore."

"Yeah, you are. I see you there twice a week. You're flippin' doin' somethin'."

"Can you keep a secret?" Chris asked.

"Yo, Doc, you're talkin' to flippin' J.J. When do I ever flap my gums?"

"Alright, look. Don't tell anyone. I'm not doing the computer work anymore, but I'm using mathematical modeling to try to find a better way to match kids up with parents."

"Oh yeah? What's wrong with the way they do it now? Everybody says Mrs. Kling does a great flippin' job."

"I know. That's true. But maybe I could help her do a better job."

"A better job? What do you know about flippin' finding parents?"

"I'm working on an algorithm."

"Uh-huh," J.J. said, dismissively, rolling his eyes. "More flippin' genius crap."

"It's math. I think it'll work."

"Will it get me flippin' placed?"

Chris smiled. "I said it was math not a miracle."

Big mistake. Major mistake. J.J. kicked Chris' bike, making him fall to the ground, and J.J. stuck the hose down the back of his trunks as Chris tried to get up.

"Ah!" Chris yelled. "That's cold! J.J. stop! It'll work! It'll work!"

"You promise?" J.J. yelled, keeping the hose right where it was.

"Yes! I promise!" Chris yelled.

"Okay then," J.J. said, releasing him. Chris

got to his feet and picked up his bike. J.J. sprayed him in the face with the hose. Chris fought off the spray and grabbed the nozzle, coming face to face with J.J. They were both wet now, but neither cared.

"Dude!" Chris said. "Don't tell anybody. I could get in a lot of trouble. It's supposed to be a secret."

"Just find me a flippin' home," J.J. said. "It's your turn to be a flippin' angel. Make that math thing work a miracle for me."

Chris picked up his bike. "I'll do the best I can. But you gotta do your part."

"That's all I ever flippin' do," J.J. said. "All day, every day. I'm no flippin' genius like you. I gotta work."

"Look, J.J., finish up and come over to the pool. We're wet already anyway. Get the trunks from my garage, okay?" Chris felt bad. Again. He always had a soft spot for J.J.

"Nah. Forget it. I ain't no flippin' flounder anyway," J.J. said, as he started to rinse the soap off the car.

"You should learn to swim. Come on, I can teach you."

"I don't wanna swim. I want a family. Just

flippin' do that for me, will ya?" J.J. yelled, returning to his work, dismissing Chris with the wave of a very soapy sponge.

Chris watched J.J. scrubbing the top of the car as if he would grind a hole right through it. "I'll try," he said, softly, and he meant it. But J.J. didn't hear him.

Chris left to rejoin his friends. As J.J. finished washing and drying the exterior of Mrs. Kling's car, and was vacuuming out the interior and the floor mats, Mrs. Kling walked out her back door and interrupted him. J.J. shut off the vacuum cleaner.

"Good Morning, J.J. My, how nice my car looks. You always do such a nice job. How were the boys for you this morning?" she asked, referring to her dogs.

"Great, as always. They're really great flippin' dogs."

Mrs. Kling winced at J.J.'s language. Not yet inured, even after two years of having J.J. run errands, his language always made her uncomfortable. The boy was gauche but guileless and as dependable as the sunrise, a worker par excellence, if taciturn, though still not quiet enough. Because on those relatively few occasions he chose to open his mouth, he instantly became his own worst enemy. That, and his confrontational demeanor, had made him the most challenging placement Frieda had ever experienced.

"You're all wet," she said.

"Occupational flippin' hazard."

"Yes, well, I need to go out again when you're finished with the car. I won't be back until late tonight, so I will take the boys with me. I was hoping you might be willing to go to the Acme for me and pick up a few groceries. The list and coupons and money are on the kitchen table, together with your check for today's work which includes an extra $20 for doing the shopping. Put the fruits and veggies in the fridge, and leave the change and other items on the kitchen counter. I'll put them away when I come home tonight."

"Sure, Mrs. Kling. No problem."

"Thank you, J.J. When you're done, you can let yourself out through the back door. Make sure to lock up, as always, okay?"

"Will do. Mrs. Kling?"

"Yes?"

"Any nibbles yet? Any new leads on placements?" he asked, as he lifted the vacuum cleaner over to the rear door of the house. He then turned to face Mrs. Kling.

Mrs. Kling smiled gently. "Well, you know, J.J., there are always a few nibbles. I am talking to people all the time. Don't worry. We'll find you a home. I promise. It's just going to take some time, but I'll find you a good home, the right home, the best home for you."

"Why does it take so flippin' long for me? All the other kids get flippin' placed, no problem."

"It'll flip...um, excuse me, dear. It will happen for you too. You just have to be patient."

"How much more flippin' patient do I have to be? I'll be twelve in a couple of months. I'm the only kid over nine years old in the whole flippin' Home. How long does it take?"

"J.J. please. Trust me. Maybe the world is saving the best parents for you. I will find you a home."

"I hope so, otherwise..." J.J. bit his tongue, remembering his promise to Chris not to divulge the placement algorithm he was working on.

"Otherwise what, J.J.?" Frieda Kling asked.

"Nothin'," J.J. said, picking up the hose and beginning to hang it over the spigot.

"No, what were you going to say?"

J.J.'s brain was on overdrive. He had to cover his tracks. And fast. Fortunately, he had a lot of experience doing so. "Otherwise, you'll be coming to me asking me to adopt some dopey flippin' kid before I even get adopted, that's what," J.J. said.

Mrs. Kling laughed. "Good one, J.J.," she said, ruffling his hair. "You're a good kid. Someone is going to be very lucky to have you as their son. They just don't know it yet. So don't you worry, young man. I have a feeling your new parents will show up any day now. You wait and see."

"That's what I've been doing."

Later that afternoon, after Frieda Kling had gone, and J.J. had purchased her groceries, collected his pay, and locked up her house, he began the four-mile bike ride back to the Home. He could have gone to the pool but he chose not to. It was no secret among his friends. J.J. feared nobody and nothing, except the deep end of a swimming pool. He had never learned to swim, and was terrified of drowning.

Passing by the last house on Mrs. Kling's side of the street, J.J. noticed roofers had gone for the day and left an extension ladder leaning against the house up to the roof. They were likely going to return Monday morning to finish their work. J.J. stopped, looked at the ladder, and looked up the block toward Frieda Kling's house. It was a bright, sunlit Sunday afternoon, and J.J., ever the businessman, knew a golden opportunity when he saw one.

As he rode back to the Home that afternoon, eating his morning hoagie, he knew he would return, when it was dark. He also calculated in his head how much money he'd make selling five-hundred, seven-hundred-fifty, or even a thousand slightly used half balls at fifty flippin' cents each.

CHAPTER 18

"Congratulations on the convictions," Captain Carroll started.

"Thank you, sir," Joe Carter replied.

"I've already spoken to Mike Mountain. I wanted to talk to you each separately about the arrests at the football game a few weeks back."

"Yes, sir."

"You know we dodged a bullet there, right?"

"Yes, sir."

"Several bullets."

"Yes, sir." Carter shifted in his seat, suddenly uncomfortable.

"Why is that?"

"Sir?"

"Why did we have to dodge bullets? Better yet, why were there bullets to dodge in the first place? Why didn't you nail down the testimonies about the knives and wallets?"

"I tried, sir. But the best we could do was to obtain corroborating testimonies."

"No contradictions?"

"All three perpetrators gave identical accounts, sir, as you can see there," Carter said, motioning to the interrogatories in Captain Carroll's hands.

"But the victim said he only saw one knife. And the witness...um..." he hesitated, flipping through the pages.

"Christopher Newman," Carter said.

"Right. Newman. His testimony doesn't agree. He says, quote, 'maybe they tossed them aside when they saw Principal Bartle coming.' But Newman was there already, right? Wouldn't he have seen them throw their knives on the ground?"

"He should have, sir."

"So why doesn't he just say that? Why doesn't he testify that he saw them throw their knives on the ground? Did you grill him on that?"

"Yes, sir, I did. Mike Mountain and I did when we arrived on the scene that night."

"And?"

"And...and...well," Carter started, not wanting to admit that he had let the Newman kid get under his skin. "We decided we would come back to it if it were necessary," Carter said. "We felt we already had enough to convict, and we did."

"Fortunately," Captain Carroll said. "It's not like you to miss important details, Carter."

"No, sir."

"I trust there won't be a repetition."

"No, sir."

"Good. That's good, Carter. Plus, you deserve a pass for your first offense."

"Thank you, sir."

"You're welcome. Be forewarned, though. This isn't baseball. You already have one strike, but you won't necessarily get three."

"Yes, sir. Understood, sir."

As Joe left his captain's office, he was steamed. That Newman kid had come back to bite him again. Of all the cities in the country, and of all the precincts in the city, why did he have to land here?

Carter hadn't felt the need to tell his captain and, in fact, he had never told anyone, not even his best friend and partner, Mike Mountain. But, when Carter had looked into Chris Newman's eyes that night at the football field, he was stunned at what he saw. The kid was not only bright, not only gifted, not only a genius, he was off-the-charts. Carter had rarely felt so overmatched. But, he felt overmatched that night.

The kid was playing him. Newman held all the cards and had orchestrated the conversation to go just as he had planned, and had gotten away with it. Twelve years old, no police record, had never been in any trouble at all and yet…and yet, he somehow knew the convictions were in the bag without having to disclose anything further. And Carter knew, and still believed, that Newman had more to disclose but had deliberately chosen not to do so. It would have been logical for Carter, or any law enforcement officer, to assume connivance, a desire to thwart, a dastardly intent. But Carter wasn't so sure. He had the distinct feeling that Newman may not have been as in control as he appeared. He may not have been the ringleader of his decisions. Perhaps he was responding to some external force, a higher power. It seemed ridiculous to Carter even to admit to such a circumstance. But, he had to. Because Joe Carter knew what he knew.

And, he knew what he didn't know. He knew that Newman was holding back, but he didn't know why. It could have been an evil intent, but Carter didn't think so. At least, now, upon reflection, he hoped not. Newman was becoming a force to be reckoned with, and Carter knew he'd rather have him as a friend than an enemy.

And, cn that front, he knew he had a lot of work to do.

CHAPTER 19

J.J. was hustling. It's what he did. Busying himself with another chore. It was late afternoon, usually a quiet time around St. Michael's on those Sundays when Chris wasn't giving a concert. J.J. could have been reading or doing his homework or watching sports on TV or playing video games, but his preferred to stay busy. Always. J.J. felt as though time was not on his side, that the world was not on his side, and that he needed to compete constantly to grab his slice of life's pie. He believed he had no special abilities. After all, he was no Chris Newman or Sam Banks or James Covington.

If there were three such special kids in his little neighborhood, he figured, there must be thousands, or even tens of thousands, of amazingly talented people out in the real world. They were his competition.

It wasn't that J.J. felt persecuted, but he did feel the need to compete well. And competing, fighting, he knew, was something he could do. Actually, competing was something he loved. It made him feel alive. He may not have the extraordinary talents his friends had, but he believed the most talented did not always come out on top. Sometimes they were off their game and, at those times, he could beat them. In J.J.'s parlance, sometimes the flippin' brainiacs could be so stupid.

At those times, J.J. would eat their lunch, because J.J. was never stupid. Over the years, dozens of potential adoptive parents had passed up the opportunity to take J.J. into their homes and, in doing so had validated, or formed, J.J.'s belief that he was somehow flawed. He could deal with being flawed.

Initially resentful and often hurt by rejection, J.J. had grown inured to it, had grown to accept it. He was, he hoped, capable of loving and of being loved, thankful for all he had and all he could do. He wasn't the sharpest tool in the shed, certainly, but he was better than some and intelligent enough to get by. What he couldn't know or see was how that good and loving kid had become encrusted over the years, under a hardened, hard-fisted mantle of loneliness, self-doubt, jealousy, and cynicism. J.J. was a jewel, really, but he didn't advertise real well. It would fall to an exceptional diviner of human hearts to one day free the anthracite-encased gem that was J.J.

He hadn't really planned on sanding the rowboat. But it needed care. Had for some time now. And J.J. needed to not be inside for lights out. Once the headmistress and Ernie locked all the doors, he would be trapped inside. And tonight, ladder fortuitously waiting, was not the night to be trapped inside. He would sand that boat and claim to be "coming, just a few more minutes," should any adults call. He had long ago learned their routine.

They would call him for dinner once, maybe twice, before figuring if he didn't come he would forfeit dinner and learn his lesson. Truth be told, though, he had learned a more valuable lesson long ago: the adults would, eventually, go to dinner without him and, when that happened, he would make his getaway on his bike, into the night. But, for this to become the long-running opportunity it had become, J.J. knew there were limits, bounds he should not cross. He couldn't stay out too long past dark and risk truly upsetting the caregivers, otherwise they would institute stricter measures to ensure his timely confinement. No, he could be, say, thirty to forty-five minutes late, after the doors had been locked at 7:00 p.m. sharp, but not too much later.

Sunday dinner was at 6:15, about sunset. J.J. was on the road by 6:20 and peddling fast. Four miles there through city traffic, and four miles back, hopefully with a ton of halfballs. That wouldn't leave a large margin of error, especially since he would have to sequester his bounty somewhere safe upon his return and knock on the front door by 7:30. Definitely no later than 7:45, otherwise he risked having the headmistress or Ernie call the police. Not that the police would search for him right away. J.J. had a reputation of going missing for short periods. Still, he knew there would be consequences if he hadn't returned before they called the cops. Although often truant, he knew not to push his luck.

His bike had been donated to the Home many years ago. He kept it in good repair and logged many miles on it. But, it was a small two-wheeler with twenty-inch wheels. He couldn't handle the larger twenty-six inch bikes that his friends rode. His legs were too short. But, as with so many other aspects of life, he more than compensated in hustle for what he lacked in ability. He pedaled much faster than anyone else. His legs were strong.

He could have made the trip blindfolded. He made this same trip on his bike from the Home to Chris' and Sam's neighborhood every morning to deliver his papers. The newspaper could have awarded the delivery route to any other kid who lived in the neighborhood, but the route was so large, with so many deliveries, it was difficult to find kids willing to take it on. This was good news for J.J. who was thrilled to have the opportunity to make so much money. All he had to do was work hard. And working hard was something he could do.

It was plenty dark when he approached his target at 6:45. He propped his bike against a tree across the larger street which ran perpendicular to Chris' and Sam's block and waited. The ladder was still in place, leaning against the end house, and reaching all the way to the roof. Perfect. Also, there were no lights on in the house and no cars parked near it. It appeared to be empty. Perfect again. Luck favors the prepared. J.J. recalled Headmistress Brennan's phrase and considered himself prepared. Every once in a great while, he thought, life could be so sweet. The ladder, the dark of night, an empty house, and a halfball mother lode.

He had to wait for a man to continue walking

his dog around the corner and up the block. Then he darted between the traffic on the large four-lane street, carrying a plastic kitchen trash bag he had "borrowed" from the kitchen at the Home folded in his jacket pocket. As he walked up the grass embankment to the foot of the ladder, he glanced quickly left, then right, to make sure no one saw him. It was dark. No one was out, and there weren't any houses with a good line of sight to where he was. With unmitigated temerity he sprinted to the ladder and immediately began his ascent, climbing strongly yet stealthily so the aluminum ladder would not rattle against the brick wall of the house, or the metal capping of the roof it leaned against. Within twenty seconds J.J. stepped off the ladder onto the roof of the house.

Looking down the flat roofs of the row houses, he saw what he expected, an unencumbered path to Mrs. Kling's roof about a third of the way up the block, maybe twelve houses down. Also, to his left, the third floor attic windows rose vertically above the roofline on which he now crouched, above the second story. The third floor attics ran only half the length of the houses, front to back, and the windows afforded a view into those smaller attics. He ignored the attic windows as he hurried over the rooftops, stepping softly so as to bring no attention from any residents who might have happened to be in the second floor bedrooms beneath him, or inside the attic windows he now hurried past.

As he approached Mrs. Kling's roof, his eyes

grew wide with excitement. He couldn't believe the sight which greeted him. Practically every square foot of Mrs. Kling's roof and the two roofs on either side of hers were inundated with halfballs. Hundreds of halfballs. Some were badly moldered due to years of sunlight, extreme heat, and acid rain. Still, many were in excellent condition. There they were. More than he could have imagined! Looking around, above the treetops, alone above the neighborhood which had been his childhood stomping ground, J.J. felt as if he were, literally, all alone on top of the world. He had never before experienced anything like this, had never been the top dog, privileged, the number one draft pick. He dropped to his two knees, raised his hands to the sky and, though not religious, gave thanks. "Thank you, James," he said, softly, knowing who was responsible for the majority of his new-found treasure.

Such a bounteous plunder did not come without drawbacks. Suddenly he knew that the kitchen trash bag he brought with him could never accommodate all these half balls. And, even if it could, he did not think he would be able to manage an overfull trash bag on his little bike. It would be too heavy, would drag on the ground and tear. No, he quickly decided, as he often did, to stick with his original plan.

He would gather up a reasonable amount of halfballs, but not too many to carry. It seemed like five-hundred would be the limit. He wouldn't be able to handle many more than that. His daydream of a thousand halfballs at fifty cents each, though fading fast, was immediately replaced by a new reality. Well, the price just went up, he thought. Supply and demand. He was nothing if not flexible.

He had the option, of course, to throw down to the ground all the halfballs he couldn't carry, and gather them up tomorrow after school. But he dismissed this idea. Fate had contrived to get him here tonight. It was going to be a long summer and fall, and many of these roofs looked like they could use some work. He liked his chances of Fate returning him once again to the top of the world. He would return to this site of conquest to claim the remaining halfballs.

Time was not on his side, so he began to work quickly. It didn't take long to gather up what he figured was roughly five-hundred decent, sellable halfballs. Ten minutes later, the bag was full, and his pants pockets were totally stuffed with halfballs. He knew he was almost done for the evening. He had to hurry back.

Picking up the last few halfballs near Mrs. Kling's two attic windows, he noticed the window to the left of the mullion was slightly ajar. It hadn't been closed all the way. He tried to push the window up. It appeared to be warped and moved only slightly. He put down the bag so he could use two hands for leverage. Pushing hard, the window suddenly shot up, with a loud screech, but stopped before opening all the way, so it didn't bang against the top of the window frame

J.J. now faced an open entrance into Mrs. Kling's attic. This was big! In all the years he had been taking care of Mrs. Kling's house, chores, and dogs, he had never been in the attic. She always kept the attic door locked and had told him that the attic was strictly off-limits and that, if she ever caught him snooping around the attic door, she would fire him and tell Headmistress Brennan. That would in all likelihood have meant relocation to a different home somewhere else, starting all over again, and having a blotch on his record that would render him virtually unadoptable. J.J. knew the attic was strictly off-limits.

He also knew the opportunity staring him in the face through the open window. He knew Mrs. Kling was gone until later that night, and he knew that Abe and Gipper were also gone. The house was empty. This was a once-in-a-lifetime opportunity. And no one knew opportunity like J.J. He had no excuse. After all, he hadn't been born a Brainiac.

Looking quickly left to right, he scolded himself. "Flippin' idiot," he said softly. "Who's gonna see you?" Thus assured, he crouched through the window, pushing a curtain aside, and put one leg through the opening before sitting on the sill and twisting to bring his other leg in. He stretched his feet for the floor and pushed off the window sill, landing softly on the floor and crouching low. An eleven-year-old cat burglar.

Not quite. After all, a cat burglar would have thought to bring a flashlight. It was pitch black in the room, very musty, and he couldn't see two feet in front of him. He stood up and placed his arms in front of him, feeling for a light switch on the wall. Halfway around the room, or what felt like halfway around the room, he had yet to knock anything over, or bump in to anything at all. Maybe the attic was empty. Finally, he felt the railing and knew this was the railing to the staircase that led down to the locked attic entranceway door in the second floor hallway. The forbidden door. He was on the other side of the forbidden door.

Suddenly, the fingers of his other hand felt a light switch on the wall. Pushing the light switch up immediately illuminated the room. J.J. squeezed his eyes shut, partially blinded by the sudden brightness. He took a moment to let his eyes adjust before turning to survey the attic in which he stood. When he did finally turn he came face-to-face with a new reality. Memories of halfballs, of getting back to the Home before 7:45, of an auspicious Fate smiling upon him, and of everything else he thought he knew rushed from his mind, replaced by a new reality. A horrible new reality.

If luck favored the prepared, his luck had just run out. Unprepared for what he now saw, he realized that his life was not sweet at all. The anthracite-encased gem that was flippin' J.J. screamed but, as a tear escaped his eye and ran down his cheek, no sound escaped his lips.

CHAPTER 20

Chris and his mother were, at that moment, returning home from St. Michael's. It was a quiet ride. Their minds were occupied by matters far distant from the car in which they sat.

Chris was concerned. He felt certain that Headmistress Brennan was seriously considering selling St. Michael's Home to a casino development company, and he knew she would do so only as a last resort. She had never said this, but Chris' latest intuition was largely based upon recent developments – particularly the arrival at St. Michael's of several limousines and well-dressed businesspeople meeting with Headmistress Brennan over the past several weeks. He had a sneaking suspicion that she was hoping he would, by some miracle, discover a way to eliminate the need to sell the Home.

She also had a team of external auditors and other consultants looking at things like expenses to see if there was a way to operate more efficiently. They were also looking at placements and revenues, as he was. She was determined to save St. Michael's.

Chris saw these professional businesspeople in their suits and dress clothes, all working at laptops in the large dining room that had been set up for their use. He did not sit with them. Mrs. Brennan had assigned him to a small study, also on the first floor. It was more like a small library, actually. It could not have accommodated the team of a half dozen auditors and outside consultants, but it suited him just fine. It was quiet. He could concentrate. The dining room was always loud, with cellphones ringing, and people talking to one another.

Chris knew that Headmistress Brennan putting faith in a twelve-year-old was a last-ditch effort, and that there wasn't much time. Given the holes in his understanding, he was worried. He feared he would not succeed. The placement results were already quite excellent, and had been for a long time. Still, he hoped against hope. He sincerely wanted to help Headmistress Brennan, Mrs. Kling, and the other placement staff if at all possible. He wasn't ready to concede to failure, but he needed to find some missing puzzle pieces and find them fast.

Some of the items he saw included press clippings in which Headmistress Brennan had been honored with various awards for her lifetime of work with underprivileged children, her successful management of a large orphanage, the exemplary placement percentage she and her team of placement professionals had been able to achieve over a long period of time, their community involvement and outreach (including the monthly concerts,) and a low rate of employee turnover. Employees were happy. They didn't quit.

Chris was interested in the press clippings, as his goal was to see if he could develop a less risky way to place orphans with the appropriate adoptive guardians. It would be difficult to beat the track record of the placement staff, and of Mrs. Kling in particular.

If it was just the positive press clippings, however, he would have finished his report and given it to Headmistress Brennan with the advice that there was nothing more to be done. But he had also inadvertently happened upon boxes of thank-you notes that Mrs. Brennan had kept over the years, from happy new adoptive parents and their adopted children, the former wards of St. Michael's Home. Just for fun – well, fun for him – he dumped all the loose thank you notes from three large cardboard boxes onto the floor. The cards were like a large pile of fall leaves, and he set to work organizing them, categorizing them, and sorting them into more distinct smaller piles based upon date, new home location, and placement volunteer. It required hours – over two evenings of one week - to do this and an outside observer happening by the doorway might have thought it ludicrous, but he had promised to leave no stone unturned in his efforts to help Headmistress Brennan, and three huge boxes of unfiled thank you notes struck him as being a fairly sizable unturned stone.

The upshot of all this sorting was the creation of fourteen much smaller piles arranged within seven imaginary circles on the study floor, one circle for each of the seven placement counselors, including one for Mrs. Kling. Within each circle he had broken the thank you notes into domestic and international, based upon where the adoptive parents lived. Each counselor's domestic pile was much larger than their international pile. Finally, he sorted all the notes chronologically, remembering hundreds of dates, as only he could.

This seemed to make sense, except for one thing. Mrs. Kling's international pile was much smaller than the other international piles. Chris found this odd, though he couldn't say why, exactly. He hoped to find an answer when he returned to the Home later in the week, because he knew he didn't have much time to get his report to Headmistress Brennan.

The thank-you notes were a gold mine in one way. Based upon the comments in those notes, he could form a picture in his mind of the characteristics that adoptive parents had favored in their adoptees, as well as how their newly-adopted charges perceived and valued their new parents and homes. Many of these characteristics were not included in the current questionnaire that prospective parents had to complete.

The current application process was paper-based too. He felt certain efficiencies and further analyses would benefit greatly from additional questions and a safe and secure online application process. As he stared out the car window on the drive home with his mom, Chris had a feeling that an online application process might be able to save some costs. He thought Headmistress Brennan might find that helpful. He hoped so.

Focused on the road ahead as she drove, Chris' mother was thinking about her boss, Mr. Lewis. Chris noticed a tear running down her cheek before it dropped to her taffeta blouse.

"Mom, are you okay?"

Aliondra Covington, at that moment, was decidedly not at all okay, but she was struggling mightily to hold herself together until they arrived home safely. Conversation with her son would have been a welcome distraction earlier but his mind seemed to be elsewhere. She figured he was thinking about the project he was working on for Headmistress Brennan, and had decided not to bother him. But her tear had leaked out and changed everything.

"Mom, why are you crying? Is something wrong?"

"Nothing this old bird can't handle. Now don't you go getting yourself all worked up over me," she said, struggling to stay focused as the tears started flowing freely "Believe you me, I have that covered enough for the both of us."

"Mom...mom, pull over. Pull over, mom. Please."

She pulled the car over to the curb, parked it, and tuned off the engine. Then she collected herself, wiped her eyes with a tissue, and blew her nose, before turning in her driver's seat to face her son. She smiled at him, gamely. But he wasn't fooled.

"Is it work?" Chris asked. "Is something wrong at your work?"

Aliondra took both of Chris' gloved hands into her own hands. "Not anymore," she started. "Mr. Lewis let me go today."

"He fired you?"

"Yes. He did."

"Well, that's okay, right? He was working you too hard anyway, right? All the extra hours and weekends and stuff?"

Aliondra smiled weakly again, but faltered momentarily before forcing herself not to cry anymore. "Chris, honey," she started. "Work I can handle. It wasn't the work," she said.

Chris looked into his mother's eyes. He was confused. She was talking the way adults talk when they're trying not to tell you something they're trying to tell you. "Mom, I don't understand…was he mean to you or something?"

"Um, well, not mean, exactly. Actually, he was nice…too nice. Let's just say he wanted me to be his, um… lady friend."

"Mom! You mean he made a pass at you?"

"Many passes."

"But, he's married, isn't he? Plus that's illegal, right? That's harassment or something. You can sue for that. You're not going to let him get away with that are you?" Chris was becoming increasingly agitated.

"Chris, Chris…" Aliondra said, squeezing his hands. "Listen to me. Listen to me now. I need you to be the strong one, okay? What I need you to do is help me in a very special way. Can you do that for me?"

"Sure, mom, anything. What?"

"I need you to let this be our little secret. I need you not to tell your brother."

"Not tell James? Well, okay, but…why not?"

"Because in a lot of ways James is younger than you, that's why. He wouldn't understand. I'm afraid he would try to take matters into his own hands, and I don't need him making the situation any worse. So, please, son, please. Promise me that you won't tell James. We can figure things out without upsetting him. Do you promise?"

"Mom, of course, but won't he notice that you're not going to work?"

"Yes, but I will make up an excuse, okay? It's alright that you know the truth, because you can handle it better, and I need someone to help me. That someone has to be you. Not James. Not this time. Maybe another time, but not now. This time, I'm going to need you to help me, to believe me. Trust your mother on this. I know my sons."

"So you're not going to tell James?"

"No, I will tell James, at some point, but not right now. Now is not the time."

"Alright, Mom, but we're gonna sue right?"

"No, we're not going to sue anybody. Lawsuits mean lawyers and we can't afford a lawyer. Plus, I'm just as happy to be out of there and away from that awful man. Trust me, Mrs. Lewis has bigger problems than I have, so keep her in your prayers."

They smiled at each other, and Aliondra hugged her son. "Plus, I'm going to find a much better job soon enough. It's about time I started paying attention to finding a job I can love rather than holding a job for the sake of a paycheck...even though..."

"No, no, no!" Chris said. "Hold that thought. You'll find a job you love. I know it."

"And how do you know that?"

"Because. I know my mom."

Aliondra turned the ignition key, pulled the car away from the curb, and continued the drive home. Chris watched her briefly before turning and looking wistfully out his passenger-side window at the sycamore trees he had ridden past hundreds of times on his bike.

First, Jack Helson and his gang, then the thugs who mugged Joey McManus, and now Mr. Lewis. Chris was glad his mother had confided in him and trusted him and sought his help. He knew he was growing up, and he felt as though he was on yet another precipice. Just a few months ago he had discovered a wonderful new world of possibility. He could travel at the speed of light! He awoke everyday thinking it had to be a dream. But it wasn't a dream. It was reality. An awesome reality. Just for him.

Now, however, he was beginning to understand the adult world might be a much less wonderful reality. He knew he had to be strong for his mother, he had to put on his game face. But, he suddenly felt that, somewhere deep inside, his heart, his spirit, and his sense of hope, had suffered a damaging blow. All adults weren't all good, noble, honest, or trustworthy. The impedimenta of his childhood were under attack, and his world was changing very, very fast. Some of the change was very good. Some of the change was...bad. Yes, there was no better way to say it. The world into which he was entering could be very bad.

As he continued to stare out the window lost in his own thoughts, he had no idea how to eliminate the bad. Suddenly, and for the first time, he had a genesis of a powerful new idea: if he couldn't change the bad, perhaps he could just leave it behind.

Chris couldn't have known it, and indeed even Fixer and Miss Portice did not know it, but it was so he could best understand and deal with such a moment as this that Mary Newman had insisted her son be born and raised on Earth.

CHAPTER 21

J.J. slumped down, back against the attic wall, and sat on the floor, staring. Caught off-guard, he began to panic, so he raised up his knees, crossed his arms atop them, buried his head in his arms, and began to rock in place, back and forth. "Think, think, think! Flippin' think," he whispered to himself, rubbing his wet eyes on his jacket sleeve.

Two minutes later, he stopped rocking and suddenly exhaled loudly. There was only one thing to do, and J.J. knew he wasn't the one to do it. It suddenly dawned on him why the world needed flippin' Brainiacs. He knew the solution to the situation staring him in the face, if there was one, would forever be well beyond his capabilities. "Doc," he said.

Getting to his feet, J.J. took one final look around the room. He didn't want to forget anything. Satisfied that the important details were forever seared in his memory, he shut off the light, and worked his way along the wall back to the open window. Turning his back to the window and placing the palms of both hands on the sill, he hoisted himself up so that he was sitting on the window sill. Pulling his right knee up to his chest, he turned and extended his right leg out the opening, before pushing his torso further through the opening to the outside.

As he did, one half ball dropped out of the left

back pocket of his jeans onto the attic floor. Very lightweight, and made of soft rubber, it made no sound when it fell and J.J. did not see it drop in the dark. Kneeling on the roof outside, he turned back to the window and pulled it down to its original position slightly ajar from the bottom of the window frame. He picked up his bag of halfballs and hurried away from Mrs. Kling's roof, confident that Doc Newman would know what to do, and that Fate remained on his side.

As Chris and his mother drove home from St. Michael's that Sunday evening, J.J. was on his bike, pedaling like crazy in the opposite direction, and away from the lone halfball, the evidence, and his fate, trapped behind in Mrs. Kling's attic, in hopes of arriving at St. Michael's before 7:45.

PART FIVE

"I suppose it's like a ticking crocodile, isn't it? Time is chasing after all of us."
  - J.M. Barrie, "Peter Pan"

CHAPTER 22 - MONDAY

On Monday, Chris went to school and returned home afterward to do his homework, as always. His homework, however, was very different from that of his classmates, many of whom didn't do any.

He was far ahead of his classmates in academics. In fact, he was far ahead of his grade level and many subsequent grade levels. However, Aliondra Covington was steadfast in her belief that he should attend class with children his own age. It had long ago become obvious that he needed little academic assistance beyond his own reading and self-study, but his mother believed, rightly, that he needed to relate to kids his own age.

He could easily have handled even post-graduate work at twelve years old, but there was more to school than academics. Aliondra knew. He needed age-appropriate socialization to become the best version of himself. Aliondra might have been surprised to learn that Chris' biological parents would have heartily endorsed her resolve concerning his academic and emotional development. They would have agreed with her game plan.

But Chris, being twelve, was getting itchy. It had been a month since he saved Joey McManus at James' high school football game, and a few months since he had learned he could "connect" mentally to the fabric of space to move at the speed of light. Since then his homework had consisted pretty much entirely of researching all he could about light travel, inhabitable planets, and the lives and findings of those scientists whose work had contributed most significantly to our current understanding of the nature of energy and light. These included Albert Einstein who lived a century ago, Joseph Faraday who lived a century before Einstein, and Emilie duChatelet, the great French female scientist who lived two centuries before Faraday.

Interestingly, Chris thought, each of these pioneering giants had overcome tremendous personal obstacles before achieving success which contributed enormously to the advancement of science, physics, and mankind.

Chris felt they were kindred spirits. Not that he had significant societal hurdles to overcome, as they had, but he had been born with significant intelligence and had struggled, so far, to make important use of it. He knew he was young, though, and had time. Given he could travel at light speed, he would likely have more time than most, because he knew that time slowed down at light speed.

If he stayed connected, constantly traveling at the speed of light, he would age infinitely more slowly than his family and friends, and would live for thousands of their years in what would seem to be a normal life span to him. But what fun would it be to travel at the speed of light all by himself, interacting with no one, and watching his mother, brother, and friends grow old and die long before him? Selfishly, it seemed pretty pointless. No, there must be another reason for him to have this ability but, as yet, he hadn't been able to discern it. It remained a significant missing piece to his personal puzzle.

As Fate would have it, though, Chris would receive his answers in time. The same as the rest of us. What he couldn't have known that Monday night as he Googled light travel and inhabitable planets, his most recent passions, was the imminent arrival of another piece to his personal puzzle.

He logged off his PC at around 11:00 PM and started downstairs to say goodnight to Aliondra. James, who had returned earlier from practice with his high school basketball team, was already in bed. There was an important tournament coming up this week at St. Joseph University out on the main line, west of Philadelphia, another world away from their inner city slum, and one step closer to James' personal goal of earning his way out of the 'hood. And Chris wouldn't bet against his older brother. James was a winner, though he had at least one personal shortcoming of which Chris and his mother, when within earshot, were aware. Chris heard James snoring loudly behind his closed bedroom door.

Downstairs, Aliondra worked on her PC at the dining room table, searching for a new job. Piles of paper littered the table, as the 11:00 PM evening news played, unwatched, on the TV in the living room.

"Hey, mom, goodnight," Chris said, walking into the dining room and stooping to kiss his mother on the cheek. "Any luck?"

"Oh, I'm getting organized: typing letters and searching the help wanted. It will take some time but, you know, the harder I work, the luckier I'll get."

Chris chimed in as she concluded, "...the luckier you'll get." He smiled. It was one of his mom's many aphorisms, and the one he most liked. "Yo, absolutely," he added, in his best Rocky Balboa deep voice. "See you tomorrow. Don't stay up too late," Chris said as he walked away.

He had yet to tell his mother of his special ability. He had wanted to tell her right away, but there never seemed to be a good time. As time went on, however, he thought it might be best to keep this little secret to himself for now, and until his mother wasn't worried about so many other things. He felt bad about keeping a secret from her. He was excited and wanted her to be excited for him. But he realized,he was thinking about himself and what he wanted. When he stopped to consider his mother and her needs, he thought there might be a better time to tell her. Plus, there was nothing she could really do. He could travel at the speed of light. Really, how could she advise him?

By telling him not to cheat or steal or spy on people? She had already taught him those things and they had become ingrained in him. He had been tempted to use his abilities to excel in baseball or basketball or half ball or in his schoolwork but he quickly concluded that he would be helping no one but himself. That seemed way selfish. It also seemed like cheating, so he decided to take some time and see if another answer, another puzzle piece, would present itself to him.

It would.

As he walked through the living room, he saw a newsflash on the TV about a row house fire about a mile away. As he stared, transfixed, at the screen, he saw flames shooting out of the roof as firefighters rushed to hook up hoses to the fire hydrants. The row house was the same as thousands of others which he had seen in his life. In all likelihood a family lived there.

In that moment, Chris knew what he had to do. He connected. Once again, all movement stopped. Aliondra was statuesque, stopped in mid keystroke as she sat at the dining room table. The TV broadcast had paused, the flames shooting from the row home unmoving, as if frozen.

He ran back through the dining room and kitchen and out the rear door of the house. He tore down the back steps, picked up his bike laying on the side of his driveway, and rode the mile to where he knew the burning row house to be. Arriving on the scene about seven of his minutes later, the sight which greeted him was surreal. Giant red and yellow flames, though stilled, reached up into the night sky from the roof of the house, and more motionless flames appeared to be inside, on both the first and second floors.

Fire trucks and firefighters were everywhere, preparing to ram the front door. Three motionless firefighters held a large fire hose, in the act of shooting motionless water through the first floor windows that other firefighters were breaking with hatchets, in the front of the house. Another fireman in a bucket high atop a hydraulic lift extending above the house from a large, red fire engine sprayed water down onto the roof from a fire hose. The water pouring from the hose was suspended in mid-air, unmoving.

From his earlier experiments with Sam in the clubhouse, he knew that when he was connected, he could pass unobstructed through a sheet hanging on a clothesline that he had set up for the purpose. That taught him that he could pass through solid matter as if he were a ghost. Only he and Sam knew this secret.

Sam had proposed the sheet experiment in the first place. He had shared his theory that, when connected, he must be pure energy to travel at light speed, and therefore not solid. So, perhaps he could pass through solid matter. Sam replied, "Let's find out," and set up the sheet-on-the-clothesline experiment.

Chris smiled at the memory. Sam would make an excellent scientist someday, if she didn't become an athlete or, knowing Sam, after her playing days were over.

He ran up the front steps, passing through the locked front door, and into the first floor of the burning row house. The flames around him flared motionless.

The heat was intense. Thick, black smoke engulfed him, stinging his eyes and obscuring his vision, so he had to hold his breath and move quickly. He soon learned that he was ill-prepared for the task at hand. The firefighters were in the midst of breaking the glass in the first floor windows, and water was streaming in, but it too was motionless in midair.

Returning back outside through the locked front door he was once again greeted with a still photograph of firefighters in action. He ran past the nearest still-frame firefighters toward the fire engine and the more distant firemen. He quickly removed the goggles and breathing apparatus from one of the firefighters who was holding them and put them on himself. It took him a minute to get comfortable with the eye goggles and breathing apparatus, but once he did he rushed back into the house.

He quickly saw there was no one on the first

floor. He went down to the basement: no one there. He ran back up the basement steps and up the main staircase to the second floor. There he found three bedrooms and one bathroom all of which were about seconds from being demolished by the charred roof frozen seven feet off the floor.

He ran back toward the front of the house and the master bedroom. There he found a woman asleep on the bed. He picked her up as best he could, and she became connected too, though she remained unconscious. Fortunately she wasn't big, and he was able to carry her back down the steps without falling. He carried her through the locked front door, put her outside the house on the front lawn, and went back upstairs to see if there were any other people there.

In the middle bedroom, he found a young girl and boy each sleeping in a different bed, with the roof suspended four feet from their faces. The boy was about five, the girl three or so. He carried the little girl out first and returned on his next trip for the boy, placing them next to the woman on the front lawn. Each had connected with him when he held them, but each was unconscious, probably from the smoke.

Chris ran back up the stairs and entered the last of the three bedrooms, the back bedroom. There was a teddy bear on the floor and, a few feet beyond that, a bassinette. In the bassinette, four feet below the roof that would have crushed her, lay an infant wrapped in pink blankets. A charred mobile that had been suspended from the ceiling now lay on her face. He removed it before her skin burned, then picked her up with her teddy bear, and carried them downstairs. He placed the baby in the woman's lap and put the teddy bear on the lawn next to them.

He felt then that his work was done. He ran back to the firefighter and returned the equipment he had borrowed. Then he ran down the block, and hid in a small alleyway outside the area the firemen had blocked off, peeking out so he could see. Then he disconnected.

The scene was truly ghastly as the roof completed its descent into the second floor, then caved into the first floor below - but before the firefighters were able to enter. None of the firefighters were seriously injured.

There was a swarm of firefighters and paramedics around the woman and children on the front lawn. The paramedics resuscitated the family members, who had all suffered various degrees of smoke inhalation. Reviving, they coughed and choked, as fresh air gradually won the battle for their lungs. The woman, understandably, soon became quite inconsolable as she watched her home go up in smoke and flame, though she gathered the three children to herself and hugged them repeatedly, kissing them, and telling them she loved them. The firemen were thoroughly confused as to how she and the children had found their way onto the front lawn, but they moved quickly to get them out of harm's way.

The fireman in the bucket continued pouring water from the big fire hose onto the collapsed roof from above. Quite a crowd had gathered. The residents of the row homes on either side of the burned out house had been evacuated. Many of them were on the sidewalk across the street, wrapped in blankets, with their hands to their mouths and faces, watching in disbelief as the firemen fought heroically to control and contain the inferno.

As Chris left the excitement behind and rode his bike home, his mind was preoccupied with many thoughts, some good, some not so good. He was happy that he had been able to save that young family in much the same way as he had saved Joey McManus a month ago. Yet his efforts to save the many children and aid workers at St. Michael's Home were coming up way short. Also, he didn't seem to be able to help his own mother in any meaningful way as she struggled to overcome her memory of abuse at the hands of her former boss, Mr. Lewis.

As he rode along the poorly lit city streets, he noticed, as if for the first time, the many front doors of the row homes he passed. What was behind those doors? Loving families with bright futures, or people suffering some kind of abuse or unimaginable hardship? Most likely, he knew, he'd find a little of both. This saddened him. Life was supposed to be happy. It was supposed to be good. What had happened? More importantly, perhaps, could he really do anything about it? He wasn't sure. Although he might be able to help a few people here and there, it seemed highly unlikely that he would ever be able to help them all or even enough of them.

The young children and their mother were safe. This was the good news. A few days later, however, the fire chief would declare the fire to have been intentionally set, an arson, which prompted police captain, Dan Carroll, to assign homicide detective Lieutenant Joe Carter to investigate and file a written report. Explaining what had happened in that house that night, and how all the occupants had survived, would once again prove to be a monumental challenge to a proud and gifted detective.

CHAPTER 23 - TUESDAY

The next day, Chris headed straight to the clubhouse after school. Now was his time, the time he used to read about things of particular interest to him, and lately that had become anything concerning outer space, space travel, jet propulsion, astronomy, light travel, inhabitable planets, and the like.

At other times, he had been deeply interested in the classics, politics, history, and calculus, but now he was consumed with learning as much as he could about predicting the number of inhabitable planets.

He sat down at the table, and turned on his desk lamp. It was getting dark earlier at this time of year. An hour later, his mother brought up some pizza for him. "Eat, Chris, please eat," Aliondra said.

"Sure, Mom," he said without looking up. He was totally engrossed in his learning, and his mother had grown used to this. She knew it was a 50/50 proposition as to whether or not he would ever even notice the food was there.

"You can't study on an empty stomach," she said, and disbelieved her own words as soon as she said them. Chris had missed many meals, but never his studies. Knowledge had always been his nourishment; its pursuit his appetite. She smiled down at him before finally realizing the hopelessness of her plea. Finally, without saying another word, she turned and left.

Was there intelligent life elsewhere in the universe? Chris was still gathering data to help him formulate his own opinion. The Scientific American and the NASA website were two of his favorite sources. He knew he could use probability, statistics, and integral calculus to derive reasonable conclusions, but the pictures and accounts in these publications were helpful to him in developing a hopefully meaningful equation.

Each night refinements arose as he learned more in school. There was so much to learn it would have taken him years had he not sometimes connected to study. He was able to learn in a span of weeks what it would have taken him years to learn without connecting.

There were so many variables to consider. There are trillions of stars with likely more trillions of planets orbiting them. Some, probably millions, of those planets likely exhibit conditions conducive to life as we know it. Some of those environments have been around long enough to support dinosaurs, and others, like Earth, are old enough to support intelligent life.

On some planets, beings probably have evolved to the point where they destroyed themselves with atomic weapons, or were destroyed by asteroids or exploding suns or failing orbits. And on a fewer number of planets, some beings may have evolved further and survived that period. Maybe only two or three planets are home to beings that have mastered space travel.

The likelihood assigned to each of these factors changed the answer of his equation from no other planets with intelligent life to about a hundred planets with intelligent life, at this point in time, throughout the universe.

This particular evening Chris was attempting to refine the factor for planet lifetimes by studying the half-lives of radioactive isotopes. He plugged in the results of the research from the latest issue of Scientific American and this reduced his equation's answer from 53 planets to 49 planets likely supporting intelligent life throughout the universe.

Not a good night. Not the kind of answer he was hoping for, but he knew his equation was a little bit more reliable now than it was before he had begun working. *Well, '49' is better than none.* With that comforting thought, he decided to call it a night.

He reached to turn the desk lamp off and go downstairs. Suddenly, he had the distinct impression that he was not alone. He felt...something. What was it? Turning around, he saw a man standing in the corner across the room, watching him.

He was a tall man, mid-forties, ruddy in appearance, with an angular jaw, slightly mussed salt and pepper hair trimmed on the sides, longer in the middle, and captivating iridescent milky-gray eyes. Dressed in a white satin blouse with gold buttons, and well-creased navy blue trousers with gold piping, beneath a long unbuttoned ivory trench coat with gold epaulettes, he also sported fine cordovan leather boots and gloves. His brilliant appearance contrasted starkly with the shadows on the far side of the clubhouse.

"Whoa! Who are you?"

The man smiled slightly. "My name is Fixer."

"Fixer? That's a pretty strange name," Chris said, frightened at the sudden and secretive appearance of a stranger in the clubhouse. Chris had risen from where he had been seated and was backing away from the man, reaching behind himself to avoid obstacles.

"Our names indicate our specialty," Fixer replied, removing his gloves and spreading his arms out slightly to either side. Chris immediately saw a pulsing series of blue lights emanating from five rings on Fixer's right hand.

"*Our* names?" Chris asked, looking away from the blue lights on the man's right hand, and up at his face.

"The Savants."

"Who are the Savants?" Chris asked,

confused.

"It is a long story, and there is not much time right now. May I sit? I have travelled a great distance to see you, and I am very tired."

"Sure," Chris responded, and Fixer settled into the arm-chair.

"So what exactly do you fix?" Chris asked.

"Actually, my full name is Amnesius Fixer. I fix peoples' memories and, many times hopefully, their lives."

Chris feared the stranger might be missing a few mental marbles, but remembering his mother's frequent admonition to not judge too quickly, and sensing that the blue pulsating rings might somehow indicate a recent, cool advance in technology, or something else important, he decided to see where this conversation might lead. "Forget things? Shouldn't you help people to remember things, if you were really being helpful?"

"Some people have painful memories, destructive memories, things they'd be better off forgetting. There's a lot of pain and suffering. That's where I come in. I can make it better."

"Can you help my mom?"

"Does she need help?" Fixer asked, choosing not to answer Chris' question.

"I don't know. I'm not a doctor, but I think she struggles with something."

"What kind of thing?"

"She never talked about it, until recently and, still, she keeps it pretty much to herself, so I don't know exactly. It might be something that happened with her former boss, Mr. Lewis. He fired her but she says he was making moves on her and she didn't want that."

Fixer was looking down now, and did not respond. Chris studied him. Fixer looked to be maybe forty years old, but his movements were slower, as though he were older.

"I feel a lot older than I am, but I'm a lot younger than I look," Fixer responded to Chris' thoughts.

"Wow, you can read my thoughts?"

"An elementary skill, really. My colleague, Miss Portice, helped me to perfect it. She's a natural. Someday you'll do it too. Most Savants can read thoughts."

"So you and this Miss Portice are Savants?" Chris asked.

"You are also."

"Me?" Chris asked, startled.

"Chris, would you mind if we connect while we have this conversation? We really need to conserve time, I am afraid."

"Whoa! You connect too?"

"Yes, all Savants connect, and only Savants connect. May we?"

"Yeah, sure, um, why not?" Chris agreed, sitting back down, facing Fixer. They both connected then.

Chris stared hard at Fixer. There was something familiar about him. "Have we met before?" he asked. "You look like someone I know, I think, but I'm not sure who. Is that possible?"

Rather than answer directly, Fixer stood and hunched over slightly, and pretended to be carrying something over his shoulder. Then he drawled, "Y'all gonna yap in there all day, or are we gonna play some dad-gum baseball?"

Chris' eyes went wide. "Billy? You're Billy-The-Trash-Picker?"

"Best dad-gum trash picker this side 'o the Pecos," Fixer replied, sitting back down, slowly, playing the part of a much older, feebler man.

"I don't believe it. You can't be. I mean, Billy is old, really old."

"Believe it," Fixer replied. "Don't be too

quick to judge, son."

"You sound like my mom. That's what she always says."

"You are the beneficiary of a wise mother," he said, seemingly referring to Aliondra but, in reality, referring to both Aliondra and Mary Newman. "We Savants have a cardinal rule: most of what is real cannot be seen."

"Like the fabric of space?" Chris' mind seemed to be on hyperdrive, as he raced to keep up with this remarkable man.

"Yes, many truths are not always obvious."

"Um, okay. Most of what's real cannot be seen. Got it. Man, you really are Billy, aren't you? I mean I can see it now: the mouth, your voice. Dang!"

When Fixer did not respond in turn, Chris broke the awkward lull, "Um, okay, so what do you mean that I am a Savant? I am a human being."

"We are the rarest of all humans," Fixer started. "Roughly just two or three humans born in any decade will become a Savant."

"So, there's you, me, Miss Portice, a few others, and that's it?" Chris asked.

"No, there are a few thousand of us actually."

"But you said two or three a decade…"

"That's correct."

"So that means…the life expectancy…" Chris stumbled, not believing where this conversation was going.

"About a thousand of your years, give or take…say, are you going to eat that pizza?" Fixer asked, motioning to the pizza which Chris hadn't touched in over over two hours. "I love pizza. Tough to find in some places."

"A thousand years!" Chris exclaimed.

"Give or take. May I?" Fixer persisted, reaching for the pizza.

"But that's impossible. We're organic. Our physiologies won't permit…"

"Ah! But that's just it." Fixer started after taking a large bite out of one of the pizza slices, "our physiologies, yours and mine, do permit it," he said, raising his right hand, wiggling his two thumbs on that hand. "You see, we are a little different. We have to be," he said, wiping his mouth with the back of his left hand. "You wouldn't happen to have any napkins, would you?"

"Sorry," Chris replied, shaking his head.

"No problem. Good pizza. Best when it's cold," Fixer said, taking another large bite.

"A thousand years old, there's no way," Chris muttered, not believing it possible.

"A thousand Savant years."

"Savant years?"

"Yes, years in a connected state. We experience a thousand years of life, activity, and accomplishments, and appear to age for a thousand years. But, in our connected state, that's about twenty million years on Earth."

"Twenty million years!" Chris shouted, dumbfounded. "There's no way!"

"It's true. Good thing too," Fixer continued. "We're a pretty busy bunch. Lots to do. Never enough time, it seems."

"This is nuts," Chris laughed. "I'm going to live to be twenty million years old? How about my family?"

"They're not Savants," Fixer replied matter-of-factly.

"So I will outlive them?"

"There are no guarantees, son. None of us can know the future with absolute certainty, of course. I can tell you, though, that unless some calamity befalls you, you will outlive not only your family and friends but this geological Earth age."

"But why haven't I ever heard of Savants, if what you say is true?"

"Savants don't advertise," Fixer replied. "There is no need. You and I will accomplish great things in our lifetimes, but most humans will never know it."

"Why?"

"It is the way it must be. There are good reasons. Let's just say that, human nature being what it is, public acclaim often gets in the way of the greater good we may accomplish."

"Because of ego?"

"Ah! Very good. Very insightful, indeed. Yes, ego – the greatest friend and foe of goodness in the known universe."

"Foe?"

"From great egos comes greatness – both for good and for bad. One of the greatest manifestations of pure ego is great evil. It is why I have been sent to you."

"Sent?"

"As a protector or guardian. Great evil exists. And one of its avowed purposes is the destruction of great good. The Savants believe you, especially, are capable of tremendous good. That also means, of course, that you may become a prized target."

"Target of who?"

"Vo...," Fixer started, then seemed to think better of it. "Better not to say here. Their hearing and senses are excellent. I'd rather not let them know where I am. In time your question will be answered."

"Okay, are there evil Savants?" Chris asked.

"Very few. Very, very few but, sadly, yes. Some have fallen and they are very powerful."

"So that twenty million years of life is only possible, not assured," Chris said.

"You should forget the twenty million. You will live in a connected state. It will seem to be a thousand years. But, you are essentially correct."

"Oh, only a thousand years, right," Chris snickered, sarcastically. "So are you, like, my guardian angel or something?"

"Not really. Just an insurance policy, so to speak. It would not be fair to you to solo in a universe where evil targets those such as you."

"Why am I a target? What did I do?" Chris was obviously worried.

"You are quite safe here, trust me," Fixer held up his hands, palms out, to reassure him. "It will likely be many years yet before you find yourself in any danger. Actually, that's true for most people. It's called growing up. As you get older, everyone has friends, and almost everyone encounters enemies in some form. In your case, you have quite a few of us watching out for you, so don't worry."

"Teamwork," Chris concluded.

"Speaking of which, could you hand me another slice of pizza?"

Chris opened the pizza box and handed Fixer a slice. "Thanks. Yes teamwork," Fixer said. "Everyone can use a little help – even the best and the brightest."

"So you're not angels. Are there guardian angels?"

"Ah! Religion. Many of us believe there are guardian angels. Most of us hope so."

"But even the Savants don't know?"

"Some things are unknowable. We are human beings too, many of us," Fixer noted.

"But you have been around a long time, right? Wouldn't you know by now?" Chris asked.

"We Savants go back eons – since before recorded time on Earth as you know it, and a few other planets, but we are of nature, as are all humans. We stake no claim on the supernatural."

"Eons?" Chris asked.

"About two hundred million years."

"Two hundred million years!" Chris exclaimed. "Oh my God! How can that be? Glacial changes on Earth would not support…"

"Life on Earth," Fixer finished Chris' statement. "You are correct. Most Savants no longer live on Earth. It is too risky: asteroids, nuclear contamination, ice ages, etc. The Savants spread risk via diversification. We live on several planets now, though we favor Maran as our home base. It is an Earth-like planet, though pristine, much larger, and very beautiful."

"How did you conquer space travel?" Chris asked.

"By doing what you and I are doing now – by connecting to the fabric of space. It is one of the greatest of all gifts – made possible only by our advanced mental capacities, and far beyond those of all other humans."

"So I was right. I am connecting mentally to the fabric of space."

"For all practical purposes. That is the colloquial term, but we all say pretty much the same thing."

"So the Savants have been around for all of recorded history?" Chris asked.

"Yes. All of recorded Earth history, and

much longer, of course."

"Why didn't you rule the world? You could've done a better job knowing what you know and doing what you can do."

"We did, for a while. Tens of millions of years ago," Fixer said. "It was an utter failure though."

"Why?"

"We are too trusting, too good, I guess. But the evil ones and their legions are very powerful, very cunning. They turned the masses against us by appealing to their baser instincts – similar to the situation in your world today. We soon understood that our evolutionary advantage is in exploration and colonization, rather than administration and domination. So, that's what we do."

"But there were no humans on earth even a million years ago," Chris challenged.

"That is correct. But there were civilization cycles prior to this one. Many millions of years ago. When a civilization cycle ends, there are no more humans coming to Maran from Earth and other home-based planets. This happens every few million years or so. But, once a new civilization cycle kicks in, nature always turns out a few Savants. Nature, it seems, likes to show off when she gets the chance."

"How modest of you," Chris replied,

sarcastically.

Fixer did not respond which spoke volumes. The Savants dealt in facts. They were beyond false modesty and political correctness.

After a short pause, and as Fixer finished off the pizza, Chris said, "I knew you were here, you know. I mean, I knew someone was here before I actually saw you."

"You are beginning to sense others' mental energy. It takes time to learn."

"Sometimes I'm pretty sure I can hear others' thoughts too," Chris added.

"Yes, it is annoying, I know, but you will learn to tune them out in time."

"My eyesight seems to be so much better than everyone else's. My hearing too."

"Supersensory perception. It is quite necessary for space travel. They are evolutionary advantages. Seeing great distances comes in handy when your nearest reference point may be several light years away."

"Space...um, travel?" Chris stammered. Fixer nodded. "Hot dang! So what exactly is the evolutionary advantage that would lead to the existence of Savants?"

"What do you think?" Fixer asked. "Is it not

obvious?"

"Continuation of the human race?" Chris ventured.

"Correct."

"In the face of glacial planetary changes."

"And, more to the point in your case I am afraid, planetary death," Fixer said.

"What do you mean?"

"The Earth is dying."

"No. Geologists predict…" Chris started, but was cut off.

"The Earth-based geologists, using Earth-based technologies, are quite wrong, trust me. Their calculations are off by magnitudes."

"How can that be?"

"Man-made pollutants, atmospheric breakdown, unrestrained nuclear testing, underground oil extraction, and an as-yet undetected cosmic event are all coming together at the same time, unfortunately."

"The Earth is dying?" Chris asked.

"Mother Earth is gasping, dying, but crying out. Do you not see the signs? Mass flooding, mass deforestation, massive mountains and oceans of pollutants, landfills, iceberg loss, atmospheric nuclear testing, a huge hole in the Ozone layer, unmitigated carbon pollution, record disappearances of whole species, irresponsible and unregulated deep-water drilling..."

"Can nothing be done?" Chris had to cut him off.

"Only a complete worldwide cessation of industry and life as it is lived. That would require all humans to live in the best interests of the planet."

"That won't happen," Chris said.

"And you understand that, even as a twelve-year-old. No, son, that won't happen. People will always act in their own self-interests or, rather, what they perceive to be their own short-term interests."

"Is there nothing I can do?" Chris asked.

"You will do much, we hope," Fixer replied.

"Any advice?"

Pointing at the blackboard, Fixer replied, "Maybe. Permit me to ask you a question first."

"Shoot," Chris said.

"Why do you undertake to solve that equation?"

"This?" Chris asked, turning to his

blackboard and away from Fixer. "Because I want to try to understand how many planets in the universe might have intelligent life living on them right now."

"And why is that important to you?"

"Why? I don't know. I guess it's an interesting puzzle. I like puzzles, especially math puzzles, and this seems to be one ginormous math puzzle."

"Why is it interesting?"

"Hey, you said one question," Chris said.

"Please, bear with me. "Why do you deem solving that equation," Fixer said, pointing at the backboard, "to be worth your time?"

If Chris had a feeling of respect before now, it had just grown markedly. He now understood that Fixer was trying to get to the heart of the matter and, in so doing, understand Chris more fully. Fixer was testing him, so Chris decided to come clean and spill the beans to this remarkable man. No one, not his mother, not James, not his science teacher, not even Sam, had ever asked him that question.

"Because...," Chris started, hesitating, "because the universe is so unimaginably huge, perhaps even beyond math models as we know them, that it may be beyond human comprehension. I mean, 350 million solar systems each containing 250 million stars and, probably trillions of planets...well, okay, we can put trillions down on paper or into a computer but for our minds to really grasp that quantity…and understand that traveling at the speed of light we will never leave the galaxy we're in, the Milky Way. I have to ask what's the sense of millions of Milky Ways? Why is the universe so large if we can never get to the end of the universe to see it?"

"And what have you concluded? What is the purpose?"

"I'm not sure, but if we can't possibly get there, to the end of the universe, it does seem like an extreme waste of effort."

"And therefore…" Fixer prompted.

"And therefore," Chris didn't hesitate with what he felt was true, "we must be able to get there."

"Even with the speed of light constraint? Even though nothing can travel faster than the speed of light?"

"Yes," Chris replied, simply. "Even though we cannot travel faster than the speed of light."

"But what if the universe wasn't designed? What if there is no reason for its size other than it's just the way it is?" Fixer asked.

"Then that would be even more ludicrous," Chris said. "Nature is efficient. It wouldn't be wasteful in that way."

Fixer smiled and said, "Bravo! You have answered my questions well." Then, pointing at the blackboard, he said, "use iridium, not plutonium in your fifth factor there. Plutonium is common here but relatively rare elsewhere in the universe. Iridium will get you closer to the answer you seek."

"But the spectra suggest…"

"Double-check the spectral readings at different times of the year and different times of day and you will get wildly disparate readings. Iridium is not as plentiful here on Earth, granted, but its spectrum is much more reliable over a distance of many light years when stellar interference is factored in – not exact, but close enough for your estimate."

Chris, still looking at the blackboard, said, "Yes, yes, I see. That's excellent, really excellent. You know, that will work. It really will!" he exclaimed as he erased the fifth factor and chalked in the correct factor and the new answer. "Hot Dang! Fifty-one planets, now we're cooking."

"You're close," Fixer said.

"Are you a scientist?"

"You might say that, yes, among other things," Fixer replied.

"How do you know this equation?"

"Let's just say it looks familiar."

"Familiar? How?"

"In my work, I have seen many similar equations."

"And what is your work?" Chris asked.

"Now that's a question. Let's see, well it is primarily helping people I suppose, though my real job involves..... astronomy."

"You're a physicist?"

"An astrophysicist."

"Do you work for the government or something?"

"Or something," Fixer replied. "Enough about me though. I see your work and I have to tell you I am impressed. It is good work and I thank you for it."

"For this? You're thanking me for my calculation?" Chris asked, waving his arm at the blackboard.

"For saving the humans in the house fire and at the football game. It is a great thing you are doing."

"How do you know these things?"

"It's my job." Chris waited for a more full explanation, but none was forthcoming.

After a slight pause, Fixer changed the subject. "Anyway, time grows short, I am afraid. Our time on Earth grows short."

"*Our* time on Earth?" Chris asked.

"Yes, your time and my time. This is actually the point of my visit. Although you may live for many millennia, your time on Earth is nearing an end. Like every single Savant before you without exception, going back over two hundred million years, you will soon decide to venture beyond Earth. To leave."

"Why?"

"Why? To survive and thrive, that's why. Your survival here is at risk because, according to our calculations, Earth will be destroyed by a near-simultaneous meteor and a series of manmade and natural thermonuclear events very, very soon. Earth is doomed."

"How soon?"

"Within twenty Earth years. That is why it is important that you leave. Important to you, certainly, but also to us. To the Savants. You see, you may very well be the last of the Savants in the current civilization cycle."

"Don't you have babies?"

"Quite infrequently."

"Why?"

"Savants represent the end of the human evolutionary chain. Biologically, there is nothing to improve. Nature is satisfied with us. She is done tinkering, so to speak. Therefore Savant births, though possible, are extremely risky and rare. Should a child be desired, we employ artificial methods which, even though most advanced, have a very low success rate. The Savant genome is infinitely complex and difficult to replicate, even for Mother Nature."

"I survived."

"But your brother and sister before you did not. They each died in childbirth."

This news rocked Chris. It was the first time he was learning he had siblings. Even though they did not survive childbirth, he felt the loss and was suddenly very sad. He filed the knowledge and hurt away, and would reflect on them at another time. He needed to use this precious time to learn what he could from Fixer.

"But why us? Why you and me and Miss Portice? Why are we Savants and my brother James and Mom aren't?" Chris asked the question, though he knew the answer.

"Come, come now, son. Self-pity does not become you. You and I have been given the greatest of all human gifts. We are not cursed, and we are not to be pitied. No, not at all. We have been given the ultimate evolutionary advantage. We are winners of the greatest lottery natural selection offers. Whatever the reason, we are the best that evolution can offer."

"The best that evolution can offer," Chris repeated, softly, reflecting.

"If you believe in purpose, it is an awesome responsibility we have been given, is it not? Why us? Who knows? I suspect every Savant who has ever lived has asked the same question. To my knowledge, none of us has received a better answer than...random selection."

"Luck of the draw," Chris summarized.

"Now," Fixer continued after a slight pause, "the only way we survive, as a species and colony, is to nurture new Savants, such as you."

"So you're kidnappers, essentially. You come and plunder our population for your own survival."

"No. Not at all. Every single Savant, for over two hundred million years, has chosen to leave Earth or their other home planets. There is no coercion. Ever. It is your choice to stay on Earth or to come with us. I'm telling you that no Savant has ever chosen to stay on Earth."

"Why?"

"Once you see the worlds and opportunities available to us beyond Earth, you will answer your own question. I am quite confident of that. Space travel is a powerful elixir for Savants. It is what we were created to do."

"So all Savants for over 200 million years have left Earth?"

"No. I said only that all Savants have desired to leave Earth. Not all have successfully done so. In fact, many do not because they do not earn the right. So, you see, we do not plunder. In fact, quite the contrary, we have set up rules to limit participation in our society. We cannot abide slackers, non-achievers. There is too much to do to support freeloaders. Every one of us pulls our own weight. Fear not, however. I see you soon receiving the assistance from us you will need to transition safely to life beyond Earth. Without our assistance, attempting to do so would be fatal."

"How about non-Savants such as Sam, James, and my parents? Will I be able to take them with me should I leave Earth?"

"In all likelihood, no."

Chris was dumbstruck as he tried to understand all that Fixer was telling him – that he would most likely leave his family, and that they and the rest of the inhabitants of Earth had only about twenty years to live. "My mom, my brother, J.J., Headmistress Brennan, Mrs. Kling, my friends, everybody will die within twenty years, and I won't be here for them. There must be some way I can save them. There has to be."

"I don't see how a twelve-year-old can save an entire planet," Fixer replied. "You won't have enough time. You'd better focus on saving yourself. But these are matters for another time. They are really not as important as what I came to talk to you about."

"What? What could be more important than the destruction of the entire planet and losing my family within twenty years?"

"It could be much less than twenty years for your brother."

"James? What about James? Is he in some kind of trouble?"

"Yes. You need to go to him. You will find him coming out of practice at St. Joe's Fieldhouse."

Chris stared at Fixer. How did he know these things? "Is there a way I can contact you? Will I see you again?"

"You will see me again. But you'd better get going. You need to help your brother. He is in serious trouble," Fixer said.

"Thank you, Fixer," Chris said, before turning to descend the steps of the clubhouse.

"Stay connected," Fixer said. "Otherwise you will be too late."

Chris, remaining connected, then ran down the steps and hopped on his bike. The ride to St. Joe's Fieldhouse was twelve miles.

Walking back to the table, Fixer picked up the last slice of pizza in the box and said, theatrically, to an imagined host, "Thank you. Don't mind if I do."

"It's not good to talk to yourself, Fixer," Senior Senator Geemez suddenly interjected from his council chamber on Maran, many light years away.

"Not good and not possible, apparently," Fixer replied, electing not to cloak his sarcasm.

CHAPTER 24 - TUESDAY

James walked out of the fenced parking lot and onto the street behind the campus. There were no parking spaces when the team bus drove to the school earlier in the evening. All the spaces had been taken by the university students, and players from the other practicing teams. So the bus driver had to park about three blocks away.

After practice and his speech to the team, James' coach dismissed the boys back to the bus. James and a couple of his teammates lagged behind, helping Coach carry the equipment. Coach had been intercepted by the tournament director as they were leaving, so he sent the boys ahead, telling them to let the bus driver know he would be along in a few minutes.

On the way back to the bus, the other boys decided to race, but James was way too tired to run after their very demanding practice.

James was far and away the best player on the team and typically worked very hard to become even better. His two teammates, on the other hand, were bench players who saw little playing time. They were apparently still full of energy and raced each other to the bus.

On a typically chilly late-November evening, James found himself lugging a string net load of basketballs through a strange neighborhood, alone. For the first time, he noticed how dark, dreary, and overcast it was as he walked farther and farther from the campus, under a canopy of trees lining the street. James quickened his pace as the bus came into view a block ahead.

Suddenly, two men jumped out of a parked car just ahead of him. One had a baseball bat. They blocked the sidewalk in front of him.

"Hey, punk, what's the hurry?" asked Bat Carrier.

"Yeah, hot shot, where you goin'?" the other one asked. As he walked past, he bumped James hard.

"Look guys, I don't want any trouble. I'm just going to my bus," James said, nervously, holding up both hands, palms outward.

"Oh yeah? That so?" mocked Bat Carrier. "Give me your money."

James backed up onto the slightly banked lawn, trying to keep both of the muggers in view.

"I don't have any money."

"Yeah you do," said the second mugger as he pushed James again.

Bat Carrier raised the bat now. "I guess I'll have to beat it out of you, punk."

Bat Carrier swung the bat at James' head. James ducked and heard the second guy say, "What the…?"

When James looked up, Chris was standing there, holding the bat, while Bat Carrier was on the ground. He had continued his swinging motion without the bat, had lost his balance, and had fallen down, sprawling.

The two muggers were paralyzed with fear by Chris' sudden appearance. Looking at the barrel of the bat, Chris said to Bat Carrier as he cowered on the sidewalk, "You hurt my brother, and it'll be the last thing you ever do." Then, looking at the other mugger, "that goes for you too."

Bat Carrier stood, and the two muggers huddled together, backing away from Chris slowly. They stared at him, frightened. He suddenly connected to cover the twenty-foot distance between them and himself instantaneously. He effectively rushed at them at the speed of light, stopped just in front of their faces, disconnected and said, "Boo!"

They both fell backward and down to the ground. "Get out of here," he said to them. "And hurry up before I have to use this bat on you." They leaped up and sprinted toward their car, started it up, and raced down the street.

Chris turned to see James sitting on the lawn embankment, stunned by what he was seeing. Chris went over to him.

"How did you…? Where did you...?" James stammered.

"A friend sent me. It's a long story. Look, get back with your team, okay?" Chris helped his brother up off the ground, then picked up his own bike to begin the twelve mile ride home. He was exhausted after the long ride from home and the confrontation with the larger muggers.

James, stunned, but beginning to regain his senses now, put his hand on his brother's arm before he could depart. "Chris, thanks for saving my skull. A split second later, I was a goner."

"That's alright, James. Glad I could help. Can't lose my only big brother now, can I?"

"But how…," James began. "Chris, what the heck is going on with you? Just what have you discovered up in that clubhouse anyway?"

"Let's talk once we're home," Chris said, looking around to see if anyone was watching them. "I'll feel safer there."

"You rode that thing all the way out here?"

"Yes."

"Why?"

"Because I like having a brother, even if it's only you."

"But, how did you know I would be mugged?"

"What? Like it's so tough to figure out that you piss off other people too?"

"Chris, come on, really…"

"Okay, James, really…we'll talk about it when we get home. I gotta get going."

"No way, Dude. You're riding on the bus with us. Come on."

"Really?" Chris couldn't believe James was inviting him to ride with the big kids.

"Really. I need you to get home safe. I think there are some things about a certain little white dude I need to learn."

"'Bout time," Chris said.

"'Bout time," James agreed, as they walked together down the narrow sidewalk to the school bus. Then, "why do you think people keep trying to hit us in the head with baseball bats?"

"Dunno. Maybe our heads look like baseballs."

James looked askance at his brother, smiled, and shook his head. "Speak for yourself…Paleface."

****

Chris looked at James and Aliondra. How much to tell them?

He and James were home, after the bus ride in which James had prevailed, over much initial objection, to Coach's insistence that he speak to Mrs. Covington about her younger son biking at night to a distant, dangerous neighborhood. Coach only relented when James promised to handle the matter with his mother and to make sure she called him the next day to discuss it.

Aliondra was fit to be tied when Chris walked in the door so late that evening with James. Much ranting and raving ensued about curfews and what Family Services might do should they ever find out, and how she couldn't have her two sons out all over the city at all hours of the night without her knowing, and how James ought to know better, and how would he like to be pulled off that team right now, and on and on and on. Chris and James had never seen their mother so angry. And, she was right, of course. As his mother railed at them both, Chris regretted letting James talk him into coming home with him on the team bus. He should have just connected, as he had originally intended, and returned home with no one, except James, the wiser for his having left in the first place.

After a few minutes, Mount Aliondra seemed to be through the worst of her eruption, and collapsed into her easy chair. When her sons apologized and went to kiss her goodnight, she waved them off. "Get to bed!" she screamed. "Both of you! Out of my sight! Now! You'll be the death of me, and I can't afford to die right now!" she shouted, pointing to the stairs.

James turned to go upstairs. Chris held his ground. "Wait, James," he said. "I promised to show you how I did what I did, and I think mom should see too," he said.

"I don't want to see nuthin' but your two sorry incorrigible ingrate butts going up those stairs, and fast!" she shouted, standing now, walking over to face down her younger son. Chris held his ground. This was important.

"I'll go under one condition," Chris stared back into his mother's angry eyes.

"That you're still drawing breath when I'm done with you? Is that your condition? Because it had better be, believe you me!" his mother thundered. "If you don't get upstairs right this minute!"

Chris demurred, not because he was afraid of what she might do, but because he knew it was in his mother's best interest. If he continued with his planned demonstration, it might scare the crap out of her and put her over the edge. She clearly was not in a state of mind right now to suffer another shock, and his demonstration would, undoubtedly, be quite shocking.

So, he said, "On the condition you know your sons would never do anything to hurt you," he said, turning and going up the stairs with James.

"Oh no you don't, Mister!" Aliondra shouted. "Down here! This minute! Both of you!" Chris and James ran back down the stairs and stood, facing their mother.

She looked at them, relenting, finally. She seemed to be shouted out. The volcano was going inactive. "I'm sorry," she began. "I'm sorry," she said, beginning to cry, plopping down in her chair. "I know you love me. I know you love me. I just don't know why," she said putting her face in her hands.

James looked at Chris. "That's easy," he said, kneeling and hugging his mother, "because you're the coolest mom ever."

"That's true, Mom," Chris joined in, bending over the other side of the chair to hug his mom.

"Okay, okay," Aliondra said, hugging them back. Then, pulling a tissue out of her pocket, wiping the tears from her eyes and blowing her nose she said, "But I didn't fall off the turnip truck yesterday. Chris, what was your real condition...and don't give me that you love me baloney...I know you love me, but I think I'd better hear what it was you intended to say."

"Mom," Chris began, "it's not important. We can talk about it later."

"We can talk about later later," she said. "We can talk about now now. Don't keep on trying to snow me, son," she said. "I don't come by gray hairs without learning a few things along the way. And unless I miss my guess, you need to tell me something I need to hear."

Chris never ceased to be amazed by his mother's intuition. She really was a remarkable woman in so many ways. Not least of all, he knew, she used to excel at basketball at Girl's High years ago. Her love of the sport had influenced James. Aliondra and James shared many fine talks over the years regarding their respective B-ball exploits. "Okay," Chris began, "but I need to tell you both. You need to be sitting when I tell you, he said, nodding at James who continued to kneel next to his mother's chair.

"Wait," Aliondra said, holding up her hands. "Is it more bad news? I don't know if I can deal with more bad news right now. I have enough on my plate as it is without you piling on."

"Actually, mom," Chris said, "it's really good news. Really good, but it is shocking. I know you're dealing with a lot of other stuff right now, so if you'd rather wait, I will wait."

"Good Lord," Aliondra said, "well if it ain't bad and it's as good as you say, I suppose I need to hear it, especially now, shocking or not. I need to take good news any old way."

James, moving to sit on the sofa, said, "Okay, I'm sitting. Shoot. Shock us, little bro."

The powerful force was back, again, compelling Chris to say nothing. Somehow he knew that he was not supposed to be telling non-Savants of his abilities. On the other hand, he had been told not ninety minutes earlier that the Earth, and his family would be destroyed within twenty years. Were that true, it was also possible that he himself would be the last of the Savants. Perhaps the "rules of the game" were changing. After all, how could a twelve-year-old like Chris be expected to save the world without help? He was growing weary of deceiving his family who had done nothing but love him, provide for him, defend him, and care for him throughout his life. Finally, he reasoned, if the Savants were infallible, perhaps the Earth wouldn't be in the condition it was in.

In that split second, Chris made a fateful decision. If the Savants wanted him to be great, then he was going to have to do it on his terms and no one else's.

"I want to show you something," Chris said. "James, give me the ball."

"Why?"

"I'm going to teach you a new move."

"You teach me? Hah!" James laughed, passing the basketball, hard, to his brother. "That would definitely be a shocker."

Chris, ignoring yet another of his brother's ceaseless taunts, said, "I need you both to stand up and defend against me."

"Chris, son, come on," Aliondra started, standing. She knew her younger son had absolutely no basketball abilities whereas James, at 14, and 6'2" tall, might already be the best young amateur basketball player in the city. The local papers already had dubbed him "Jesse James" for his jump shooting accuracy. The living room was small, barely 14 feet wide, less three feet for the staircase along one side wall, and two feet for the straight-back piano and piano bench along the other side wall. It was highly unlikely that twelve-year-old Chris, at 5' 6", who couldn't dribble well, could maneuver in a nine-foot wide space between two high school standouts. "What are you doing?" Aliondra asked.

"You need to stop me," Chris replied, "from getting past you. But, once I succeed, you have to promise not to freak out and to sit down with me to figure out a few things, okay?"

"You dribble past me?" James laughed. "That ain't happening, little bro."

"Mom?" Chris looked at his mom, once again ignoring his annoying brother. "Promise?"

"I promise," Aliondra said, standing next to James, confident there was no way Chris could beat them. "I won't freak out, and I will talk to you," she said, taking a deep breath, collecting herself, and assuming a defensive posture.

"Ready?" Chris asked, as he checked the ball to James.

"Bring it on, hotshot," James responded, tossing the ball back to him.

"Don't try this at home," Chris responded.

"Big talk from a little man," James replied.

"Okay, stop me now," Chris said, beginning to dribble the ball, hoping for the best.

Immediately, so as to most dramatically prove his point, James lunged for the ball. Chris connected, and James and his mother immediately froze. Chris walked the ball between them, sat in his mother's chair with the ball in his lap, and disconnected.

Seeing his mother and brother from behind now, Chris heard James say, "What the...?" and saw them both look side to side and at each other before turning to see him sitting in the chair. Aliondra stumbled, in shock, but did not faint, as James rushed to hold her up. Staring at him in disbelief, Chris said matter-of-factly, "I can travel at the speed of light. Pretty great, huh?"

Their subsequent family talk went way into the evening. Aliondra was as good as her word. She did not go hysterical or faint. All things considered, she handled the shock amazingly well. When Chris told her so, she replied, "I guess having two sons will do that to you."

Chris did not tell his mother everything, however. He did not tell her about Fixer or how Fixer had told him to save James. He said he had a feeling James was in trouble and had rushed to save him. He could not bring himself to tell her the Earth would be destroyed in twenty years. She was in no condition to hear news like that. But, later, upstairs in his bedroom, he told James everything. So now James and Sam knew everything. Chris knew he risked angering Fixer and Miss Portice, whoever she was, but it seemed to him to be the right thing to do.

The reality of seeing his older brother almost murdered began to sink in for Chris, as he replayed the mugging in his mind. James was also getting goosebumps knowing how close he had come to death.

Several minutes went by before Chris broke the silence. "So, what are you going to do in the twenty years you have remaining?"

"Twenty years. That's such a crock," James replied. "I'm putting my money on you, Mr. Fifth Level Quadratic Rubik's Cube Master Lightspeed Newman #1."

Later, as Chris laid in his bed, before falling asleep, he smiled. It sure felt good to have Jesse

James on his side.

CHAPTER 25 - WEDNESDAY

Detective Carter's trips to Captain Carroll's office were becoming painful.

"You really expect anyone to believe this?" Captain Carroll asked Carter, waving the report in his hand. "I suppose it's good to know that if you ever decide to retire from police work, you'd be able to find a job as a comedy writer. I mean, this stuff is pretty funny."

Carter had submitted his written report concerning the row house fire in North Philly a few hours earlier. The Fire Department brass suspected arson. Carter had been sent to investigate the possibility of attempted murder by arson.

"Were you trying to be funny?"

Carter was confused. "A family lost their home in that fire. What's funny about that?"

"Nothing is funny about that, Carter. There's nothing funny at all about what happened. Just your reporting of what happened."

"I guess I don't see the humor, sir."

"Well, let me help you there. Don't you think it's funny that a sleeping family could escape a raging inferno by somehow going out through a locked front door?"

"Funny? No. Fortunate, yes," Carter replied.

"Fortunate and impossible. Carter, it is not possible to escape through a locked door."

"Sir, I did not say that they escaped through a locked door."

"No? Well what does your report say?"

"It reports the facts. The family escaped and the front door was locked."

"Oh, I'm sorry. So what you're telling me is that I've misread your report, is that it? Maybe you're right. Guess I assumed that since they were found on the front lawn, and all the windows were locked shut, and the door was locked shut, and they didn't jump off the roof, that they went out through the front door. Is that a bad assumption, or was there another exit route not mentioned in your report?"

"There was no other exit route."

"So, how did they get out?"

"I don't know."

"Humor me, speculate."

"I assume they went out through the front door," Carter said.

"Now you see, that's what I thought too. But you don't find it funny that a family could walk, as nicely as you please, through a locked front door?"

"Odd, not funny."

"Look Carter, you can play semantics all you want, but this report is crap!" the captain shouted. "For god sakes man, you are a trained homicide detective. How can you overlook such details? And you, the detail expert!"

"I didn't overlook anything, Captain. I reported the facts."

"Carter, we cannot go public with this report. It isn't credible. It casts doubt over everything you have reported here. Is that what we have trained you to do? To investigate and, apparently, overlook pertinent facts?"

"Sir, what facts have I missed?"

"I don't know, Carter. I wasn't there. I didn't investigate. You did. I don't know what you missed, but you must have missed something."

Carter did not respond. He did not blame his captain. Carter had gone over every square inch of the fire scene searching for answers, but came up empty-handed. The conclusion was not believable, unless the laws of nature had somehow changed during the course of the fire. The woman did not remember how she came to be on her front lawn with her children. She did not even remember waking up or coming down the stairs.

She reported putting her children to bed, going to bed herself, and being revived on the front lawn with her children as firefighters fought the fire raging all around. That was it. That's all she remembered. She revealed no other details when he visited her in the hospital where she and the children were being treated for shock and smoke inhalation. It would be several more days before Carter could talk to her or her children again.

The children had recounted the same scenario. The last thing they remembered before waking up on the front lawn was going to bed. The firefighters had no idea how she and her children had gotten there. The front door was securely locked. It was a mystery.

Carter was stumped, but he had reported his findings honestly and accurately. It made no sense, but so be it. That's what he had found. Now, however, he had to deal with the wrath of his captain. He had been dreading this confrontation, but he knew it was inevitable. So, he had resigned himself to taking his lumps. He was coming to believe that no matter how qualified or trained he was, and no matter how diligently he searched for clues or answers, sometimes there were no answers.

"Okay, look, I see that it will be several days before we can talk to the family again," the captain continued. "Maybe they'll recall something that will turn this report into something other than the fairy tale it is now. I will have to stall on releasing our, uh your, findings. At least you were able to determine that it was arson. That's something anyway. Any leads on who might have done it?"

"Not yet. We're tracking down the estranged husband. There's a history of domestic violence. We're also talking to family, friends, neighbors, anybody who might have seen someone leaving the scene or anyone suspicious hanging around the past few days," Carter replied.

"Alright, Carter. I guess that will have to do for now. Keep me posted on developments."

"Yes, sir. Is that all, sir?"

"For now, I guess, but I'm worried about you, Carter."

"Sir?"

"First the mugging at the high school and now this. Your work is getting sloppy. You're missing details, critical details, and I can't live with that. I'm warning you right now that you had better step it up, or there are going to be consequences. And I mean severe consequences. I don't want to see any more reports from you that are missing critical details. If I wanted sloppy work I could hire any slob off the street. There's no need to keep pouring time and money into someone who can't do the job right. Do I make myself clear?"

Carter continued to believe in himself and in

his abilities. Captain Carroll was being vituperative, yet again, and had the upper hand for the moment, but Carter knew life was a marathon, not a sprint. Given his age, experience, and abilities, he still liked his chances at coming out ahead.

"Crystal clear, sir."

CHAPTER 26 - WEDNESDAY

At the same time Detective Joe Carter was affirming the crystal clarity of his captain's threat, Chris was riding to St. Michael's Home on his bike to meet with Headmistress Brennan regarding his report and findings. He propped his bike against the wall near the front door and went in through the ballroom to his little study.

He carried the report in an envelope, sitting down at the desk and reading it through one more time. Mrs. Brennan arrived a few minutes later, but Chris was surprised when Mrs. Kling entered with her. He had yet to master the poker face so many adults had had a lifetime to perfect, and his surprise was apparent. He stood to greet them.

"Christopher!" Mrs. Kling said, in that treacly manner she employed whenever greeting someone. Chris smiled. He couldn't help it. She was always so positive, always so happy to see him. Plus, she was very pretty. It was obvious why so many people would like her and why she would be so successful in sales and fundraising and anything that involved getting people to give of themselves.

Hurrying to hold Chris' gloved hands in her own hands, smiling at him warmly, she immediately put Chris at ease. "My goodness! But what brings you to St. Michael's on such a lovely afternoon? Shouldn't you be out playing football or something like that, outside in the sunshine and crisp fall air, with your friends?"

Chris smiled, and was ready to respond, when Mrs. Brennan interjected, "Chris has been so kind as to volunteer to help me find ways to improve things around here," she said.

"Isn't that lovely! Just lovely! What a wonderful thing to do. Well, I know that St. Michael's will be forever blessed to turn out such an upstanding alumnus as Christopher Newman!" she beamed, still holding his hands. "And in addition to all the help down the hall here..." Frieda started, referring to the team of auditors who had seemingly taken up residence the past two weeks.

"Yes, Frieda," Mrs. Brennan interrupted. Chris thought she seemed annoyed. Apparently the costly professional help was a sore spot. "I can use all the help I can get, and I am very anxious to see what Chris has to tell *me*," she said, looking at her friend, emphasizing the 'me' and that this was to be a closed-door meeting between herself and Chris. Mrs. Kling, ever in tune with her client, didn't miss a beat.

"Well, then, I hope you two find whole bunches of things to help this wonderful old home. Chris, before I leave and since I bumped into you today, I wanted to tell you that I have decided to have my old roof re-tarred on Saturday. The roofers will set up Friday night so as to get an early start

Saturday morning.

Now I know you and your young friends like to play halfball behind my house, *which has afforded me hundreds of hours of viewing pleasure over the years through my kitchen window,*" Frieda said parenthetically to Mrs. Brennan, though Chris did not believe she really enjoyed watching the games. "Therefore, I suspect you might be the beneficiary of a good many halfballs. That's what you call them, I believe?"

"Yes, ma'am," Chris said.

"Good I have told the roofers to throw them down onto the driveway when they are up there. I trust you and your friends will then retrieve them and once again put them to good use entertaining yourselves, and me?"

"Yes, ma'am. Thank you, Mrs. Kling. That'll be great."

"Yes, well, there may not be as many up there as there were a week ago, you understand?" she said.

"Ma'am?" Chris said.

Mrs. Kling looked at him, somewhat oddly Chris thought, before continuing. "I mean with the wind and all. Some must have blown off by now."

Chris looked at Mrs. Kling, then at Mrs. Brennan. He wasn't sure what to say. "Um, I suppose a few blow off the roof all the time," he said.

"Yes, well, good, then. They're all yours. Enjoy!" The bubbly Mrs. Kling had returned, apparently. "And good luck with your work here."

"Thank you, ma'am," Chris said.

"Goodbye, Maxine," Mrs. Kling said. "I'll see you tomorrow." She turned and walked to the front door. Chris and Mrs. Brennan watched her leave.

"Well, shall we discuss what you have found so far?" Maxine Brennan said, closing the door to the study. They didn't see Frieda Kling greet J.J. out front as he was coming in from working on the lawn.

Later that evening, from her house, Frieda Kling was on the phone.

"It was J.J.," she said.

"Are you sure?" asked the man.

"Yes, I'm sure."

"How about the Newman kid?"

"No, he doesn't know anything."

"Okay. Good."

"Just make sure you're here this weekend. Everything is riding on this."

"I'll be there," he said.

CHAPTER 27 - THURSDAY

Chris was practicing on the piano in the living room, as he did just about every weekday after school. He no longer took lessons. He had progressed, technically, far beyond what anyone was able to teach him. He was technically perfect.

His former teacher, Dr. Hampton, played for the Philadelphia Orchestra. He loved listening to Chris perform, as everyone did, but elected to resign as Chris' teacher because he never cared for Chris' interpretative style. He said Chris was "too immature and unrealistically optimistic."

Chris did not care, however. His own feeling was that Mr. Hampton was an okay teacher but "too serious, too dour."

Aliondra Covington agreed. "That man never had a good day in his life," she would say. "His glass is definitely half empty."

An objective observer would probably have agreed that Chris was an innate optimist who still had some maturing to do as an interpretive artist. Though gifted, his outlook on life, and depth of feeling, were certainly that of a twelve-year-old.

Aliondra Covington and her friends in the neighborhood couldn't have cared less. Listening to Chris practice was the highlight of their day. And there they were again, gathered around the living room, all seventeen of them, men and women, enjoying a free concert. Today Chris had selected the works of Prokofiev, and although the sheet music was on the music stand in front of him, he didn't need it. He played entirely from memory.

No one enjoyed his performance more than his mother, sitting straight and attentive, craning her neck, on one of the dozen or so folding chairs that had been set up for her and her friends. She was proud of Chris, of course, very proud, as any mother of a musical savant would be. It was beyond her how any human being could play so well. Especially a twelve-year-old. And, most especially, *her* twelve-year-old.

Suddenly, as he began playing Peter and the Wolf, which had been requested by Mr. Matwechuk, Chris had an overpowering thought *regarding...regarding...what exactly?* He was losing focus on the piece he was playing, as muscle memory in his fingers took over, saving him from embarrassment.

In his mind, he struggled to resolve the uninvited thought while he also tried to pay attention to his music. *Big Al...Al...Apple – ah! That must be it. The Big Apple. The Big Apple what?* He continued struggling to resolve whatever it was which was intruding on his concentration as he trilled on the keyboard with his second index finger and middle finger of his right hand.

The Big Al...Al...ter. No, not Apple, alter. The Big Alter? What the heck is the Big Alter? Ar...ter, Big Al...ar...ar...ter. Big Arter? Big Garter? What the heck! Chris continued to struggle uncharacteristically, as his brain tried to process many simultaneous, yet incongruous thoughts vying for his attention.

Big...no, not big...bic...yes, bic..ar...ter...Bicar...ter...carter...Big...alter...carte r? No...big..al...carter. Big Al Carter! Big Al Carter? Who is Big Al Carter? Chris continued to tussle mentally, narrowly avoiding making his first keyboard mistake in years.

Then, suddenly, he knew. *Big Al. Detective Carter.* Detective Carter was in some kind of trouble at Big Al's. Chris didn't know how he knew this, but he was never so sure of anything in his life. Detective Carter was over at Big Al's store on Rising Sun Avenue. More than that, Detective Carter needed Chris' help.

Immediately, Chris connected and stopped playing. Fixer was standing next to the piano.

"Was that you putting those thoughts in my mind?" Chris asked.

"No, son. You are beginning to sense others in need. The thoughts are strictly yours, whatever they are. I am just here to help, if necessary," Fixer replied.

"Um, okay. Something about Detective Carter at Big Al's Cigar store. He may be in some kind of trouble. I think I need to get over there pretty quick."

"Guess you'd better go check it out. Be careful."

"Do I have time to disconnect?" Chris asked.

"Yes, initial precognitions usually give you a few minutes advance notice, but hurry. You may only have five or ten minutes. You might want to take your bike."

Chris disconnected, continuing exactly where he had left off in Peter and the Wolf, and then stopped playing. "Sorry, everyone. I remembered that I have to meet someone. Please come back next Thursday and I will finish. I promise. Bye," he said as he got up from the piano bench, ran between his seated neighbors, and darted out the front door.

"Boy has a lot of energy," said old Mrs. Clarke and all the adults nodded in agreement.

Aliondra Covington, at the window, saw Chris race away on his bike. "Keep him safe," was her silent prayer. Greatness demanded action, she knew. She wouldn't have her son for long.

****

Lieutenant Joe Carter arrived to see the place surrounded by patrol cars and police with weapons drawn. A large crowd had gathered on the periphery and traffic was halted in all directions. The focus of attention was a small retail storefront on Rising Sun Avenue, Big Al's Cigars. Carter ran low, and quickly joined Lieutenant Mike Fenton, the man in charge, taking cover behind a patrol car.

"What do we have here, Mike? Looks pretty exciting."

"Yeah, it's a real thrill show. Suspect's a Caucasian male, early twenties, name's Turner, Brian. He's got a record: petty theft, burglary, assault. Troubled kid, local, broken family. He's armed and he's got Big Al as a hostage."

Carter knew Big Al well. A Vietnam vet who had started this little retail store almost twenty years ago. Al sold cigars, cigarettes, candy, newspapers, comic books, and lottery tickets.

"How did all this start?" Carter asked.

"Officer Lonerghan walked by on his regular foot patrol and witnessed an attempted armed robbery. The creep shot at him right through the door. He's stunned and lucky to be alive. Vest saved him."

"Thank God. So what's the deal here?" Carter asked, motioning for Fenton to surrender his megaphone.

"He wants to talk. He's demanding a deal to

release Al. We've got sharpshooters all over the place, but no clear shot yet."

"Okay, thanks, Mike. Why don't you see if you can move this crowd back some more? I don't want to see anybody getting shot."

"Sure, Joe. Goes for you too. Be careful."

"I always am."

Lieutenant Fenton motioned to several other officers for assistance, then retreated quickly to move the crowd. Carter placed the megaphone above the hood of the patrol car stationed near the storefront.

"Turner. Brian Turner. This is Lieutenant Carter of the Philadelphia Police Department. Surrender the hostage and put down your weapon."

The gunman responded by shouting through the broken plate glass front door. "You want him? Then I get what I want first."

"Turner, you are surrounded by police and every one of them has you in their sights. You cannot escape."

"Then Big Al's going with me."

"Why don't you let me in so we can talk?"

"Talk about what? There's nothing to talk about."

"How about you getting out of this alive?"

"I shot a cop."

"He's okay. He wasn't hurt. Come on out while you still can, before somebody does get hurt."

There was a pause then. Lieutenant Carter saw the hundreds of onlookers and the dozen or so sharpshooters positioned strategically. A police helicopter buzzed overhead, and a news crew was nearby in the street. Although it was cold outside, he found he had to wipe his brow. He often did in these situations. As experienced as he was, these standoffs were never easy for him. Lives were at stake, and these things did not always come out well.

Down the sidewalk to the right he saw the Newman kid, but Carter's attention was suddenly diverted back to Big Al's by the gunman.

"Okay! I want to talk!" shouted the gunman.

"You'll have to let your hostage go first," Carter replied.

"No deal. I let him go and I'm a dead man."

"You'll be okay. You haven't hurt anyone yet." There was silence as the gunman weighed his options.

After a few seconds, he responded, "We talk in here. One-on-one."

"You release the hostage," Carter said.

"You come in first. Then I release him."

"Don't do it, Joe." It was Lieutenant Fenton standing next to him. "This guy is psycho and armed. He'll make a wrong move and we'll pop him."

"Look, Mike, we can still get out of this without bloodshed, and that's what I intend to do. Tell you what, though; if it starts going bad, make sure you're not far behind, okay?"

"Yes, sir. Good luck, Joe. Be careful with this kid though. Some are better off dead. He's one. You're not."

"Yeah, well, neither is Al."

Then Lieutenant Carter turned his attention back to the storefront. "Okay, I am standing up now. I will come in by myself, just me. Just you and me, but you have to let the hostage go when I come in."

Mike Fenton breathed a silent prayer for his comrade under his breath.

As Carter approached the storefront, he glanced to his right and noticed Chris standing behind the bright yellow crime scene tape. The boy smiled and gave him the thumbs up sign. Refocusing, and facing straight ahead again, Carter walked slowly, cautiously, up to the front door and peered through the broken pane. The gunman was standing behind Big Al with an arm around his neck, well out of the line of sight of the sharpshooters.

Lieutenant Joe Carter opened the door slowly and stepped inside.

"Your sicko cop buddies can't see me back here, can they?" Turner sneered.

"Okay, Turner, it's just you and me now. Let him go."

"You step inside more and move away from that door first. Over here," he motioned with the pistol for Carter to come closer to the sales counter. "Put your hands up where I can see them. And no sudden moves, I'm warnin' ya. No signals to your friends with the rifles." Carter did as he was directed. "Now remove your gun and throw it over here on the floor."

"Let him go first," Carter said.

"I'll let him go after you lose the gun."

"You're changing the deal…"

"Look, no deals. Throw away your gun. Now!" Turner yelled.

"Okay, Brian, calm down. Look, I'm removing my gun."

Carter removed his gun from his shoulder holster and slid it across the floor. "Your turn. Let him go."

The gunman held his gun to Big Al's temple. "Okay, fat boy, listen good. I'm going to let you go now. You go straight over to the door and go out. Don't turn, don't walk into anything, and don't look back. Got it?" Al nodded his head and the gunman let him go, keeping his weapon trained on Big Al's back. Big Al did as he was instructed and left the store. Carter sighed ever so slightly with relief, even though he was still in peril.

The gunman turned to face Joe Carter. "Put your hands on the counter where I can see them and leave them there. I don't want any sudden moves out of you. In case you haven't noticed, I don't have much to lose, so don't give me an excuse to pop you, because I will. I should've popped that fat slob, but you had to play the hero. Big mistake. Big mistake, unless I get what I want."

"And what is it you want, exactly?" asked Carter.

"I want you to shut your mouth. Don't talk to me unless I tell you to."

"Whatever you say. You're the boss."

"That's right, and don't forget it."

The gunman was agitated. He walked around the back of the store, out of sight from anyone outside. He ran his hand through his hair repeatedly, never taking his eyes off Carter. He was in a tight spot. Finally, he spoke to the detective, "I guess they're out back too?"

"Yes, this place is surrounded."

"You're lying."

"Poke your head out there if you don't believe me."

"Funny. You're pretty funny for a guy who's about to die."

"You thinking about killing me?" Carter asked.

"Bingo, genius."

"What good would that do? I'm your only ticket out of here."

"Yeah, right, like there's any way out of this," Turner challenged.

"There is, just surrender. You won't be harmed."

"How about you and me take a walk?" Turner countered.

"And go where?"

"To the airport. You get your buddies to get us a car to the airport and a plane out of here."

"It won't work. Too many people out there want a piece of you. I can't guarantee your safety, if

I'm a hostage."

"Man, you don't get it. I'm the one calling the shots here." the gunman screamed as he waved his pistol wildly in the air.

Carter tried to reason with him. "Turner, look, how old are you, twenty-one, twenty-two? You have your whole life ahead of you. Don't throw it all away…"

"Shut up. Shut up!" the gunman screamed.

Carter could see this was not going to be easy; he was sure he had lost this kid.

"Don't tell me about throwing anything away. You don't know anything about me," said Turner. "You think it'd be better to go back to my pathetic, meaningless life. You are so wrong, man. That ain't gonna happen. Ain't no way I'm going back. No way. And if I can't get a break here, then maybe you can't either. Yeah, why not you too? You wanna see what it's like to be dealt a losing hand? Well do ya? No, of course not. Well, neither did I, but guess what? I didn't get a vote. How's it feel not to get a vote, Lieutenant Hero? How about I pop you for the heck of it, huh? I do unto you before you do unto me. That's my religion. That's what I believe. And after I do you, I'm gonna do as many of the other little pigs that come in here, before they take me out," he continued screaming.

Then he raised the gun, pointed it at Joe

Carter's face, and said softly, "And know what? They'll be doing me a big favor. Doesn't look like it's gonna be a good day for either of us. Goodbye, Lieutenant Hero."

And he pulled the trigger.

Carter flinched, sensing his own death. There was a flash of light and a tremendous explosion from the gun barrel.

Carter's heart raced for one split second, to almost double its normal pace, from the adrenaline rush. But that was all.

Opening his eyes, he saw the upraised arm of the gunman, and a cloud of gun smoke, but the gun had disappeared, vanished. The crazed gunman was clearly confused.

Carter tackled and cuffed him. At that moment the other officers burst through the front and rear doors with their weapons drawn.

"Don't shoot! Don't shoot!" yelled Carter. "Everything's under control."

Carter spun Turner around and grabbed his shirt, facing him nose-to-nose, looking him straight in the eye. "Enjoy your R & R, creep. You're going away for a long, long time."

Carter was shaken by what he saw in Turner's eyes. He could swear that he saw nothing but icy cold, bottomless blackness, and pure evil. It chilled him. In all of his years working homicide on the force, he had never seen anything like it. Was Turner even human? The guy clearly had no fear, but did he have a soul?

Carter was not so sure. "You are one sick dude," he said under his breath.

The other officers took Turner away from Carter and escorted him out to a police wagon for the ride to police headquarters, the Roundhouse.

Carter too was stunned by all that had happened to him in the past ten minutes, and was making a verbal report to Lieutenant Fenton when he noticed the bullet on the sales counter and the gunman's pistol on the floor nearby, next to his own gun.

"How did these get here?" Carter asked. In a state of shock, he picked the bullet up with tweezers and placed it in a plastic bag for Forensics. He was having a hard time believing what he thought he had just experienced. As the full import hit him, he lost his balance slightly and sat shakily in the nearest chair.

"You okay, Joe?" Lieutenant Fenton asked him, but Joe Carter was tracing his fingers over his forehead in utter disbelief. How was he going to write up this police report?

Carter walked outside. The crowd was still there and they cheered when they saw him. He noticed that the kid was still there too, in his same spot behind the police tape. Carter smiled weakly and gave the boy the thumbs up sign. The boy returned the gesture once again.

There was something different about the kid, though. A small thing, a minor detail, perhaps, but minor details had helped Carter stay alive this long. *What was it? What was different?*

Chris watched everything that transpired. But what was this? Was Carter talking to him? No, Carter's lips weren't moving. Chris was hearing Carter's thoughts. He quickly cupped his hands over his ears so he could concentrate. Chris now clearly sensed Lieutenant Carter's mental anguish regarding how he would explain what had happened to his superiors. Apparently, Chris surmised, things had not been going well between the lieutenant and his superiors. *Interesting. He still needs my help. Lieutenant Carter really needs my help.*

CHAPTER 28 – THURSDAY NIGHT / FRIDAY MORNING

"Oh, come on, Mike, did you hear a shot or not? It's not a tough question."

Captain Carroll was not happy. He was grilling Lieutenant Mike Fenton and Lieutenant Joe Carter about the robbery attempt at Big Al's. "This jerk Turner's gonna walk within a year or two unless you guys come clean! What the heck happened in there?"

"Captain, I've already told you..." Fenton started.

"Oh, yeah? Well humor me, because Ballistics is telling us something totally different. They're saying that kid couldn't have fired a shot at point-blank range and missed, without leaving some evidence. Other than the bullet on the counter, and the one fired at Lonerghan, no other bullets were found on the whole crime scene. Now don't you think that if Brian Turner had fired and missed we would have found some evidence of that?"

"But Captain, we heard the shot. We all heard it. That's when we rushed in. It wasn't just me coming in the front door. I had already given orders to crash the place if any shots were fired, and that's what we did. Everybody heard it."

"Then where's the bullet?" screamed the

Captain.

"You have it," Carter said calmly.

The Captain walked around behind his desk, sat down in his chair, and put his face in his hands. After a few seconds he raised his face to address his two officers.

"Carter, don't tell me one more time that the bullet you picked up off the counter was the bullet that was fired. That's about as crazy a thing as I have ever heard."

"In the first place that bullet never hit anything. You ever hear of a fired bullet that never hit anything? Even total misses land on the ground and show some impact evidence. This bullet was nearly pristine. It wasn't damaged at all. Secondly, this kid was packing some serious heat, not a defective pop gun, because that's what it would've taken for that bullet to leave the gun and land on the counter – a defective pop gun. Is that what he pointed at you Carter, a pop gun?"

"No, Captain..." Carter began.

"You're right! It wasn't! It was a .38 semi-automatic. Had he fired that weapon as you described, the bullet wouldn't have bounced off your head, no matter how hard-headed you are, and floated down to lay as pretty as you please on the counter waiting for you to pick it up. No, siree. That bullet would have passed through you like a hot knife through butter and you would not be standing there right now making a mockery of this investigation! By dad-gum no! You'd be deader than a doorknob!"

"But, Captain, how about the empty casing? How do you explain that? Plus the barrel marking on the bullet itself. That bullet was definitely fired," Carter said.

"The empty casing was from a prior firing in all likelihood. As for the bullet, there was no impact damage. None. I don't know how to be any clearer than that. Can you say for certain it wasn't on the counter when you walked into the store? Maybe the kid placed it there and staged this whole affair to make us look like raving lunatics!" The captain's volume was increasing. "And if he did, he did a pretty good job, because that's what I'm looking at, a couple of madmen. Did you really think that I, or headquarters, was going to buy this malarkey? Because that's what it is: malarkey, a big fairy tale. No one in their right mind can buy what you two are selling."

The Captain stood again and walked around in front of his desk. "And let me tell you, right now I'm pretty tired of talking to a couple of loons. So, until this investigation is through I am relieving you both of your present assignments. Fenton, you are to assume desk duty for the foreseeable future, pending the result of this investigation. Carter, I am placing you on mandatory R&R for two weeks. I don't want to see your handsome, intact noggin in this place before then. Gentlemen, do I make myself painfully clear?"

"Yes, sir," they both replied.

"Good day!" said Captain Carroll as he sat in his desk chair and placed his face in his hands one more time.

Carter and Fenton left their captain's office. "I'm sorry, Mike. Honestly, I don't blame him. I'm beginning to wonder if I really believe it myself."

"Joe, look, why don't you go home and rest up? This thing will blow over soon enough."

"No, not soon enough," corrected Carter.

"I'll be behind a desk around here somewhere in the meantime. If I can do anything for you, you let me know, okay?"

"Sure, thanks, Mike. You know. There is one thing you can do for me."

"Just name it."

"See if you can get me a copy of that helicopter surveillance tape. I have an idea. Do you think you could get a copy over to my house?"

"Do you really think that's going to show anything? All the action took place inside the store. You're not going to see any of that on the helicopter tape."

"I know, Mike, but I'm more interested in seeing what was going on outside."

Fenton regarded his friend quizzically. He knew Carter was an ace detective with a keen power of observation. He saw things that most people routinely overlooked. Nonetheless, in Fenton's opinion, Carter was not going to see anything on that surveillance video that would help him to explain what happened inside the store. He was pretty sure of that. The only thing he was absolutely certain of, however, was that if there was evidence outside the store, Carter would find it. And only Carter could find it.

"Okay, Sherlock. Consider it done."

Lieutenant Fenton delivered the surveillance videodisk later that evening. He stayed with Carter as he loaded the disk into his home computer and uploaded the video.

The picture from the helicopter was okay, but not great. The resolution was somewhat grainier than Carter would have liked, but it was serviceable. Also, the picture was shaky in some sequences, not steady, which made for a difficult study. But it was all he had to go on, so he was not complaining.

Mike Fenton had already studied the video and was pointing out certain details to his colleague. "There's Big Al's right there, in the middle of the block. You can see the alleyway in the back and Rising Sun Avenue in the front. Clearly, though, you won't be able to see what's going on inside Big Al's. And there you are, right there, approaching the storefront. Now you're going in. That's pretty much it for a couple of minutes before we crash the place." They watched the video for two minutes more and, indeed, nothing of interest happened until the police rushed in through the front and the back doors.

"I've watched this tape a dozen times. Can't even see a gunpowder flash from this angle. Sorry, Joe. I wish there was more here for you, but it looks pretty inconclusive I'm afraid."

Carter didn't reply. He was studying the tape closely, but he wasn't focusing on Big Al's. He was engrossed in another area of the tape, where the crowd stood nearby. He searched for the boy, Chris Newman. He could not spot him. "Can we zoom this in, Mike?" he asked.

Fenton reached over and took control of the mouse. "How's that?" he asked as he zoomed in to a magnitude of ten times.

Carter didn't respond. He kept his eyes on the tape as he took back control of the mouse. He started to re-center the digital picture on the spot where Chris Newman should have been standing. Nothing. The crowd was very dense. The taller adults obscured the line of sight between the helicopter camera and the shorter Chris Newman. "What can we slow the frame progression to?" Carter asked.

"One frame at a time," Fenton answered.

"Nice."

"Nothing but the best for Philly's Finest. What are you looking for?"

"I'm not sure. I'm hoping I'll know it if I see it," Carter said softly as he concentrated intensely on the video.

Mike Fenton stood up. "Gotta go, Joe. Let me know if you find anything, okay?" No response. "I'll let myself out. Let me know if you need anything else, Joe."

Carter, focused on the screen, never heard him leave.

****

The next morning, Friday, Chris was helping J.J. with his route again. "Buon Giorno, Chris." Pop sat at the table, playing chess with Luigi, as Chris entered Luigi's Bakery.

"Buon Giorno, Pop. Hey, Luigi." Chris laid the paper on the counter. "Hey, Ben. Paper."

"Hi, Chris," Ben replied. "Holy Cannoli?"

"I'm a little short."

As Chris turned to exit the bakery, he noticed

that Pop and Luigi were engaged in an advanced game of chess. The chess board consisted of two horizontal clear Lucite layers, stacked one above the other. As always, Pop and Luigi did not appear to have made a move in quite some time. Chris decided to watch them, and Ben walked over with a damp cloth.

"What time did you get started, Luigi?" Chris asked.

"At the signing," Luigi grumbled, not looking up.

"Another epic struggle," Ben joked, wiping down a nearby table.

"Shh!" Luigi shushed him.

"Hear that? He's got a leak," Ben said to Chris.

"Benjamin, please! I cannot concentrate when…"

"You're asleep."

Chris chuckled. "You'd be asleep too, Ben, if you'd been around at the signing of the Declaration of Independence."

"Great, Ben! Encourage *him* now!" Luigi barked, motioning at Chris. "It's not enough to have one idiot…"

"Doing the work around here. You're welcome, by the way," Ben quipped, rolling his eyes.

"Maybe we should sell tickets and invite the whole neighborhood. Give away popcorn and door prizes! As if it's not noisy enough in here already!" Luigi thundered.

"Luigi, please," Pop interjected. "Calm down."

"Don't tell him that, Pop. If he were any calmer making his moves, he'd be dead."

"This is not checkers!" Luigi yelled again. "It demands attention."

"Speaking of dying," Ben replied, ignoring Luigi, "remind me again, if you two die at this table do you want to be buried together with the chess board?"

"Very funny," Pop grumbled at the apparently overused joke.

"It'd be so much easier," Ben replied as he moved away to wipe the table tops. "We could have the whole ceremony wrapped up before the morning rush."

"Actually, maybe we could go back to a time limit on moves," Pop said.

"You only ever mention that when it's my

turn," Luigi grumbled.

"I wonder why that is," Pop grumbled back.

"Because with your limited IQ you cannot see ahead…"

"Fifteen moves. Uh-huh, I know," Pop interrupted. "But you only need to make one."

"Yes! The right one!" Luigi thundered in reply. "Not some simple, jackass, brain dead, poor excuse for a paperweight-inspired bumbling backwoods…"

"Bishop to L-2-6," Chris interrupted.

"What?!" exclaimed Luigi, suddenly reconsidering the board.

"Unless you make a wrong move, that'll give you what you need sixteen moves from now," Chris said.

After fifteen seconds of renewed scrutiny by Pop and Ben, Luigi laughed, "You know, that'll work!"

Luigi moved his bishop. Pop said to Chris, "Thanks a lot."

"Sorry, Pop," Chris shrugged.

"No, I'm being serious," Pop replied. "Thank you very much. Maybe I can find something else to do with my day now that Luigi has finally won a game."

"Finally!? Finally? Why, do I have to remind you that you have never beaten me?"

"It's sad when their memory goes, too," Pop joked, grabbing his cane to stand.

"Well, there are sixteen moves still to be made correctly before checkmate," Chris replied.

"Even Loser Luigi won't screw them up," Pop said.

"Watch your mouth, *Poop*," Luigi retorted.

"Alright boys, play nice," Ben called from across the store. "Don't make me give you a time out."

Pop said to Chris, in Italian now, "So you play too?" They each continued to converse in Italian.

"A little."

"A little, huh? How little?"

"Very little, actually. I've never played two-level chess."

"Then how did you know what move Luigi should make?" Pop asked, as he and Luigi focused on Chris for his answer.

"I...I...don't know," Chris replied. "It just looked right to me, I guess."

"It looked right, but you've never played chess before, let alone two-level chess?"

"Um...yeah, I guess. Is that okay?"

"Okay? Sure," Pop replied. "Just a little depressing when I find out a beginner is way better than I'll ever be."

As Pop balanced himself with his walking stick, he pushed his chair back under the table. Luigi also pushed his chair back and said, "Ah, it's the residual effects of the Holy Cannoli I gave you a few weeks ago. And since you came to my aid, I will return the favor. Wait here," he said as he hurried into the walk-in refrigerator at the back of the store.

A minute later he returned, holding out a cannoli wrapped in pastry paper for Chris. "Here, please, have a Luigi's Holy Cannoli."

"Um, Luigi, I don't have a hundred dollars," Chris replied, in English now.

"Not necessary. It's not necessary, my dear boy. You owe me nothing. I, on the other hand, am indebted to you, and Luigi always repays his debts. Now, here, take it. I insist," Luigi said, handing the Holy Cannoli to Chris.

"Hot dang!" Chris said. "Thanks Luigi. I love your Holy Cannolis. They're the best."

"Of course they are. Not to toot my own horn," Luigi replied.

Pop then tooted the bicycle horn on his walking stick loudly. HONK-HONK. "Don't mind if I do," Pop said. He, Ben, and Luigi high-fived each other half-heartedly, their hands not coming close to meeting.

Chris took a bite of the cannoli. "Awesome," he said. "Well, I'd better get back to my papers. "See you Pop. See you Ben," he said, turning to walk out the front door.

"And don't slam..." Luigi began to call after him.

"Got it," Chris said, suddenly returning to grab the screen door before it slammed shut, closing it quietly, and taking another bite of the cannoli.

Luigi, Pop, and Ben all stood in the middle of the store, watching Chris leave. "Remarkable," Ben said, holding a broom. "Yes, he is." Pop and Luigi agreed as Chris honked his bicycle horn and drove away.

In the corner of the bakery, a patron sat at a small table. He folded down his morning paper, picked up his cup of coffee, stood, and walked toward the three men. "Any chance I can get one of those Holy Cannolis?" he asked.

"Certainly," Luigi replied, hurrying to the

back room and returning with a Holy Cannoli. He held it out to the man.

"That's a hundred dollars, correct?" the man asked, taking the bills out of his wallet.

"Free of charge to our men in blue," Luigi said. He could have added, "to those in need." Luigi would never sell a holy cannoli, and never intended to sell any. The steep price was a test. He knew anyone willing to pay a hundred dollars for a cannoli likely needed a break.

"Well, thank you very much, Mr. Luigi. That's very kind."

"Not at all. I insist. Now, please, enjoy it in good health and may good fortune be with you," Luigi replied.

As the man approached the front door to exit, Luigi called after him, "Please be careful out there, Lieutenant. Thank you for all you do."

"I will, and you're welcome," Joe Carter replied.

After Carter left, Pop, Luigi, and Ben stood together, looking after him.

"Nice job, Luigi," Pop said. "The boy and the lieutenant are two lucky people."

"Yes, they are now," Luigi agreed.

CHAPTER 29 - FRIDAY

Chris went straight home after school. His mother sat at the dining room table working on her resume. "Hi, Mom."

"Hi, Chris. How was school?"

"Way too long. I'll be in the clubhouse."

"Okay. Dinner's at six. I'll text you."

"Thanks, Mom," he said as he picked up a bag of potato chips from the kitchen pantry, and headed out the back door to the clubhouse. He had a lot on his mind and had to figure out a few things. Flipping on the light switch, he ran up the steps to the clubhouse, threw his bag of potato chips on an easy chair, and promptly dismissed them from his mind as he began to write an equation on the blackboard.

Earlier, at school assembly, a city councilmen addressed the students. Chris noted the woman on the side of the stage signing for the deaf students there, and this gave him the idea he was now transcribing into differential calculus on his blackboard. Ten minutes later, he was so engrossed in his work that the sound of a ripping potato chip bag startled him, but he didn't turn around. He knew who it was.

"Ah! Sign language to text. Very nice," Fixer

said, standing perfectly erect next to the easy chair, enjoying a potato chip. "Not as great a discovery as cheddar cheese potato chips, but not bad. Not bad at all. Goodness! These are quite good. I'd almost forgotten. Tough to find a good potato chip in some places."

"Do you ever knock?" Chris asked, without turning around. "Or bring your own food?"

"Do I overstep my bounds? Have I erred in thinking this snack was the furthest thing from your mind and, as such, would not be greatly missed? Are guests proscribed? Or, perhaps, it is a simple matter of admittance by invitation only, hmm?"

"No. Sorry. I have a lot on my mind." Chris said, putting the chalk on the ledge and turning around to face Fixer.

"In that case, I accept your proferred sop," Fixer said, placing another potato chip in his mouth as he smiled at Chris. "So, what's on your mind?"

"People."

"People?"

"Yeah, there are a lot of bad people. Adults mostly. Caz, the creep who hurt Joey McManus; Jack Helson and his gang; Brian Turner, the psycho who tried to kill Lieutenant Carter; the arsonist who tried to kill the little kids and their mom in a house fire; my mom's boss, Mr. Lewis…to name a few in the last few months."

"There will be others," Fixer said.

"You sound like you know something I don't know."

"I know a lot of things you don't know. It's called living. You haven't been around long enough, yet. You're just starting out, but you'll see. There are a lot of bad people," Fixer said, matter-of-factly, before putting another cheddar cheese potato chip in his mouth.

Chris looked at Fixer eating the potato chips, slouching in the chair, with one leg draped over one of its arms. "And a lot of good people too, right?" Chris asked. Fixer kept eating, looking at him, but did not respond. "Right?" Chris pushed for a response.

"If you say so," Fixer replied.

"I do say so," Chris said, looking down and beginning to pace back and forth in front of where Fixer was sitting. "There's Headmistress Brennan, mom, James, Sam, J.J., my friends..."

"Only two of those are adults," Fixer interrupted. "No men."

"Okay, um, there's Ernie, and Mr. K, Luigi, Pop, and Ben, Mr. Schwartz, Big Al, Principal Bartle." Chris looked at Fixer for some sign of agreement, but none was forthcoming. "I think they're good men," Chris said.

"You're entitled to your opinion."

"You're not a big fan of humans, are you?" Chris said.

"Let's just say I've been burned enough to know what I know. If I can help you, I will, but I won't lie to you. No, I'm not a big fan of non-Savants."

"Wow. Then you must've pulled the short straw to get this assignment."

"No. Your mother was a great lady, a great lady. Miss Portice and I, and many others, by the way, would do anything for her...anything to honor her memory. She wanted you to be raised here, and that's that. Miss Portice and I volunteered immediately. No questions asked. Although neither of us understand her desire to have you raised on this godforsaken planet."

Fixer popped the last potato chip in his mouth, crushed the empty bag into a ball, and tossed it into a nearby waste basket. "Thanks for the chips," he said, standing and brushing the crumbs off the front of his cordovan leather bomber jacket.

"I don't know, either," Chris said, dropping to sit in the other easy chair.

"What don't you know?"

"How to make a difference here. If it's as bad as you say, if there are no good people…"

"I didn't say that," Fixer interrupted. "There are some."

"Some. Yeah, but not many, right? That's what I'm going to learn as I grow older, isn't it? It's what you're trying to tell me without being too negative. You think making this world a better place is a fool's errand. That there aren't enough good men, right?"

Fixer took a deep breath. Even he, a centuries-old Savant, one of the most gifted of a gifted race, appreciated how quickly Chris assimilated truths. How quickly he was to learn even what he had yet to experience – an important attribute of all the greatest Savants.

"The sad part," Chris continued, staring at Fixer's tan aviators, "is that I am beginning to agree with you."

"Not to pile on here," Fixer said. "But it's likely to get worse as you grow older. Yes, you will find some good, indeed you already have, but you will encounter much evil. Much evil. Especially you, I am sure. You will become a prime target."

Chris leaned forward, elbows on his knees, gloved fingers of his two hands intertwined, and exhaled deeply. He looked down at the floor. He was beginning to understand, really understand the truth of what Fixer was trying, without being too hurtful, to teach him. His analytical brain fired on all cylinders as he raced, calmly, to calculate the probabilities embedded within the life lesson Fixer was imparting. Finally, taking a deep breath, he looked up at Fixer standing in front of him. "The 'some good' you mentioned I have already found, have I mentioned them?"

"No."

"Lieutenant Carter?" Chris asked.

"He's not my cup of tea, as the saying goes. Too brusque. Too taciturn. And, of course, so painfully burdened with a non-Savant mentality. Still, I have to agree with Miss Portice – there is something there. He's not a Savant, of course, but there is something there."

"How do you know?"

"I've seen it. The night you were born, Miss Portice and I abducted you from the hospital so that we could raise you as a Savant needs to be raised in the first three years of life. Carter, though only of Earth, pursued us so doggedly for three years the only way we thwarted him was via the galactic portal, the access to which only Miss Portice can provide. Many nights he was actually standing in the same room with us though, of course, he could not see us. We were shielded by the portal. Nonetheless, this human spent a significant portion of three years of his life to save you from abductors – me and Miss

Portice – whom he could sense only, but never see. His motivation? The truth. To do the right thing. He is one of the few Earthlings to be recorded in the history books on Maran. I have never seen anything quite like it, and I doubt that I ever will again. Three years. He never stopped caring about you, even though he had never laid eyes on you. Remarkable. Truly, to give him his due, remarkable."

Chris looked down at the floor. "Any others?"

"Sorry, kid. You're asking the wrong guy."

"One. One adult. Wow. Seems like a waste of time," Chris said, looking up at Fixer for confirmation.

"You'll get no argument from me."

"Can I go with you then?"

"To Maran? Certainly. Our agreement was to raise you here until you were 12 ½, which you are now. You may leave at any time."

"Through the galactic portal?"

"Yes."

"Where is it? If I was there for three years, why can't I recall it? I remember the day I was born my mom telling me to trust you; that you are a good man, yet I cannot remember anything about the portal…" Chris hesitated, recognition dawning, and looked up at Fixer. "You…"

"I had to, Son. It would have been too dangerous for you if you were able to recall the portal. And we needed Detective Carter to leave us alone."

"So you relieved me of the memory."

"Only of the portal location. Nothing else. Otherwise you, like every Savant, remembers everything you ever experienced."

"Even on the day I was born."

"Yes. Even then. Of course, you also retained your excellent Savant education."

"Which I received from you and Miss Portice?"

"Yes."

"Thank you, Fixer. Thank Miss Portice for me also, okay?"

"I will, and you're welcome. Like I said, it was our pleasure. You were a wonderful charge and student and we couldn't be more proud of you. Still, I suspect the day you will be traveling to Maran with Miss Portice and me is not long off now. You can thank her yourself when you see her. Here," Fixer continued as he stood and placed his hand on Chris' head, "remember… now."

Instantly, all the memories of his first three years in the apartment on Rising Sun Avenue flooded, like a movie, into Chris' mental vision. But the storefront was not vacant. It was furnished as a beautiful, modern, clean and bright apartment. It smelled wonderful. It was warm and safe and Chris remembered it all. Fixer removed his hand from Chris' head. Chris looked up at him again and smiled.

"I smelled gingerbread."

"Miss Portice and I love to bake. Gingerbread men were your favorite."

"It was like Christmas morning."

"Get used to it, kid. You're gonna love life on Maran. The Savants do it right."

Then, walking over to the blackboard, Fixer picked up the piece of chalk. Chris stared at the blue lights, which continued to pulse rhythmically, sequentially, as before, on the fingers of Fixer's right hand. Fixer studied the board before putting the chalk back down. "No," he said. "You're doing fine. I'll let you get back to it."

"Will I see you again?" Chris asked.

"Yes. I'll be back. I don't suppose you might happen to have any sour cream and chive potato chips?"

Chris smiled. "I'll see what I can find."

"Later," Fixer said as he connected and disappeared.

Chris leaned back in the easy chair. His phone buzzed with a text message from Aliondra saying that dinner would be ready in five minutes. He responded that he would be there and connected to spend a Savant-hour equivalent of a fraction of an Earth second thinking about everything he had just learned.

But, it was one thought which dominated his thinking.

Three years.

Lieutenant Carter had spent a good portion of three years trying to save Chris. A picture formed in his mind of the scale of human good versus evil, similar to the scale of justice. On one side of the scale were all the adult criminals who had come into his life in the past month. On the other side of the scale was Lieutenant Joe Carter. The scale was in balance in Chris' mind. Which way would it tip?

Lieutenant Joe Carter had spent three years trying to save him.

One very good man.

And all these years, Chris never knew.

CHAPTER 30 - FRIDAY

That Friday evening after dinner Chris was working in the clubhouse when J.J. and Sam came up the steps.

"Hey, Doc," J.J. said.

"Hey, J.J. Hey, Sam," Chris said.

J.J. and Sam plopped down in the two empty easy chairs and watched Chris as he knelt on the floor in front of his blackboard, putting the finishing touches on a monster equation.

"Whatcha workin' on there, Doc?" J.J. said. "Formula for flippin' fat-free potato chips?"

"Been there. Done that," Chris said.

"There's a flippin' shocker," J.J. said, looking over at Sam for confirmation. She nodded.

Chris continued to complete the equation which was sprawled across the entire blackboard from the upper left-hand corner to the lower right-hand corner, where he now wrote the last parenthesis and put the chalk down on the ledge. The equation was seven lines long. Chris clapped his hands together to wipe off the chalk which formed a white cloud in front of him.

"No, really, Chris, what is it?" Sam asked.

"It's something I thought up a little while ago. It can be used, I think, to program sign language into text."

"Like on a PC screen?" Sam said.

"Yep. I think I could build a glove or something with transmitters in the fingertips. Someone who understood how to sign could then use the glove to sign and this algorithm here," he said, motioning to the board, "should be able to translate the finger motions into text which would then appear on a screen."

"Cool," Sam said. "So someone who can sign but can't speak could use it to communicate with someone else who doesn't understand sign language."

"Which is just about flippin' everybody," J.J. said.

"Exactly," Chris said. "I think it could have wide application."

"Sweet," Sam and J.J. said together.

Sam's cellphone rang. "It's my mom. Gotta go," she said, getting up. "We have relatives coming for dinner tonight and I have to help her set up."

"Don't forget about tomorrow," J.J. said. "Next weekend's flippin' Thanksgiving. The papers tomorrow will be flippin' full of ads. You said you would help Doc and me with the papers. 5:30, bright and flippin' early at Stan's Deli."

"I'll be there," Sam said, going down the steps. "If I'm late, get started without me."

"I'll wait for you out back here until 5:20, Sam," Chris said. "If you're late, we'll leave a delivery list with the papers at Stan's."

"Got it," she said. "See you tomorrow. Bright and early," she said as the door at the bottom of the steps closed behind her.

"Know what else is flippin' sweet?" J.J. said, as Chris sat in the chair vacated by Sam. "I pulled about five-hundred flippin' half balls off of Mrs. Kling's roof last weekend."

"Really? How?" Chris said.

"Some roofers left a flippin' ladder up at the corner house Sunday night. I went up the ladder, across the rooftops with a bag, and picked up as many flippin' halfballs as I could, that's how. Gotta be worth 75 cents each, right?"

"Sounds a little steep for used halfballs," Chris said, and immediately regretted it, as J.J. jumped up.

"Steep! What the flip'," J.J. started. "Let's see you go up a flippin' ladder in the flippin' dark without breakin' your flippin' neck, and haul fifty flippin' pounds of flippin' halfballs four flippin' miles on a flippin' 20-inch bike with the flippin' bag draggin' all the way on the flippin' street!"

"Okay! Okay," Chris said. "75 cents is fine. Calm down."

"Me calm down? How about you flippin' calm down?" J.J. was not happy as he paced back and forth between his chair and the blackboard. "Flippin' geniuses, that's what I'm surrounded with. Writing some flippin' equation on a board that nobody can flippin' understand to convert flippin' sign language nobody can understand. Why? So we can all know that some guy that can't talk has to flippin' poop. You know what? You gotta flippin' poop, go poop! Don't flippin' sit there signing at me so I have to read on a flippin' PC screen what everybody in the flippin' room with a flippin' nose already flippin' knows."

Chris was covering his mouth to hide his smile. He knew if J.J. saw him laugh, he'd get a black eye for his trouble.

J.J. looked at Chris. "So, Einstein has a sense of humor, eh? Let's see how flippin' funny you think this is." J.J. turned and began erasing the blackboard, quickly.

"Okay! Okay!" Chris said, standing, laughing. "Tell you what. I'll give you ten bucks for ten half balls, okay?"

J.J. immediately stopped erasing the board, but the damage had been done. He turned and faced

Chris, eraser in hand. "You're gonna pay me more than you flippin' have to? Why?"

"Well, that's a pretty impressive advertisement for your services I just heard there. Considering all the work you did, I'd say a dollar apiece is a steal."

"Flippin' A., it is," J.J. said, calming down. After a minute, he continued. "But that's not the best news."

"Really?"

"Yeah. Listen to this. Mrs. Kling tells me she's gonna have her flippin' roof tarred tomorrow. The ladder's already up down there. I passed it on the way here."

"So, you planning on going up again? Are there more halfballs up there?"

"Yes and yes, but there's something else."

Chris started to worry whenever J.J. stopped using his universal flippin' modifier. "What?"

"When I was up there last week, Mrs. Kling's flippin' attic window was open a little, so I pushed it up and went into her flippin' attic."

"What? J.J. that's illegal!"

"Only if I'm flippin' caught. Don't worry. Nobody flippin' saw me. Plus, you'll never guess what I flippin' saw. I know why she keeps that flippin' attic locked all these years, I can tell you that," he said, conspiratorially.

"Do I want to hear this?" Chris said.

"Well, you're gonna flippin' hear it."

"That's what I'm afraid of." Chris didn't know if he could stand to learn that Mrs. Frieda Kling, whom everyone loved and respected almost as much as Headmistress Brennan, was doing something illegal. The scales of justice flashed in his mind. They were teetering.

"You know how Headmistress Brennan had to spend all that flippin' money to have a flippin' alarm system installed?"

"Yeah."

"And you know how everybody blamed me for taking things all these years when I never took flippin' anything?"

"No. I didn't know that."

"Well, they did. They thought all those thefts were a flippin' inside job. I overheard the security guys talkin'. That's what they called it. An inside job. So, Headmistress Brennan had to pay all this money to find out who was flippin' ripping off St. Michael's Home. They thought it was me. I'm not sure why. Look at this flippin' face," he said, pointing at himself. "Is this the face of a flippin' thief?"

"Um…no, no it isn't," Chris lied, opting for discretion over valor.

J.J. smiled at Chris, looked side to side, and whispered softly. "It was Mrs. Kling."

"What'" Chris exploded. "J.J. what are you saying?"

"I'm saying, genius, that Mrs. Kling's whole flippin' attic is full of stuff she took from St. Michael's. I'm saying that all the money Headmistress Brennan wasted on security was caused by Mrs. Kling. And I'm saying that tonight, you and me are going to go up there on the ladder, and you will see for yourself, that's what I'm saying."

"No, J J. No," Chris said. "I'm not going to break into anyone's house. That's nuts. Just call the cops."

"I already thought of that. We can't call the cops."

"Why not?"

"No probable cause, that's why not. It'd be her word against mine, and nobody's gonna believe me. They need to get a search warrant. But they need a reason, probable cause, to have a judge issue a search warrant. That could take days, and by that time she could move all the stuff and get me in trouble for being on her roof in the first place. I'll get screwed and she'll get off, like always. I'm getting tired of getting screwed and her getting off all these years. But, if you come with me tonight, then you can back me up, and it'll be two against one. Then the cops will have reason to request a search warrant. Plus, nobody's gonna see us anyway. All you have to do is see it. One minute and we'll be outta there. Nobody'll ever know. Trust me."

Chris was really worried now. J.J. just rattled off about a dozen sentences without using one "flippin'." That could only be major league bad.

J.J. looked at Chris. "Sorry about erasing your equation."

Chris smiled. "Don't worry," he said, tapping his temple with his finger. "You didn't."

J.J. shook his head. "Yeah, I kinda figured."

Later that evening, after dark, with great trepidation, Chris did go with J.J. He suffered no delusion that this would proceed without complication, but he was acting as a friend.

He cared for J.J., who had always been there for him when he needed protection or help. This was Chris' way of partially repaying the many favors from over the years. Plus, Chris knew, he could employ his special ability should they need it.

J.J. had already assured Chris that the house

was empty, because all the lights were off and Mrs. Kling's car wasn't parked in its usual spot in the street in front of the house. Up on the roof, in the dark, J.J. showed Chris how the one window was slightly ajar, and the attic pitch black, just as before. J.J. forced the window up and went into the attic. Then he turned to Chris. "Come on. There's nobody here. One more minute and we'll be outta here."

Chris climbed inside the window with J.J. "Over here," J.J. said, pulling Chris' arm. "The light switch is along this wall."

"I don't know, J.J. This isn't right, man."

"Don't wimp out now," J.J. said. "We're almost done anyway. Just stay next to me near this wall. Come on."

Chris stayed close behind his friend, as they both used the wall as a guide around the perimeter of the room. Once they reached the light switch, J.J. said, "Here it is. I feel it."

That's when all heck broke loose.

Suddenly the attic door at the bottom of the stairs opened, and somebody turned on the lights. J.J. and Chris, both frightened out of their wits, made a beeline back to the window but someone outside slammed the window shut. Chris and J.J. stared through the pane as a man laughed contemptuously as he hammered the window shut from the outside. Two large, growling pit bulls charged up the steps, ran across the room bearing their fangs and leaped at Chris and J.J., huddled together with their backs to the window. J.J. covered his face with his hands and screamed. Chris connected.

Immediately the two large dogs froze in mid-air, right in front of the boys faces. The hammering stopped. Chris stepped aside, and turned to see the now inanimate man outside. He retrieved his phone from his pants pocket and began to take pictures.

He took a few pictures of the man's face through the windowpane. Then he took pictures of many of the items in the room. J.J. was right. There were dozens of articles that had once adorned St. Michael's Home. Mostly artwork, which Chris figured was probably quite valuable, but also vases, carpets, china, silverware, tapestries, a grandfather's clock, an old roll-top desk, a crystal chandelier, many knick-knacks, and some jewelry boxes. Chris opened these and took pictures of the jewelry inside. He also took some pictures of the whole room from an angle which did not show J.J. and the dogs. Hopefully, this would be proof enough for the police to identify the room as Mrs. Kling's attic.

Then, putting his phone away, he walked over to J.J. "Sorry, J.J. I have to do this. We need to get out of here," he said, and he took hold of J.J.'s hand.

J.J. who had resumed his interrupted screaming, suddenly stopped. When he saw what new reality now engulfed him, he screamed again. "AAAAHHHHHH!!"

"J.J.! J.J.! It's okay. It's okay," Chris said. J.J. stopped screaming, turned and looked at Chris with wide eyes and said, "It is?"

"Yes, it is. Come on. And don't let go of my hand. We have to get out of here."

"Wait," J.J. said, refusing to move. "What's going on? Those dogs are hanging there, in mid-air."

"It's a flippin' genius thing," Chris said. "You wouldn't understand."

"Oh, why didn't you say so?" J.J. said, starting to walk with Chris, looking backward at the dogs.

"That dude out there nailed the window shut," Chris said. "We have to go downstairs and out through the front door."

"You see all this flippin' stuff?" J.J. said, pointing to the purloined goods. "You see it?"

"Yeah, I see it. I already took pictures. You were right. Come on. Let's get out of here. I think we have enough proof if we live through this." They hurried down the steps.

"Don't let go of my hand," Chris warned.

"Ain't never flippin' gonna happen, Doc.

Trust me."

"Don't say 'trust me' anymore after this," Chris said.

"Right. Sorry about that."

As they went through the attic door at the bottom of the steps, they saw Mrs. Frieda Kling holding the door open with one hand. Her other hand was on the light switch at the bottom of the steps. She was the one who had turned the lights on and let the dogs up into the attic. Chris and J.J. looked at each other, but didn't say anything. Of all the reality they were experiencing right now, this was the worst. Their beloved Mrs. Kling had tried to kill them. Chris pictured the balanced scale of human good versus evil come crashing down as Mrs. Kling leaped joyfully away from the scale she shared with Lieutenant Carter, Aliondra, and Headmistress Brennan to join Jack Helson, Brian Turner, the thugs and arsonist on the opposite scale.

"Mrs. Kling had this all planned. She set the trap by telling you about the ladder and you bought it. You do know she set you up, right?" Chris said.

"Yeah, she sure did. I can be such a flippin' idiot."

They continued to run along the upstairs hallway to the steps. They then hustled down the steps to the first floor which was dark, except for a blue light coming from the kitchen.

As he reached for the front door, Chris said, "Wait. I want to check this out. It might be important."

"Doc, come on, man," J.J. said, not budging. "Let's get out of here." He was clearly scared and wanted to put all this behind him.

"No, J.J.," Chris said. "Something tells me this is important. I'm going into the kitchen and you're coming with me. Come on."

"Okay, you're the doc." J.J. went to the kitchen with Chris.

Chris saw exactly what he thought he would see. The light was an LED light coming from a laptop in the middle of the kitchen table. A chair had been pushed back from the table. A cozy cup of hot coffee sat on the table on one side of the laptop. On the other side was a checkbook, and two printed boarding passes for a USAirways Saturday afternoon flight to Miami.

"Always nice to sit and have a hot cup of coffee as you're murdering children," J.J. said.

Chris looked at the computer screen. As J.J. held his left hand, Chris sat in the chair and navigated through the screen by using the mouse in his right hand. It was a bank statement which showed many large deposits into Mrs. Kling's account. Ten thousand dollars each, for the most part. But the deposit amounts did not command

Chris' attention. The deposit dates did. There was a pattern here. No one else would have seen it, but he couldn't miss it.

He then his phone from his jacket pocket and began to take pictures of the deposits on the screen. He also took pictures of the boarding passes and of the dates and amounts of the deposits which had been recorded in the checkbook.

"Doc, what are you doing?" J.J. asked.

"Evidence," Chris said.

"Evidence? How much flippin' evidence do you need? There's a whole attic full of evidence upstairs."

"This is different," Chris said. "It might be important. Come on," he said, putting his smartphone away. "Let's get out of here."

Chris and J.J. exited through the front door and closed it. As they walked back to Chris' house, Chris remained connected and J.J. continued to hold his hand to remain connected with him. "You're gonna sleep over at my house tonight," Chris said. "I'll have mom call Headmistress Brennan and tell her."

"How about the rest of all this? How did you get those dogs and the man and Mrs. Kling, and these cars...,"J.J. said, pointing at the stilled traffic. "How did you make everything stop? Are you going to tell me that?"

"Everything is still moving. It's just that we're moving faster," Chris said.

"How much faster?"

"The speed of light."

"Whoa, cool. No kidding? How? No, wait. Let me guess. It's another flippin' Brainiac thing, right?"

"Yes."

"Oh man! This is so cool. We're doin' all this stuff in like a split second, right?"

"Right," Chris said, as they continued walking in the dark, down the sidewalk, under the umbrella formed by the bare branches of the fifty-year-old Sycamores lining the street.

"You know what this means?"

Chris was afraid to ask. Apparently, J.J. the entrepreneur was already dreaming up some commercial scheme. "It means a lot of things. What's it mean to you?" Chris said.

"It means we can do the flippin' papers in two seconds, duh," J.J. said.

Chris smiled at his friend, but didn't say anything.

"We are still doing the flippin' papers tomorrow, right?" J.J. said.

"Yeah. I think we need to keep on with our lives as if this never happened. First chance we get, after the papers tomorrow, we'll call Lieutenant Carter."

"The basketball cop?" J.J. said.

"Yeah."

Their sneakers made little sound as they continued walking. After a bit, J.J. agreed, "Makes sense."

"Yes. Plus, he's a winner. A good guy. And he'll believe us."

After walking along a few more steps, J.J. said, "So, the guy in the window looked familiar to you too?"

"Yeah, he did."

PART SIX

"Our business was done at the river's brink...And what's dead can't come to life, I think."
   - Robert Browning, "The Pied Piper of Hamelin"

CHAPTER 31 - SATURDAY

On Saturday morning, Chris came out the back door at 5:20, where Mink waited for the bowl of cat food he placed on the back deck. When J.J. followed him out, Mink ran away.

"What's his flippin' problem?" J.J. asked.

"He doesn't know you," Chris said. "He's hyper cautious. It's how he survives out here. He'll come back once we leave."

They walked down the back steps, picked up their bikes, walked to the alleyway, and waited for Sam.

"Look," Chris said, nodding his head down the alleyway.

"Look? At what? Can't see nuthin'. It's too flippin' dark."

"The ladder. It's gone."

"The ladder at Mrs. Kling's? You can see that far in the dark?"

"Yeah. It's gone."

"Think they took the stuff outta the attic?" J.J. said.

"Not yet," Chris said, padding his jacket

pockets. "Not overnight. Dang! I forgot my phone."

"Go get it," J.J. said. "I'll wait."

"No. I don't need it to do the papers. It'll be okay in my bedroom 'til I get back. Glad we took those pictures last night. Even if they clean out the attic today, at least we have some proof. Come on," he said. "Let's get started. Looks like Sam overslept. She can catch up to us."

They biked the six blocks to Stan's Deli, riding side by side most of the way, the early morning darkness punctuated only infrequently by yellow sulphur street lamps. As they approached Stan's, J.J. said, "Hey, the flippin' light's out. Mr. K usually keeps the front light on."

"Maybe it burned out," Chris said. "Look, the papers are there."

"Flippin' hawk eyes you got. You can really see 'em? Oh, yeah, I see 'em now," J.J. said, as they covered the last hundred feet or so and then dismounted to begin the work of removing the plastic ties that secured the papers in bundles of twenty each. As they knelt on the ground working, two assailants approached from behind and simultaneously applied chloroform-soaked gauze pads over their noses and mouths. The boys' unconscious bodies slumped down into the waiting arms of their attackers. The two men quickly carried J.J. and Chris to a nearby parked car, placed them in the trunk before closing the trunk lid, hopped into the front seat of the car, started the engine, and drove off, headed east.

Neither of the men saw Sam recording the entire episode on her phone from behind a hedge across the street from Stan's Deli. Horrified, Sam was momentarily frozen before hopping on her bike and peddling as fast as she could after the departing car. She had the strongest legs of any kid in the neighborhood, except James. She was going to need them now as she struggled mightily to keep the car in sight up ahead.

She knew it was a late-model white Lexus with a New York license plate and a New York Yankees logo on the back window. She lost sight of it periodically as it drove over another rise far ahead, but she always regained sight of it once she raced over the rise. She was practically flying, going airborne and landing roughly in a perilously awkward manner, though always maintaining her balance and pushing forward, always forward and very, very fast.

Her legs were burning up, but she never noticed. The ball was headed for the alley. Sam had been there many, many times before. She was a pro who never took her eye off the ball. With Sam in centerfield, her glove was where doubles and triples in the alleys went to die.

This time, however, her friends were in grave danger of going away to die. No way would she let that happen. "No flippin' way, J.J.," she said as the wind whipped her face and blew her long, blonde hair wildly behind her. Sam was a girl possessed. *What self-respecting female athlete from Philadelphia would let a couple of stupid Yankees fans beat her?*

Not this one she thought, pushing on heroically, even though they were quite a long way ahead of her. Fortunately, however, she was able to make up ground when they stopped at a red light at Roosevelt Boulevard. *If they cross the boulevard and turn left, they're headed to the dumps or, O God, no...* Sam thought. The light turned green when Sam had approached to within a long block of them. The Lexus crossed the boulevard and turned left. Sam flew through the red light and narrowly missed being killed two times by cross traffic, but she couldn't stop. She wouldn't stop. *Five more minutes,* she thought. *Come on, girl, push!*

She patted her rear jeans pocket covering her butt raised way off her bike seat, as it had been the whole trip. Her phone was there. Her mind raced. Should she call 911? Dismissing the thought, and all other thoughts, she focused on the task at hand. She couldn't let that ball hit the ground. *Focus, girl! Focus! Push now. Push! White Lexus. Yankees. Don't stop! Don't stop! You're the best! You're the best! Win! Win!*

Fortunately, there was not much traffic this early on a very dark Saturday morning. Friday night, the bars did a lively business. Early Saturday morning, people were sleeping in. Sam was able to keep the red rear lights of the Lexus in view. The driver seemed to be taking his time, which helped – and hurt at the same time. Sam figured he did not want to attract undue attention. This allowed her to keep up. But, were a cop to stop him, it would be even better. It didn't look like such help was forthcoming, though. Once again, Sam would have to cover the alley alone.

Five miles into her race now, and Sam's legs were ablaze. Only afterward would she be conscious of the damage she inflicted. Right now she thought of nothing but Chris and J.J. being tossed around in that car trunk. It was anger that fueled her now, and anger that blinded her to the extreme demands she was placing on her extraordinarily muscular legs.

Sweating profusely in the early-morning cold, she refused to waste time wiping the sweat from her eyes. She would lose sight of her prey every once in a while and her heart would speed up with anxiety until, she cleared the next bluff, and regained sight of the Lexus.

She was typically three to five blocks behind it, rarely getting close enough for the occupants to notice her. Finally, fifteen minutes after the adventure had begun, it became clear to Sam that they were not going to stop at the dumps along State Street, which paralleled the Delaware River. Instead, they crossed State Street, next to St. Michael's Home and drove to a nearby dock where a motorboat awaited. They were going to be taking that boat. Once this became obvious to Sam, she stopped her bike on the other side of State Street from the river, dismounted, cropped to her knees behind a hedge, and pressed the speed dial to call Lieutenant Joe Carter.

Sam was nearly out of breath, panting heavily. "Come on, come on," she said as the phone rang.

****

Joe Carter studied the helicopter surveillance tape most of Friday, late into the night. Unfortunately, although he had nearly memorized the tape from watching it repeatedly, dozens of times, it showed absolutely nothing that happened inside Big Al's. It showed the outside crowds and traffic, police and sharpshooters only. And they were all outside.

After a long night of focusing on his PC screen, and a very, very short night of sleep, he was awoken at 5:30 Saturday morning by Mike Mountain who stopped by on his way to work. Mountain had been switched to the day shift a few weeks ago by Captain Carroll. It was department policy to switch up the detective pairings periodically.

"How's your review going, Joe?" Mountain said. "Any luck?"

"No, not really," Carter said, as he served Mountain a cup of coffee at the kitchen table and sat down with a cup for himself.

Mountain saw that his friend was bleary-eyed, likely due to an extreme lack of sleep. "What time did you get to bed last night?" Mountain asked.

"Dunno. Late, I guess," Carter said. Mountain figured he might not be hanging around long enough to finish his cup of coffee at this rate. Carter was less talkative than usual which, for him, was saying something. Mountain was scrambling for something to talk about.

"That garden of yours looks great out there under the floodlight, Joe. No surprise."

"Thanks," Carter said. "Feels good to do something constructive. Takes my mind off things."

"I see you cleared out all the dead plants that used to be beside the steps out there. Looks like they up and disappeared."

"Well, they had some....," Joe paused. "...help," he finished, suddenly looking up at Mountain, apparently having lost interest in studying the deep recesses of his coffee cup. Carter then repeated Mountain's last word. "Disappeared," he mumbled. "No, not disappeared...," he shot up, grabbed Mountain's face in his hands, and kissed him on the head. "Not disappeared, Mike!" he shouted. His face broke into a huge smile.

"Appeared! They didn't disappear, they appeared! That's it!" he exclaimed as he went running upstairs to his PC, leaving a befuddled Mike Mountain all alone at the kitchen table.

"Looked like they disappeared to me," Mountain said to the now empty chair across from him.

Joe Carter turned on the computer in his bedroom "Come on, come on," he said as it booted up. A minute later he was back to looking at the surveillance video. He centered the picture on the spot where Chris Newman must have been standing. He zoomed in as far as he could, until the picture was a big blur. Then he began to run the film slowly. Two minutes later, he pointed at the screen and said, "There!" He stopped the film, re-wound it about fifteen seconds and ran it forward again, this time frame by frame. He saw it again. "Yes!" he exclaimed, stopping the video and running it in reverse, one frame at a time, and saw what he was looking for.

"Mike, I've got it!" he shouted. Then, to himself, "Holy cannoli, Luigi."

Mountain ran into the room. "What Joe? What is it?"

Joe Carter smiled a big Cheshire grin, sat back in his chair with his hands behind his head, closed his eyes and said one word: "Proof."

Just then the phone rang. The caller ID said it was coming from Samantha Banks. Carter and Mountain each saw the message before looking at each other.

Carter picked up the phone. "Detective Carter," he said.

"Detective Carter, this is Sam Banks. I'm at St. Michael's Home, across the street. You have to get here. Chris and J.J. have been kidnapped. They're unconscious. Two men are carrying them onto a speedboat on the Delaware."

"Stay there," Carter said, getting up. "Stay out of sight. I'll be there in ten minutes."

Carter hung up, hurried to retrieve his service revolver and shoulder holster from the floor board of his bed.

"What's up?" Mountain asked.

"Game on, Mike," Carter said, hurrying out of the room.

Mountain watched him leave and shouted after him, "Need me to come with you, Joe?"

Carter ducked his head back through the open doorway. "Yes, but you better not. I'm on probation. You need to keep your nose clean." Then, Carter turned and hurried along the upstairs hallway. Starting down the steps, he looked up to see Mike Mountain standing in the bedroom doorway. "Help yourself to the fridge, Mike."

Mountain smiled broadly. "Go get 'em, Fey-Man!"

CHAPTER 32

Sam watched as the two men parked the white Lexus near a small wooden pier. Although they moved quickly, fluidly, they did not appear to be rushed or agitated. *OMG, they've done this before*, Sam thought. The truck lid popped open as the two men got out of the car, one on either side. Moving to the rear, they retrieved one boy each, hoisting their limp bodies up and over their shoulders before walking briskly to the pier.

Sam then ignored Lieutenant Carter's admonition to stay put, opting instead to run across State Street and down an old row of arborvitae running along the outside of the black wrought iron fence which bordered the campus of St. Michael's Home. At the end of the row she got down on her belly and crawled on the ground between the last two arborvitum, took her phone from her back pocket and started taking pictures of the Lexus license plate and of what was going on down at the pier. Even though it was very dark and foggy on the riverbank, and the pier was at least fifty yards away, Sam hoped that the police computers would be able to magnify and enhance whatever she was able to capture.

The men placed the boys in the speedboat. Then one of them started the outboard motor and its sound cut through the pre-dawn stillness and drowned out the soft murmur of the running river, the same river song Headmistress Brennan loved so much. The two men shook hands, and laughed about something. One of them left the pier, and walked quickly back to the car.

Sam snapped pictures of his face like crazy as he came closer, though never closer than twenty-five yards, got back in the car, started the ignition, and backed away from the pier.

Sam buried her face in the ground as the glow of the brake lights found her briefly before passing by. Sam had gotten a good look at the man's face, but she had no idea who he was. She had never seen him before, but he was in good shape. Probably forty years old or so, she thought, and good-looking, not the scruffy, creepy, long-haired weirdo she had envisioned as she chased him on her bike earlier.

Suddenly, Sam saw that the man in the boat was using an oar or pole to push the boat out into the river and away from the pier. He then dropped whatever he was using to shove off and went to the back of the boat to man the outboard motor. Two seconds later, the engine roared and the boat departed quickly, headed out into the heart of the river before turning right and heading south, down to the airport and meat-packing plants of South Philly. Sam sprang from the hedge and ran toward the pier to get a better look at where the boat was headed. When she arrived at the pier ten seconds later, the boat was already far down-river, practically invisible in the fog. Even though she had excellent eyesight which came in handy when tracking sky-high baseballs in a sunny blue sky, she wished she had Chris' eyesight which seemed to be custom designed for low light conditions such as this.

And his extrasensory hearing. Concentrating as hard as she could, clutching the piling at the end of the pier to keep from falling into the river, she could have sworn she heard a distant splash coming from the direction of the boat. Was it possible? Did she hear something splash?

That's when she became aware of the headlights on State Street. She ran back across the lot, waving her arms, "Lieutenant Carter! Lieutenant Carter! Over here! Over here! Come quick! Hurry!" she shouted.

The car drove across the gravel road toward her and came to a screeching stop, gravel flying, as Joe Carter jumped from the car and ran with Sam to the pier.

"How long ago did they leave?"

"Five minutes. A speedboat. It's way south there," Sam said, pointing.

"How many?"

"Two men. One man in the boat. The other guy came back and took the car. A white Lexus. New York license plate ACL-310. It had a Yankees sticker on the rear window."

"I think he stopped," Sam continued, turning

back toward the boat. "I think I heard him throw something in the river about a minute ago."

****

Chris and J.J. were in a bad way. Laying in the bow of the boat, they were crumpled, but not uncomfortable, because they were still unconscious. Their abductor had his right hand on the rudder as the boat sped away from the pier, over and through the river waves, leaving a strong wake fanning out, cutting through the rapid river current. Soon he turned right and headed south down the river.

Almost every summer the mighty Delaware claimed the lives of children as it ran through the densely-populated city of Philadelphia. Whether from capsized boats or inner tubes, or from ill-advised Tarzan swings on the banks, or from rising creeks and streams in poor drainage areas during torrential summer storms, some very few children would, through a tragic turn of fate, find themselves sucked down and under the surface of the water by riptides and very, very strong undercurrents. Some adults also. But few ever survived to tell the tale.

More often than not their bodies were found by police or Port Authority personnel trawling the river bottom with large nets. Other times the bodies would wash ashore in the mammoth city aquifers or be found weeks later in the Delaware Bay well south of the city.

J.J. was to be first. The man cut the engine to idle, picked J.J. up in his arms and carried him to the rear of the boat. The man did not know that the boy, even when conscious, could not swim. And he did not care. He had a job to do and was being paid handsomely to do it. The river would take the body down almost immediately anyway, whether he could swim or not. So much the better. No evidence.

The boy moaned and began to stir in the man's arms as the chloroform began to wear off. The man heaved the boy overboard and there was a loud splash as he hit the frigid water and began to sink almost immediately. The idling boat continued to drift south with the strong current.

The man went back and picked up the second boy and repeated the process, throwing him overboard a good five yards south of the first, who had now completely disappeared beneath the surface. The second boy began to sink. Seeing this, the man said, "Goodnight boys. Sleep tight." He then sat, turned to face forward in the boat, clapped his hands together, and said, "time for breakfast." He gunned the engine once more to speed south down the river to where another accomplice was waiting for him in a black Cadillac parked at a predestined rendezvous point near the river bank about three miles further south.

****

Back on the shore at the departure point, Sam and Lieutenant Joe Carter heard what sounded like a second splash. Though very, very faint, they both heard it.

"Oh my God! Oh my God!" Sam screamed. "He threw them overboard. He threw them overboard! J.J. can't swim. They're both unconscious! We have to save them!"

****

Chris began to regain consciousness as soon as he hit the icy water. Within five seconds he was sinking beneath the surface and about to lose consciousness again as water rushed into his nose and throat. Suddenly, he was wide awake, though sinking fast and being drawn down. He did the only thing he could think to do. He connected.

The water stopped pulling him. He swam quickly to the surface, popped above the water line and began to violently cough water out of his throat, nose, and lungs, and began breathing in air as fast as he could. Though still panicked, he was able to make out the dim form of a boat pointed downriver away from him, and the shadowy form of a man facing away from him as the boat was now stilled, its getaway monetarily interrupted.

Chris doggy paddled in place a few seconds more, trying to stabilize his breathing and get the rest of the water out of his respiratory system. The water was very cold and he knew he had to get out of it as fast as he could, otherwise hypothermia would kick in.

He looked around. He was a long way from the shore. He was a good swimmer and he knew he could make it and was about to try when he saw a halfball on the surface of the water near him and he suddenly remembered. "J.J.!" he screamed and coughed at the same time.

Panicked for the life of his friend, he remembered that he was connected. "Everything's stopped. Calm down. Calm down. You have time. You have all the time you need. Think."

He looked at the river. "Okay, okay. It's going south. To the bay. The ball must've been north." He began to swim north. "Hang on, J.J. I'll get you out of this," he said as he swam. He put his face into the water as he swam and used his keen vision to see through the murky water. He was surprised how well he was able to see in the dark. He could actually see better than in the light of day. *I'm nocturnal*, he thought to himself.

One Savant-minute later he saw J.J.'s lifeless body in mid-tumble about twenty feet under the surface. Chris immediately dove down, wrapped his arm under one of J.J.'s arm pits, and swam quickly back up to the surface with his friend. When he broke the surface of the water, J.J. remained unresponsive, so Chris wrapped his arms around J.J.'s chest and tried to force the air out of his lungs.

When that failed to revive J.J. after thirty seconds, Chris tried the mouth-to-mouth resuscitation he had been taught many years ago by Fixer and had re-learned in middle school health class. No luck. J.J. was still unresponsive. He wasn't breathing.

Chris began to swim toward shore with his friend, near death, in tow.

After twenty Savant-minutes he approached the shore. His body ached terribly, but he couldn't stop. He had to save his friend. Up ahead, through the dark and the fog, he saw an unmoving Sam and Lieutenant Joe Carter on a pier. He swam toward them ever so slowly, almost out of strength. His toes and fingertips were near-frozen. His thighs had both cramped up, his arms were weak from straining, and he still struggled to breathe as he carried his friend almost a half mile through the icy river.

At long last, Chris felt the river bottom against his numb feet. He stumbled to stand up and drag J.J. with him up onto the shore and out of the water. Falling down onto the ground next to J.J., Chris disconnected and immediately heard Sam in mid-scream, "We have to save them!"

"Look!" Carter shouted, suddenly seeing the two boys magically appear out of thin air on the shore.

"Chris!" Sam screamed, as she and Carter ran to where Chris and J.J. were now sprawled, unmoving, on the shore.

Chris looked up into the face of Joe Carter peering down at him. "J.J. first," he said. "He can't breathe."

"How are you, son?"

"C-C-C-Cold. So…so… c-c-c-cold."

"Sam, there's a blanket on the back seat of my car."

"Got it!" Sam said, turning and running to the car. When she returned, Joe Carter was performing CPR on J.J. Sam covered Chris with the blanket, and then rolled him first on one side, then the other, to tuck the blanket under him in an attempt to insulate him.

"Take off his shoes and socks," Carter said. Wrap his feet and his head, too. When you're done, go start the car and turn the heater on. We're going to have to warm them up fast."

She kept an eye on Carter as he tried to resuscitate J.J. It didn't look good. Sixty seconds later, J.J. was still unresponsive. After she had finished removing Chris' shoes and socks and wrapping him like a mummy in the blanket, Sam ran up to the car, started it and turned the heater on as Carter had told her to do.

When she ran back over to Carter, he was lifting J.J. from the ground. "I can't help him," Carter said. "We have to get them to the hospital.

You get in the backseat. You'll need to hold J.J. He's small enough. He'll need the body heat. I'll lean Chris against you. You'll have to prop him up."

He didn't want to give Sam the bad news. J.J.'s pulse was very weak.

After he had belted the three kids in the back, Carter hopped into the driver's seat and put the car in gear. When the car started moving Chris experienced a lucid interval. "Is J.J. breathing?" he asked.

"No, we need to get him to the hospital."

"No!' Chris shouted and immediately started coughing. Carter braked to a stop.

"To Welsh's. Take him to Welsh's," Chris said.

"The vacant storefront on Rising Sun?" Carter said.

"Yes. They can help him," Chris said. "Please, trust me. They can help him there."

Carter was in a tough spot. Any delay could jeopardize not only J.J.'s life but, possibly even Chris' life. If he took them to a vacant storefront and they died, he could be charged with a whole host of crimes. He was, at that moment, staring at many years of prison time.

He knew he would never be criticized if he took them straight to the hospital. But, he also knew, this Newman kid was special. That was good and bad. Every time Carter tried to do the right thing when this kid was involved, he had nothing to show for it but a lot of grief. On the other hand, the kid had appeared out of thin air. He saw it with his own eyes. Plus, the police surveillance video at Big Al's also proved this kid was way, way special.

All these thoughts ran through Carter's mind in a split second. It was his special gift which he couldn't put into words: the sixth sense that had always guided him. And, for better or worse, Carter knew what he knew, and he had to follow his heart. He immediately threw caution to the wind, overruled his natural concern for his own well-being, and put his full faith in this remarkable kid. "Okay," he said. "Welsh's."

"Wait!" Chris said. "Here, Sam, hold my hand and put your other hand on Lieutenant Carter's neck. Let's see if we can speed things up." He connected.

Immediately, they were all connected, but no one realized it, because there were no points of reference to indicate that anything had changed. But Chris knew that time was of the essence for J.J. If he could get him to Fixer in one second rather than in fifteen minutes, then that's what he would do.

Carter drove out on to State Street and back through the city streets in the pre-dawn dark. "Wow. Nobody's moving," Carter said after a few minutes.

"It's weird."

But, he really didn't appreciate the full weirdness of it until he arrived at the heavier-trafficked Boulevard and all the cars were stopped. No one was moving. Carter stopped at a red light, but Sam told him to keep going, that it was okay to cross the Boulevard. "What's going on?" Carter said.

"Keep going," Sam said. "Don't stop. Chris will explain later."

Chris opened his eyes at that. He fought to maintain consciousness, shivered uncontrollably, and came close to passing out a couple of times. Sam continued to squeeze his hand to keep him awake.

Eight Savant minutes later, a split second in Earth time, they arrived at Welsh's. Carter parked the car in the rear alleyway, remembering that only the rear door offered access to the vacant storefront, and hopped out of the car. Chris disconnected. They were now back on Earth time and had to hustle. There was no time to lose.

Carter opened the back door and took J.J.'s lifeless body from Sam, so she could exit the car. "Sam, you'll have to carry J.J.," Carter said handing J.J. back to her. "I'll carry Chris." He bent into the rear of the car and pulled Chris, who had slumped over onto the seat, into his arms. Standing again, he turned, approached the rear door, and forced it open with his foot as he had so frequently done many years ago. He entered into the dark, vacant interior, carrying Chris. Sam followed, carrying J.J.

Walking into the dark, dank, dusty abandoned building, Carter suddenly began to doubt the wisdom of what he had done, and worried anew for his well-being. He looked down at Chris in his arms. The boy was slipping in and out of consciousness, trying valiantly to stay awake.

"Don't worry," Chris said to Carter, his voice a barely audible whisper.

But Carter was worried. "Hello!" he called loudly into the gloomy darkness. "Hello!"

"Don't shout," Chris said softly. "They're here."

Carter was spooked now. The boy was clearly delusional. "Sam, look," Carter said. "I've made a big mistake. We've got to get them to the hospital. Let's go," he said, turning on his heel to head back to the door. "This is nuts."

"No!" Sam shouted. Carter stopped, turned and looked at her. "No, Lieutenant Carter. You have to believe in him. It's the only way."

"Sam," Carter said, "there's no one here…"

"Hold hands," Chris said suddenly. "Sam, hold Lieutenant Carter's hand."

Sam, carrying J.J., walked back and held one hand out to Joe Carter.

"This is no time for Kumbaya," Carter said.

"Hold my hand, Detective Carter," Sam said. "Trust him. Please."

Carter sighed deeply, resigned. He slipped his hand into Sam's.

Chris connected.

Lieutenant Joe Carter couldn't believe his eyes.

CHAPTER 33

Suddenly they all stood, not in a dingy, dark, vacant storefront, but inside a beautiful, modern, gleaming apartment which, he was certain, could win any interior design award anywhere in the world. It very well could have been the only six-star interior on the planet.

"Um...," he started, not knowing what to say. "What just happened?"

He and Sam turned to face what, until a few seconds ago, was the front of the empty storefront. Now it was a grand living room. To the right, on one side wall, was a large floor-to-ceiling brick fireplace. An Asian woman sat there, near the fireplace, apparently sipping tea from a china teacup held in her right hand. On each hand she wore white gloves. Five small, blue lights, arrayed in a row along the knuckles of her right hand, blinked in a syncopated wave. She wore large, black opaque glasses which led Carter to think she might be blind.

Beautiful red and gold flames leapt from burning logs, casting an additional welcoming light onto the Persian rug covering the parquet hardwood floor and inlaid dark oak design around the perimeter of the room. A marble staircase with a gold-turned wrought iron railing wound up to a second floor balcony.

A tall, stately gentleman stood in front of the bow window, which was partially obscured by ivory colored drapes, in the front wall. He wore a long ivory trench coat. Blue lights emanated from small lights on the fingers of his right hand, even though both hands were covered by soft brown leather gloves. Tan aviator glasses shielded his eyes from view. He had close-cropped salt and pepper hair.

"Welcome to the portal," he said. "My name is Amnesius Fixer. My colleague, there," he said, nodding to the left, "is Miss Portice."

Carter and Sam walked toward him, into the middle of the room, carrying Chris and J.J.

"Nurse Fixer and Doctor Portice," Carter said, remembering.

Fixer bowed his head. "At your service, Lieutenant. It seems your diligence has been rewarded."

"Help them," Carter said, motioning to the boys. "Can you?"

Fixer looked across the room at Miss Portice, who remained seated. She indicated nothing, or so it seemed. But Fixer said, "Miss Portice approves." He strode up to Carter, stopped when they were very close, as if he were studying him, and looked down at Chris.

"Hi, Fixer," Chris said, lying in Carter's

arms, looking up through half-closed eyes.

Fixer smiled slightly, then placed a gloved hand over Chris' face and said, "Be well. Now!" Immediately, the cold left Chris' body. He warmed immediately. His teeth stopped chattering, he regained feeling in his hands and feet, and his energy returned. He was able to breathe clearly and was now wide awake.

"I'm good," Chris said to Carter. "You can put me down, but hold my hand. You too, Sam. Don't let go of my hand." Carter stooped so that Chris could stand on the floor. Chris now stood between Carter and Sam. All three held hands.

"Thank you, Fixer," Chris said, "but J.J.'s in critical condition. He can't breathe. Please save him."

"Son," Fixer started. "You are my charge. I have done what I can for you, as I would do for any Savant, but I am restricted from meddling directly in the affairs of humans."

"But you've already saved James and Lieutenant Carter," Chris said.

"No. You saved them, I merely pointed out that they needed help."

"Fixer, that is a distinction without a difference," Chris said. "Please don't split hairs. My friend's life is in peril. Only you can save him. I can't. If you don't save him, he will die."

"Son, it is not allowed. I cannot," Fixer said. "I am sorry you wasted your time coming here and have chosen to disobey our most fundamental law, of which you are no doubt aware."

"Telling humans?"

"Yes. I will have to relieve them of the memory. They cannot be permitted to remember any of this."

"Fixer, please! J.J. will die."

"He would've died last night in the attic if you didn't save him. He's living on borrowed time as it is."

Chris couldn't believe what he was hearing. All this time he thought Fixer was concerned for his welfare. "I am concerned for your welfare," Fixer said, clearly reading his thoughts.

"But not that of my friends?"

Fixer did not respond, but he didn't have to. Suddenly, Chris understood why his mother insisted he be raised on Earth. "Yes, she cared," Fixer said, still reading Chris' thoughts, walking back over to Miss Portice, holding her hand. "Your mother cared deeply about humans. We miss her so much. So, so much. She was a great woman, with many, many fine qualities. But this!" Fixer turned to face Chris. "This we have never understood."

"That she cared for humans?"

"Yes. If it weren't near-sacrilegious to even suggest it, we might think it was...well, I won't suggest it."

But he didn't have to. Chris understood. "You think my mother was flawed because she cared..."

"Please, don't..."

"...about humans? No, Fixer, that's not a flaw."

"It is your opinion," Miss Portice spoke for the first time. "A worthy debate between two planets. Between two life forms. Regardless, we cannot interfere."

Chris looked at J.J. He was near death. "Then why are you here?"

"You would play chess with us, boy?" Miss Portice said bitterly. "You have no idea who you are up against."

"I will answer your question when you answer mine," Chris said. "I asked first."

"Very well. We are here to honor your mother's wish to have you be born and raised on Earth."

"And why did she want that?"

"Ah! That is the question, is it not? We have been asking ourselves that for a very long time but, truthfully, we don't know."

"Interesting that you invoke the truth twice in a span of thirty seconds, yet you yourself are not truthful…"

"Be…"

"Oh, I am quite careful. And I know as well as you do. First, you mention two lifeforms, but there is only one, isn't there? Savants are "of Earth" as you like to say, aren't they? It's just that they started here millions of years ago, before pioneering space and finding more suitable planets. Therefore, it would seem that humans and Savants are not two lifeforms, but one: human.

Now, I am sure this may fly in the face of your elitist self-image but it is nonetheless true. Your second lie was to say you do not know why my mother wanted me to be raised here. But that cannot be true because Savants know everything, isn't that right?

She wanted me not to be starved of empathy as you apparently are. I suspect it is what drove her from your pristine, perfect world and back down to our messy, complicated, imperfect little Earth, where I can experience hatred, prevarication, death, avarice, betrayal, love, caring, self-sacrifice, teamwork, and all the other messy, illogical experiences of real humans. Finally, I think you can see that I know who I am "up against," as you say, so I have answered your question."

"And I'll tell you one more thing. I know why. I know why my mother wanted me to experience all these human emotions and messy situations. It's because you need leaders on Maran. Good leaders. Great leaders. Well-rounded leaders. It's because there are evil Savants and they need to be dealt with. Well, you better go back to your current leaders and tell them if you do not save my friend here, right now, the deal is off. You'll have to find someone else to help you out of your universal conundrum."

"But..." Miss Portice started.

"It's nonnegotiable. Save him now, or leave and don't come back. This is our planet, our world. You are guests here. You don't come here with your rules."

"But why is he so important to you? He's not even a decent representative of a lower lifeform," Miss Portice said. "I could see if it was somebody with some potential, albeit limited. But this one..." she said, motioning toward J.J.

"This one..." Chris said, looking at J.J., "is a human being!" he shouted, irate. "That seems unimportant to you. Thanks to my mother, and your efforts on her behalf, it is of paramount importance to me, and I thank you for that. But, be warned, you ignore my request at your peril. Choose carefully."

Fixer and Miss Portice looked at each other. After a minute, they each nodded. Fixer walked over, looked at Chris, and then down at J.J. laying in Sam's arms. He placed his gloved hand on J.J.'s face. "Be healed. Now," he said.

Suddenly J.J. began to stir, then he coughed violently and water gushed out of his mouth and all over Sam. "Ugh!" she said, putting J.J. down, helping him to stand. "Don't let go of my hand!" she yelled as he tried to pull away.

"Whoa!" he said, looking around. "Nice place. Sam, you're getting water all over the flippin' floor," J.J. said. Then, seeing that he and Sam and Chris and Carter were all holding hands, he said, "Ain't this flippin' cozy?"

"J.J.!" Sam and Chris yelled, as they moved to hug J.J., Carter trailing, still holding Chris' other hand. "Geez, a flippin' group hug," J.J. said.

Fixer watched Chris smile broadly as he hugged J.J., looking up at Fixer as he did so. "Thanks, Fixer. Thanks for everything."

Fixer shook his head in response. "Don't blame me."

Chris laughed. "There's hope for you after all."

"A rare risible error of judgment on your part. I'll chalk it up to adolescence," Fixer said.

After the hug, J.J. attempted to get up to speed. "So, where are we? What is this place? Who are the dudes with the blinking hands?"

"It's old Welsh's Hardware," Chris said. "This is Amnesius Fixer, and that is Miss Portice," Chris said.

J.J., initially perplexed, looked around, then at Chris. "Is this more speed of light flippin' Brainiac stuff?"

"Yes."

"Thought so. You said you'd find me a home someday. Is this it?"

Chris looked at Fixer and Miss Portice. "What do you say? Is there room on Maran for J.J?"

"Well, I don't think…" Miss Portice began.

"What's Maran?" J.J. said.

"It's the planet they're from," Chris said.

J.J. looked at Fixer and Miss Portice. "Oh, yeah? So where's your spaceship?"

"No spaceship," Miss Portice said. "You go through the portal," she said, motioning up the stairs with her arm. "With us, of course. You couldn't survive it without us."

"Wait, Chris," Carter said. "We need to

return J.J. to the orphanage."

"So, let me ask you," J.J. continued to address Fixer and Miss Portice, as if Carter hadn't spoken, "tell me about this flippin' Maran place."

"Well, it's very beautiful. Very beautiful," Miss Portice started.

"And much bigger than Earth," Fixer said. "Plus, there are only a couple thousand of us there, so there's plenty of elbow room. You could get a nice house with a yard as big as Pennsylvania, if you wanted."

"And there's no crime," Miss Portice said. "We live in peace."

"What kind of job could I get? Could I have a paper route?"

"Oh, no," Miss Portice said. "We do not have money. There's no need. Everybody has whatever they need. There's plenty to go around. Of course, you could be whatever you want – a farmer, anything."

"No money, huh?" J.J. said.

"That's right. There is no need."

"How would I buy a house or feed a family?"

"You would have whatever you needed."

"Are there kids there?"

"No."

"No?"

"We do not have children."

"That's flippin' baloney. Chris was born."

"Nature has made it difficult, as your friend can attest in the case of his own mother. We are totally evolved. There is nothing for nature to improve upon."

"So you're all, like, flippin' Brainiacs...no offense, Doc."

"We are all Savants."

"Um, in that case, no thanks," J.J. said.

"J.J. are you sure? It sounds perfect," Chris said. But Carter breathed a sigh of relief. He did not know how he would explain a missing J.J.

"Perfect for you, maybe, but I'm no flippin' Brainiac and I couldn't stand to be surrounded by Brainiacs all day long. I'd go flippin' nuts. You have no idea how much work it is to keep up with you. Plus, no kids? No thanks. I always wanted to be the dad I never had. I'm gonna be the best flippin' dad ever. I'm gonna adopt as many kids as I can. And I like work. I'm gonna work and I'm gonna make money. I like money. I don't need everything just given to me. It don't seem flippin' right, know what I'm sayin'? And we still got some bad guys we gotta catch. Don't think I forgot about being thrown in the river and almost drowning. They can't get away with that. Somebody's gotta catch the bad guys. Maybe I'll be like Lieutenant Carter here someday."

Joe Carter smiled. "I wouldn't doubt it. Not for a second."

"That reminds me," Sam said. "We'd better get moving. We have a lot of work to do."

"Before you leave," Fixer said, "I must relieve you of the memory of me, Miss Portice, this portal, and all you've seen and heard here today. But, don't worry, it doesn't hurt. I place my hands on your head. And you won't lose any other memories."

"Whoa! Wait a minute," J.J. said. "Why?"

"Because humans cannot know of Savants," Fixer said.

"Yes," Miss Portice said. "It's been the way for millions of years. You cannot know of us."

"Seems stupid," J.J. said. "Who we gonna flippin' tell?"

"You could tell anyone," Miss Portice said.

"Why would we do that?" J.J. said. "Who's gonna flippin' believe us?"

Fixer and Miss Portice looked at each other.

"That's a good point," Sam said. "Look, it would be helpful for us, as we try to catch the creeps who tried to hurt them, to know that Chris can do what he does and to understand why. Plus, like J.J. said, we won't tell anybody. It doesn't do us any good to let other people know, and they wouldn't believe us even if we told them."

Miss Portice and Fixer looked at each other and then turned to face them.

"What do you say, son? Is this something you want?" Fixer asked.

"Yes. I think it's a good idea," Chris said.

"Okay," Fixer said. "We're willing to give it a shot. But one strike, you're out. Deal?"

Chris looked at Carter, Sam, and J.J. They all nodded.

"It's a deal," Chris said. "No mistakes."

"With that, we will bid you a good day," Fixer said, as he and Miss Portice began to walk up the stairs, "and good hunting."

Chris then disconnected. He and Sam, Carter, and J.J. now stood in the middle of a dirty, dark, abandoned storefront.

"That was flippin' intense," J.J. said.

"Where do we go from here?" Carter said. "Do you have any idea who tried to kill you?"

"Yes," Chris said. "We have an idea."

"A rea_ good flippin' idea," J.J. said, looking at Chris.

"Okay, let's get going," Carter said, as they all headed for the back door.

CHAPTER 34

When they were outside, Lieutenant Carter said, "Okay, Team, where to?"

"I still gotta do my papers," J.J. said. Incredibly, after almost drowning an hour ago, J.J. was back to being a businessman. "I bet two or three of my customers have already called the home office complaining about late delivery."

"Right," Chris said. "It's important that we get back to our regular routine."

"No, I disagree," Carter said. "Look, these guys, whoever they are, think you two are feeding fish in the Delaware. I think it best that you lay low for a while so they don't try something again. If they think you're dead, let 'em keep on thinking that."

"How do we flippin' do that? I gotta do my papers."

"Can't do your papers if you're dead, J.J.," Carter said.

"Good point," Sam said.

"Sure I can. Might take a little longer is all," J.J. said. Sam rolled her eyes.

"Look," Chris started. "I'll do the papers. I can connect, do the papers, and go get my phone in less than a second, unseen, and then we can meet somewhere secret. Can't be the clubhouse, my house, or Sam's house though. They might see us: too close to Mrs. Kling's house."

"Right. Good thinking, Chris…" Carter said.

"Get used to it," Sam said.

"Flippin-Ay," J.J. agreed.

"Alright, we'll meet at my house. It's a few blocks over from your street," Carter said. "They have no reason to think you'll show up at my house. You can call your folks from there, so they don't worry, and we can figure out next steps. Okay, everybody hop in," he said, opening the driver side door and getting into the car. Sam and J.J. got in the back.

"It'll be faster and safer if I connect and leave from here," Chris said, "rather than chance having someone see you drop me off at Stan's."

"Okay, we'll wait for you at my house. 812 Longshore," Carter said.

"Uh, yeah, about that…I'll be waiting for you. Later," Chris said as he connected and disappeared.

"I'll never get used to that," Carter said to Sam and J.J. as he started the engine.

Chris delivered J.J.'s papers using the

customer address list accompanying the bundles of newspapers still laying on the sidewalk outside of Stan's deli. It was about 7:00 AM, still pretty early on a Saturday, so there was still time, Chris knew, before the customers would start to call and complain. One and a half Savant-hours later, or one fraction of an Earth second, Chris had completed delivering the larger pre-holiday newspapers, had ridden home, guiding J.J.'s bike with one hand, ran up to his bedroom to retrieve his phone, and sent his mother a text message saying he was helping J.J. with the oversized papers. He then rode the four blocks to Detective Carter's house on Longshore guiding J.J.'s bike, sat on a patio chair on the front porch, disconnected, and waited another eight Earth minutes for Lieutenant Carter to arrive with Sam and J.J.

"Wow! You done already?" Carter said, walking up.

"Yep. If you'd left your lawnmower out, I could've cut your lawn. What took you guys so long?" Chris said.

"Flippin' Brainiac humor," J.J. said. "Could you imagine livin' with a whole planet of 'em?" he said to Sam.

"I could handle it," Sam said. "I still can't believe you didn't go. Maran sounded wonderful."

"Yeah, everything that sounds wonderful ain't always so great," J.J. said. "Like farts."

Carter, Sam, and Chris stopped walking up the sidewalk to the house and looked at J.J., who turned and saw them, staring at him.

"Looks like you've given this some thought," Carter said.

"Where do you come up with this stuff?" Sam said.

"I'm sure he didn't mean it," Chris said. "I'm sure he meant to say flippin' farts, right J.J.?"

"Like I said, flippin' Brainiac humor," J.J. said, turning and continuing to walk up to Carter's front door.

Inside, seated at the kitchen table, they got down to business. First, Chris gave his phone to Carter so he could see the pictures from Mrs. Kling's attic. Chris and J.J. watched Carter closely as he stared at the phone in disbelief.

"Does the man in the window look familiar?" Chris said.

Carter, looking at the cellphone, was clearly stunned. "Yes," he said softly as he continued to look at the other pictures Chris had taken.

"We thought so too," J.J. said. "He's one of your teammates, right? He's the guy we see yelling all the time at your P.A.L. basketball games. The hothead."

"It's my captain. Captain Carroll. I...I...don't believe it."

"Believe it," Sam said, handing her phone to Carter. Carter watched the video and looked at the pictures Sam had taken, becoming more agitated the more he saw of the boys being manhandled and thrown roughly into the trunk.

Later, at the river, the man walking back to the Lexus was clearly Captain Carroll. Carter stood and paced, running his fingers through his hair. Agitated, he would, at times, seem to calm down long enough to sit down, then would stand right back up and resume pacing. He said nothing but, clearly, his mind was racing.

"You okay, Lieutenant?" Sam asked after Carter sat down and got up a third time.

"No, not really," Carter said.

"Why not?" J.J. said. "We know who he is. You can arrest him, right?"

"It's not that easy," Carter said, finally sitting. "Look, you know what happened last night and this morning, and I know what happened, but it is going to be very, very difficult to arrest anybody."

"Why?" Sam said. "It's right there in the pictures and in the video."

Chris understood. "Because we're not dead, right?"

"Yes, that's right," Carter said. "I hate to say it, but that's exactly right."

"And there's no proof we were actually ever hurt."

"Right again," Carter said. "No medical records at all. Look, if I go after the captain with these photos and videos, he'll claim they were somehow doctored or photoshopped. I'm on probation right now so he could claim that my motivation is revenge; that I am trying to make him look bad. It would drag out in court. In the meantime, I would be fired. Which, truthfully, would be okay. I'll survive. That's not what concerns me though.

What concerns me is that this evidence, I believe, is credible, but it might take the courts two or more years to bring this to trial. A trial for child abduction. If he loses, then the best case is the captain will be forced out at that time, and he will see some jail time, but the judge could go easy on him, depending on who the judge is. Worst case, the photos and video are determined to be inadmissible in court, and a jury would never even see the only evidence we have. In that case, the captain would be reinstated, would likely sue me for defamation, and might even win."

"But we could testify," J.J. said.

"Probably not," Carter said. "First of all, you're kids. Kids are not great witnesses, especially on cross-examination. How are you going to explain that you got away from the dogs, got out of Mrs. Kling's house without being caught, or didn't drown this morning? How are you going to explain that you suffered no injury at all? You can't talk about Chris moving at light speed and such. No one is going to believe that and Chris has promised not to tell anyone. No. We need more than this. Is this it, Sam? Chris? Is there anything else?

"There are the things in Mrs. Kling's attic that she stole from St. Michael's," J.J. said.

"Right, and I will get a search warrant this morning. Hopefully the articles are still there and we can return them to St. Michael's. Mrs. Kling will be charged. Maybe, *just maybe*," he emphasized, "Mrs. Kling will be dismissed from St. Michael's or be forced to make restitution if some articles are missing, but nothing ties her to your abduction or attempted murder. In fact, the same can be said of the captain. Even if a jury finds him complicit in the thefts and, possibly, your abduction, he may be dismissed also, but nothing ties him to the attempted murders. Plus, the captain is a very powerful man, well-connected politically. He has a lot of powerful friends who could make life for you and your parents very, very difficult. Maybe even dangerous again. No, I really think we need something, *something* more incriminating. We need rock-solid verifiable proof. I don't suppose you have anything like that, do you?"

"You have all we have," Sam said. "There on our phones. That's all we can prove."

"Oh, come on!" J.J. shouted. "Those dudes threw us in the river! They tried to kill us!"

Carter looked at him before looking down. "Come on, J.J.," Chris said. "He knows that, but there's no proof."

"No proof? Look at the flippin' pictures. Yeah, I guess it'd be nice if I had taken a picture of the guy throwing me in the flippin' river but, from what I'm hearing, it probably wouldn't be allowed by a judge anyway. What a crock! How much flippin' proof do you need?"

"J.J., we have proof – of abduction by the captain and of theft by Mrs. Kling, but that won't get them out of your lives forever," Lieutenant Carter said. "A few years, tops. Then they'll be back. These people are cold-blooded killers. They'll stop at nothing. They've already proven they will drown kids in the river. I want proof that will put them away for a long, long time."

Then they all fell silent, as if they had been defeated. After a couple more minutes, Carter stood. "I guess I'll get a search warrant. At least we can get those stolen articles back to St. Michael's Home. By the way, Chris, why did you take pictures of Mrs. Kling's checkbook and bank statements? What was that all about?

"Oh, yeah, that. I'm doing some work for Headmistress Brennan. I noticed that a lot of the dates of the $10,000 deposits to Mrs. Kling's account are very close to the dates of Mrs. Kling's flights to Miami."

"Flights to Miami?"

"Yes. She flies there several times a year to accompany orphans to their new parents, who usually fly to Miami from other countries."

"What countries?"

"I don't know. All's I know is that the adoptive parents fly to Miami and meet Mrs. Kling there with the orphan."

"How long has this been going on?"

"A few years, I think. Maybe three or four years. Something like that, near as I can tell from the records at the Home."

"And you say these trips to Miami happen at about the same time that $10,000 deposits are made to her bank account?"

"Yes. Most of the time it's $10,000. Sometimes it's more."

"Hmm. I wonder what that's all about. That's a lot of money."

"I don't know. I guess I need to ask

Headmistress Brennan. It's strange, though."

"What's strange?"

"Well, whenever any of the other placement counselors place a child overseas, they usually receive a thank you note from the parents and from the child a few days or weeks later."

"What's so strange about that?"

"Nothing. What's strange is that Mrs. Kling almost never receives thank-you notes when she places children overseas."

When he heard this, the psychic Fey-Man alarm went off in Lieutenant Joe Carter's mind. Acting on that, as well as on years of experience dealing with criminals, he immediately placed a call to a friend he knew who had helped him many times in the past.

Carter listened to the phone ring. "Steve Rand, FBI," said the voice.

"Steve. Joe Carter here. I need your help."

CHAPTER 35

Chris, Sam, J.J. and Lieutenant Carter got right to work on a plan. There was no time to waste. It took about an hour for them to decide on a course of action, and it took another half hour for Lieutenant Carter to think about, and plan for, everything that could go wrong.

"No doubt about it, I ought to be shot for even considering this hair-brained idea," he said. "It's a big risk."

"Big risk, big return," J.J. said. Everybody looked at him as if he was speaking Chinese.

"Yeah, I read that somewhere."

"Pretty shocking," Sam said.

"What? That I would say something like that?"

"No," Sam said. "That you read something."

"You know, if you weren't a girl..." J.J. said.

"You may be eating a knuckle sandwich depending upon what you say next," Sam warned, holding up a fist.

J.J. looked at her, saw she was serious, and reconsidered, "...um, you'd be a lot less pretty?"

"Better," Sam said.

"Pretty smooth, Bud," Lieutenant Carter said, smiling.

"I think we should go for it, Lieutenant Carter," Chris said. "Don't forget, I can use my ability in case we run into trouble. Plus, we don't have any more time. According to the airline tickets I saw last night, Mrs. Kling's flight is in three hours. She's probably at the airport already with one of the orphans."

It was this last statement which spurred Lieutenant Carter into action. Based upon the information Chris had uncovered about the timing of the big deposits and airplane flights, and lack of thank you notes, and even though he could not bring himself to voice his fears to Chris, Sam, and J.J., Lieutenant Carter thought the orphan was in grave danger of being sold into slavery by Mrs. Kling when she arrived at the airport in Miami. She had likely sold other young orphans into slavery over the past several years. The large deposits into her bank account were likely her share of the sales of the children, and he guessed that the people who took the children from Mrs. Kling and sold them into slavery certainly wouldn't send thank you notes to Mrs. Kling.

"Can any of you act?" Lieutenant Carter asked.

"Yeah, J.J. can," Chris said. "He's a thespian,

right J.J.?"

"Flippin ay," J.J. said.

"Chris too," Sam said.

Carter looked at them. "I hope so. Okay, let's go."

Chris and J.J. figured out what they would do once they got to the airport and rehearsed their lines. Lieutenant Carter was on the phone with Steve Rand and Lieutenant Mike Fenton to coordinate next steps. Timing was critical. The sting would be very, very risky. He knew he should have his head examined for involving the kids but, once again, his Fey-Man impulse was now guiding him as loudly and clearly as it ever had. Usually, however, he only ever placed himself at risk, not his partners on the force and certainly not inexperienced children.

On the other hand, a young child was about to be sold into slavery to criminals in another country. Also, this plan was primarily the brainchild of twelve-year-old Chris Newman. The boy was brilliant, no doubt. If he ever decided to go into law enforcement, the bad guys all over the world would do well to turn themselves in now or find something else to do. Sure, Joe Carter was the Fey-Man, but he knew he had limitations. He doubted Chris Newman did.

They arrived at Philadelphia International Airport, parked in the short-term parking garage, took the elevator to the terminal floor, proceeded through security, and approached Gate B-16 where passengers awaited their direct flight to Miami. They all walked into a retail store in the terminal building to finalize their plans.

"Sam will wait here, and I will be sitting on that bench over there," Carter said, pointing to a metal bench in the hallway where travelers and their families hurried past. We will keep an eye on the hallway to make sure you are okay. When you're finished, come back this way, walk past us without looking at us and head back to the car in the parking garage. Sam and I will be behind you to make sure you don't run into any trouble and will meet up with you back at the car. Got it?"

"Got it." Chris said.

"Got it." J.J. said.

"You both okay?"

J.J. and Chris looked at each other, before J.J. looked up at Carter. "Yeah, we're good."

"Man, I sure hope she thinks you're dead," Carter said, worried.

"Don't worry. She does," Chris assured him. "Let's do this."

"Okay, get going. Good luck."

Chris and J.J. bumped fists. "Showtime,"

Chris said. The boys turned and walked down the hallway. Carter walked over to the bench, sat down, pulled out his cellphone, and called Steve Rand who then conferenced in Lieutenant Mike Fenton.

Carter looked over at Sam in the bookstore, pretending to read a Sweet 16 magazine, and watched Chris and J.J. walk further down the hallway, mixing in with the crowd.

The sting was on.

Chris and J.J. walked and talked their way past Gate B-16, going with the flow of the crowd. J.J. was the first to see Mrs. Kling sitting in a seat with a small child next to her. He nudged Chris and nodded his head in Mrs. Kling's direction. They kept walking forward, as planned. Once they were out of sight of anyone in the gate area, they turned and headed back.

"That's Jose with her," J.J. said.

"I know," Chris responded. A few steps further along Chris said, "Play ball."

Immediately J.J. started laughing and Chris laughed along with him, pretending to be enjoying the funniest joke ever. "Hey, look. It's Mrs. Kling," J.J. said, a bit too loudly.

"And Jose," Chris said, loudly.

"Hey, Mrs. Kling. Hey, Jose," J.J. said.

Chris saw right away that Mrs. Kling looked as if she were looking at two ghosts. She was shocked, he knew. And, being as cunning as she had been all these years, she attempted, badly, to cover up her surprise. "Chris? J.J.? I don't believe it."

I bet you don't, Chris thought, still smiling as he approached her.

"Hey, Jose, what's up?" J.J. said, hugging the smaller boy. "Going to your for-real home today, huh?"

"Si!" Jose said, smiling. "I can't wait."

"So…so, um, what are you boys doing here?" Mrs. Kling said.

"Oh, we're here with Chris' mom and brother," J.J. said.

"Yeah, we're going to visit my mom's family in Alabama," Chris said.

"They invited me along too," J.J. said.

"What time's your flight?" Chris asked, as rehearsed, and right on cue.

"We'll be boarding pretty soon," Mrs. Kling said.

"Why does it take so long?" Jose said. "We've been here a long time."

"Ah, just a few more minutes, Jose," J.J. said. "Then you'll be flying home. You ever fly before?"

"No," Jose said, shaking his head.

"Me either," J.J. said. "I can't wait. It'll be fun."

"Si," Jose said. "I can't wait too."

"What time's your flight?" Mrs. Kling asked.

"About a half an hour," Chris said. "We better get going. See you, Jose. Good luck," Chris said, hugging Jose.

"Yeah, take care, big guy," J.J. said. "I'll miss you at St. Michael's. Don't forget to write. And send pictures too, okay? Of your bedroom, your parents, everything."

"Si, J.J. I will."

J.J., kneeling and looking eye-to-eye at Jose, suddenly started to tear up. "You be good." J.J. stood and said, "See you, Mrs. Kling. I'll see you back at the Home."

"When?" she asked, and the question caught J.J. off-guard.

Fortunately, Chris was ready. "We're coming back Wednesday. Just three days. See ya," Chris said, pulling J.J. to walk with him.

But Mrs. Kling held out her arms to them. "No hug?" she asked.

The last thing Chris or J.J. wanted to do was have her touch them. They wanted nothing more to do with this devil-lady who tried to have them killed. They felt terrible that they had to leave Jose with her, but it was part of the plan, and they still had parts to act out.

"Sorry, Mrs. Kling. Gotta run," Chris said. "Good bye, Jose."

"Bye, Jose," J.J. called back as he hustled away with Chris.

As they continued to walk rapidly down the hallway and past Lieutenant Carter on the bench to the left, they saw him give them a surreptitious thumbs-up. Sam, in the store on their right, said, "Academy Awards." Her eyes smiled at them over her magazine as they continued down the hallway.

Mrs. Kling continued to hold Jose's hand as she watched Chris and J.J. hurry away. Once they were two gates down she stood where Jose couldn't hear her and placed a frantic phone call.

"Dan!" she said softly but angrily. "Frieda. You'll never guess who I just saw."

"Who?"

"Chris Newman and J.J."

"Where?"

"Here. At the airport."

"That's not possible. They're dead as rocks on the bottom of the Delaware."

"Dan!" It was all she could do not to scream. "Did you see them go down?"

"No. Like I told you, Ed did it. He saw them."

"I don't want to argue with you. We have a problem. I'll call you when I get back and this had better be fixed." She hung up. At that moment, Mrs. Frieda Kling, no dummy, knew she would never be returning to Philadelphia. It was too risky now. In fact, she knew she would be leaving the country as soon as possible after she arrived in Miami. Her life in the United States was over.

Unfortunately for her, and fortunately for Jose, Steve Rand, Special Agent for the FBI, and Lieutenant Mike Fenton of the Philadelphia Police Department had authorized phone taps and heard every word of the phone conversation. A search warrant was issued. FBI agents out of Philadelphia arrived at Frieda Kling's house and recovered all the items stored in her attic. These were held in storage pending an insurance company investigation.

Warrants were issued for the arrests of Frieda Kling, Captain Carroll, and the owner of the white

Lexus with New York license plate number ACL-310. Two FBI agents arrived at Captain Carroll's house as he was having a cookout in the back yard for friends and family who were stunned to see him being led away in handcuffs. Mrs. Frieda Kling was arrested as she sat in the airport terminal in Philadelphia with Jose Aramis, a five-year-old boy from St. Michael's Home who that day escaped being sold into slavery in Ecuador by about three hours.

Two FBI agents escorted Jose back to St. Michael's Home. The owner of the white Lexus, Ed Hughes, was arrested as he exited a restaurant in the Port Richmond section of Philadelphia. A very nervous man, his plea-bargained testimony serendipitously facilitated the FBI's subsequent, several-month successful effort to prosecute his partners in crime.

Captain Carroll, Ed Hughes, Frank Oliver, the owner of the black Cadillac, and Mrs. Frieda Kling were each charged with multiple felony counts, the most serious being conspiracy, abducting a minor, endangering the welfare of minors, wire fraud, and theft. Each of the defendants would spend between fifteen to twenty-five years in federal prison.

The most serious sentencing, as it turns out, was for wire fraud - the crime which, because it occurred across state lines, permitted the FBI to get involved in the first place. Joe Carter suspected wire fraud based upon Chris' photos of the bank account and the airline tickets. He figured Frieda Kling was being paid to deliver orphans into slavery. The large deposits she made whenever she made a trip to Miami tipped him off. Combined with the absence of thank-you notes, Joe Carter had a pretty good idea of what was going on. Sam, J.J., and Headmistress Brennan were stunned by this development. But, none were more distraught at this news than Chris.

"I should've known," J.J. said, as he, Sam, and Chris sat together eating pizza in Chris' kitchen, as Lieutenant Carter and Steve Rand conferred in the living room with Aliondra Covington, Mrs. Banks, and Headmistress Brennan.

"Why? Why should you have known?" Sam asked.

"It's a crappy world, that's why. Look around. Everybody's in it for themselves. Eat or be eaten. Survival of the fittest. I should know."

"I don't know, J.J.," Sam said. "There're a lot of good people too. Like Lieutenant Carter and Agent Rand and Headmistress Brennan and us."

"Yeah, yeah, I know. I'm just sayin' I'm not surprised is all. I'll never be surprised at how bad people can be. I may not be the brightest guy in the world, but I don't have to be thrown in the river twice."

Sam looked at J.J. and wondered if his glass

would always be half empty. She couldn't blame him if it were. He really did have to fight for everything. Just yesterday he had to fight to stay alive. No, she would never blame him.

But learning that the seemingly kind-hearted Mrs. Kling was evil threw Chris, especially, for a loop. As he sat there with his friends, and later that evening when he went to bed, his mind raced with the implications of all he had been through the past several months. He wanted to believe that there were some bad people in a good world rather than some good people in a bad world. He knew what Fixer's and Miss Portice's opinions were and, since they were Savants who had been around for millennia, their opinions could not be taken lightly.

Still, he wasn't sure. He knew he had a lot to learn about human nature. He hoped he had time. If not, if the Earth tremors he sensed foretold an imminent cataclysm for mankind, he would have to learn how to lead millions of children to safety. But he couldn't do it alone. He was glad to have Fixer, Miss Portice, Lieutenant Carter, Sam, J.J., and James on his side.

PART SEVEN

"There could not have been a lovelier sight, but there was none to see it except a little boy who was staring in at the window. He had ecstasies innumerable that other children can ever know, but he was looking through the window at the one joy from which he must be forever barred."
- JM. Barrie, "Peter Pan"

CHAPTER 36

The next Saturday, Thanksgiving weekend, Chris asked Sam, James, and Lieutenant Carter to meet him and J.J. in the clubhouse at around 9:00a.m., after they had finished delivering papers.

It had been a whirlwind week. Lieutenant Carter and Agent Rand seemed to be everywhere, meeting with Aliondra, Mrs. Banks, Chris, Sam, J.J., and Headmistress Brennan several times each, as well as coordinating with the District Attorney's office, the police department, the FBI, and the Department of Families concerning the many crimes committed by Frieda Kling, Captain Carroll, and their accomplices.

Headmistress Brennan was horrified to learn the truth about her longtime friend, Frieda Kling.

"I only wish I had hired you sooner, Christopher," Mrs. Brennan said. "For the sake of the children, I only wish I had hired you sooner."

"It wouldn't have mattered, Headmistress Brennan. I only thought to look at placements in the first place because Mrs. Kling said there were no perfect placements. That's what gave me the idea."

"I'm so glad you did! But, if I may, how did you think to sift through and sort hundreds of thank you notes? None of the professional consultants thought to do that."

"I don't know. I was coming up dry in other areas, I guess, and I wanted to make sure I didn't miss anything. The thank you notes hadn't been filed away, and as I picked through them it struck me as an interesting sort of puzzle. Who was receiving the most thank you notes and who was receiving the least, and why."

"But then you went a step further and sorted them into domestic and international placements. How come?"

Chris had spent some time thinking about this also. He certainly could have sorted the notes based into boys versus girls, or by age, or by state, or any number of other ways. Yet, he distinctly remembered having a rather intense predisposition to proceeding as he did, and he was pretty sure it was the same advanced type of intuition which recently permitted him to sometimes hear peoples' thoughts or anticipate what they might say.

Fixer was right, it could be annoying, and he hoped he could figure out a way to keep others' thoughts from intruding on his own. But, he said none of this to Mrs. Brennan. Rather, he simply said, "I guess I just had a gut feeling. It seemed like a good and easy thing to do, so that's what I did."

"Well, I am certainly glad you did. I never noticed that I was receiving fewer international notes and letters from Mrs. Kling's placements. Of course, I received all the follow-up correspondence from the parents and their adoptees, and I never thought to group the notes and letters as you did. Also, three or four years ago Mrs. Kling asked if she could handle her own international correspondence. I agreed because I was thankful for the help, being swamped with so many other things. I never suspected the real reason. I should never have agreed to let Mrs. Kling manage her foreign correspondence. But, she was my friend. I trusted her all these years.

"Don't beat yourself up, ma'am," Lieutenant Carter said. "We trusted our captain too."

"Yes, thank you Lieutenant. I suppose we have each suffered a betrayal."

"Fortunately, we have them both in custody. They should be put away for a very long time."

"I have to be honest, Lieutenant," she said. "I often wondered why the police were unable to find the thieves all these years, especially after we had the surveillance system installed."

"Yes, I guess Captain Carroll really thought that they were going to get away with pawning off your artworks. It would've been a cool payday had they pulled it off," Carter said.

"Thanks to you and your young posse of St. Michael's alums, we won't have to worry about that, will we?"

"No ma'am. We won't."

The bad news was that St. Michael's Home would need to find a new placement professional. But this paled in comparison to the good news. Mrs. Kling would never again ruin the life of another child. Headmistress Brennan thought that Aliondra Covington would make a fine placement employee and hired her on the spot. For her part, Aliondra was thrilled to be able to spend her days performing meaningful and necessary work without fear of harassment.

The return of the stolen artwork resulted in an immediate reduction in St. Michael's hefty insurance premium. Mrs. Brennan would now be able to sell some of the artwork at auction to support the mission and would no longer be pressured to sell the property. And Chris' new placement algorithm would help her reduce her placement expenses and improve results markedly.

The he day after the arrests and the first day of Aliondra's employment at St. Michael's Home, when she, Chris, and James sat down to dinner, James commented on her gold angel pendant. "That's pretty, Mom," he said. "Is it new?"

"Yes. I stopped by Schwartz's on Rising Sun after work today and bought it in honor of my new job. It's St. Michael the archangel," she said, fingering it so James and Chris could get a good look at it. "It will remind me always how God sends us the help we need." Then she got up from the table, walked to the hutch cabinet, took down a small wrapped box and handed it to Chris. "While I was there, I mentioned to Mr. Schwartz how you invented a new algorithm to better match orphans and parents," she said to Chris. "He wanted you to have this," she said, handing the box to him.

"For me?" Chris said, surprised. He excitedly tore off the gift wrapping and opened the box. Inside was a brand new Timex watch with a leather band. He loved it and hurried to put it on. His first watch! "I can't believe it!" he said.

"Mr. Schwartz said you and he had a deal. He said you should have a watch to commemorate whenever you do something great."

"Actually, mom, that wasn't really the deal. It was more like his idea to have me go into his store and buy a watch to commemorate when I ever did anything great."

"Son, let him do this for you. He wants to. Learn to accept kindnesses as well as to give them. But don't forget to thank him personally."

Throughout that week, Chris had a lot of time to ponder what the events of the previous week and month meant, for him, and for many others also. He had learned so much about human nature, probably more than he wanted to know, and he had struggled to understand the implications. And although nothing fascinates Savants more than a great puzzle, mathematical or otherwise, they prefer solvable puzzles. But Chris was learning that human beings are so complex that perhaps there is no solution to them and the evil of which they are capable.

Something deep within him, however, accepted this only as a possibility; not as a given. There had to be hope, hadn't there? He wasn't sure, at first. But he had the past week to think about it and reach a conclusion.

It was this conclusion which he now wanted to present to his friends. He wanted to know what they thought, so he called for a meeting in the clubhouse.

"So, what's up, Hotshot?" James started things off once everyone had gathered in the clubhouse. "It better be good. I'm giving up basketball practice for this."

"Right," J.J. agreed. "I need to get back to the Home. Gotta help Ernie clean the floors."

Chris smiled. "Sam, anyplace you have to be?"

"I'm tutoring and babysitting, but I'm just on call."

"Lieutenant Carter?"

"Golf, but I stink, so no worries."

"Well, anyway, thanks for being here. Um…a lot happened to us last weekend and before then. I think I owe you all an explanation. J.J.

practically died, Sam raced her legs off halfway across the city, otherwise the bad guys would never have been caught, Lieutenant Carter got the FBI involved and helped us to catch all the criminals. And James? Well, James is just James but, still, he needs to understand what's been going on."

"He means how he automagically appeared out of thin air to save me from being killed," James said, for everyone's benefit. "I owe you, big time, so I won't sweat missing basketball practice."

"Right." Chris began. "So, as J.J. likes to say, it's a Brainiac thing. I have been gifted with an advanced brain. Apparently I can sense the fabric of space and can connect to it, mentally. That enables me to either move at the speed of light or transpose, I'm not sure."

"What's transpose?" J.J. said.

"It means going from one place to another without traveling through space and time."

"Automagically," James said.

"Yes," Chris agreed. "Automagically is a good way to say it."

"So, how do you go from point A to point B without traveling?" Lieutenant Carter said.

"I don't know enough yet," Chris said. "I'm still learning, but it's definitely a mental connection."

"So, can anybody do it?" James asked.

"I don't think so, James. Nobody can do it, except me and the Savants. They're people on another planet named Maran."

"Whoa! Aliens?"

"Yes and no. They are humans who started out on Earth millions of years ago but they all have a brain like mine – very advanced."

"So, like, in a million years we will all evolve to be able to move automagically?" James asked.

"Maybe, if we survive that long," Chris said.

"No guarantees there," Lieutenant Carter said.

"Except a bad one," Chris said. "It seems to me that human beings are not built to survive millions of years due to ice ages, meteorites, super volcanoes, and stuff like that."

"But the Savants survived," Sam said.

"Yes, that's true, but not very many. Only a few thousand. And only because they are able to travel to other planets."

"And they can only do that because they're Brainiacs," J.J. said.

"Right. Only one human every decade or so

becomes a Savant. It's evolution or, actually, mutation. Every once in a while Nature kicks out a Savant just to keep the species going."

"Okay, you seem to have figured out a lot," Sam said. "What's the problem?"

"The problem is the Earth is dying and I don't know if I can move humans off the Earth, or if I should even try. J.J. had the chance to leave, but he chose to stay. It seems the Savants wouldn't be everybody's cup of tea. They don't seem to care for humans very much. They seemed to have lost some of their humanity over millions of years of living on other planets."

"Yeah, it's like they're better than we are," J.J. said.

"That's because they are better than we are," Sam said.

Chris wasn't going to argue, but he wasn't so sure that intelligence beat empathy or love. This was what he had been trying to understand. It was a puzzle, for sure, but it was a human puzzle and that's what made it so frustrating and so fascinating. Maybe there wasn't one right answer. Or maybe there was. And maybe that answer could only be found on Earth, among humans.

"If the Earth is dying, how long do we have?" James asked.

"I'm not sure," Chris said. "Maybe one more generation, but I don't think much longer than that."

"Why not?"

"Just a hunch." This was true, but it was based upon a lot of study. Chris knew humans were polluting the Earth at an alarming rate. He also knew that, over the millennia, the Earth tended to take care of itself, and he was certain that process had begun. The Earth was in the early stages of ridding itself of humans. Once the caretakers, humans were now an infestation, a cancer, expendable.

"So, do you really travel at the speed of light?" Lieutenant Carter asked. "I thought that was impossible. How do you do it?"

Chris stood. "For that, I'd like to demonstrate. Could you drive us?"

"Sure," Lieutenant Carter said. "Where are we going?"

"Fun Time."

"The indoor play park for kids?"

"Actually, to the batting cages they have out back," Chris said.

"Are the batting cages even open this time of year?"

"Yep. As long as it's not snowing."

"I'm surprised you would know about the batting cages being open this time of year," Carter said.

"Well, then you don't know him very well," Sam said.

"You'll know me a little better in a few minutes," Chris said, picking up his red batting helmet from a side table. "Come on, let's go," he said, starting down the steps. "Everybody hits. My treat."

"He really likes baseball, eh?" Carter asked Sam.

"I don't know anyone who loves baseball more than Chris," she said.

"Is he any good?"

"Why don't we let him show you?" Sam said, heading down the steps.

Everyone piled into Joe Carter's car. It was a ten minute ride to the batting cages, about two miles away through city traffic. When they arrived, Chris kept his promise and purchased pitching machine tokens for everybody. Carter, James, and J.J. took their tokens and headed right for the batting cages outside, in the rear of the complex. They each grabbed bats from the racks and batting helmets which were required for safety reasons.

There were two dozen individual enclosed

hitting areas situated in a cartwheel formation around the pitching machines clustered in the center of the wheel. Each individual hitting area was enclosed on the top and sides by heavy rope netting. A playground-type fence extended around the perimeter of all the hitting areas, forming the rim to the cartwheel. Each of the individual hitting areas had its own entrance gate in the fence.

Lieutenant Carter put on his batting helmet, picked up a bat, entered one of the hitting areas, and closed the gate behind him. He selected the 'medium' speed pitch setting, and dropped his token into a nearby vending machine. Then he took his place in the painted batter's box next to the painted home plate on the concrete floor and prepared to hit the first pitch from the pitching machine facing him about sixty feet away.

James did the same in another batting cage on one side of Carter, and J.J. similarly prepared in the cage on the other side of Carter. J.J., a reasonable fellow, chose the 'medium' pitch speed. James, the athlete, chose the 'fast' speed setting. No one chose the 'professional' setting. Chris and Sam chose to be spectators outside the hitting areas.

"Aren't you going to hit, Sam?" Chris said.

"No. It's off-season. I don't feel like pulling a muscle. I'm not in baseball shape right now. How about you?"

"Not yet," Chris said. "Let's watch."

So they watched. What they saw shouldn't have been too surprising. Each hitter received twenty-four pitches. J.J. struggled with the 'medium' speed pitches, about 55 miles per hour because he hadn't warmed up, and because he really didn't play baseball much. But, he was a good sport and enjoyed himself, even though he swung and missed at more than half the pitches and only hit one well. James struggled with the 'fast' pitches (65 miles per hour) because he was not in baseball shape and had not warmed up. Still, he was obviously talented and managed to hit three out of every four pitches, although he only hit two or three well. The others were weak hits or foul balls. Lieutenant Carter was a very good hitter. He hit most of the medium speed pitches pretty well, but whiffed completely on a half dozen or so.

When James, J.J., and Lieutenant Carter came out of their hitting cages they all agreed that they probably should've stretched or warmed up first. "You really think it would have helped?" Sam asked. "Probably not," Carter confessed and they all laughed.

"How about you two? You going to hit?" Carter asked.

"I'll pass," Sam said. "I'm not that great when I'm warmed up. I don't feel like making a fool of myself, thank you."

"Sam, what are you talking about? You're a

good hitter," James said.

"Maybe. In season, but not now." Sam then looked to deflect attention from herself. "How about you, Doc? You gonna hit?"

"Yes," Chris said, putting his personal batting helmet on, the one with 'Newman 1' stenciled on the back.

"You have your own helmet?" Carter asked.

"Yeah. Custom-made. Brainiac size," J.J. said. "Ain't that right, Doc?"

Chris smiled, but did not respond. Instead he asked Carter, "Do you remember the question you asked me?"

"I asked you how you travel at the speed of light."

"Exactly. Well, let me show you." Then he asked everybody to step up to the fence which formed the backstop behind where the batter stood. They were on the outside of the fence, so they couldn't get hit. A thick canvas mat was draped on the fence to prevent damage to the baseball and to the fence when the batter swung and missed which, for most customers who tried, was most of the time.

"Have any of you ever seen a professional fast ball up close?" Chris knew that almost no one, except the infrequent college baseball player, ever chose the 'professional' speed setting of 90 miles per hour.

"Oh, come on Chris," James said. "What are you talking about? You can't hit pitches that fast."

Chris looked at each of them and said, "Keep your eye on the ball." Then he picked up his bat, walked into the cage, closed the gate, put his token in the machine and selected the 'professional' setting. "Oh brother," James said. "What a waste of money."

Chris did not step into the batter's box immediately. Rather, he turned to his audience behind the fence, pointed at the pitching machine and said, "Watch." Immediately the first pitch raced like a rocket right out of the machine and slammed, one half second later, into the mat right in front of Sam and J.J. The ball exploded into the mat with a loud "POW!" All four spectators were so startled, they took a reflexive step backwards. J.J. stumbled backward so suddenly, his feet became tangled. Sam had to catch him to keep him from falling to the ground.

"Dang!" J.J. said. "What was that?"

"Chris, come on, get out of there. You're gonna get killed," James said. Chris looked Joe Carter in the eye and said, "Watch." He then stepped into the batter's box.

The next pitch exploded out as fast as the first one. Chris connected as the ball approached.

The ball hung in mid-air in front of home plate. He eyed the ball and swung the bat hard to hit it as he disconnected. Of course, no one saw him connect. All they saw was Chris swing and crush that pitch on a line drive right back at the pitching machine. The same ball that came in at 90 miles per hour went screaming back at the machine at 120 miles per hour off of Chris' bat.

Chris did not have to turn to see the expressions of shock on the faces behind him. Rather, he prepared for the next pitch. He hit the next twenty-one pitches as aggressively as he hit the first, spraying line drives all over the batting cage. He owned every single pitch. He was a hitting machine.

There was now just one pitch remaining. Chris faced the machine one last time in a hitter's stance. This time, however, when the ball approached and he connected as he had for all the pitches, instead of hitting the pitch he put his hand up, caught it as if he were plucking a floating feather out of the air, and disconnected. He then turned for the first time to see the stunned expressions of his audience who had just seen him reach up without a baseball glove and, quick as lightning, snatch a 90 mile-per-hour fastball as if doing so was the easiest thing in the world.

Once again, Chris stared at Joe Carter, making eye contact. "That's how I move at the speed of light," he said.

Lieutenant Joe Carter suddenly understood. "You saved me in Big Al's didn't you?"

"Yes. How did you know?"

"You waved to me…" Carter appeared to be lost in thought, remembering as he spoke.

"I waved to you?"

"Yes. As I was going into Big Al's, I looked over, saw you standing in the crowd beyond the police tape, and you waved to me. Then, when I came back out, you waved to me again, except…"

"The gloves," Chris, now understanding Carter's line of thought, interrupted.

"I couldn't put my finger on it," Carter said. "I guess I was in shock or something but I remember thinking something wasn't right, something was off-kilter. I mean, trying to rationalize having not been killed at point-blank range demanded all my attention. Still, there must've been some unconscious recognition that…that…something was different…about you. Something impossible, I thought.

But, I didn't know what it was until I saw the crime scene video shot from the overhead police helicopter. And, even then I almost missed it. It happened so fast…in one frame, instantaneously: a glove appeared on your hand. When you waved at me going into the store you weren't wearing gloves.

But when I came out two minutes later and you waved to me, you were wearing gloves. I didn't consciously make this connection but subconsciously I suppose I did. So I decided to take a look at the crime scene video to see if it would help me in some way. I never expected to see a glove appear on your hand instantaneously. That's why it took so long for me to see it even after studying the video all night."

"Yes," Chris said. "I wear my gloves almost all the time to hide a physical deformity. But, I had come from a piano recital. I don't wear my gloves when I play. Then, when I knew I would be catching the bullet, I decided to put my gloves on so that..."

"So that you wouldn't leave any fingerprints, just like when you tossed the knives aside at the football game."

"Yes," Chris said sheepishly, looking down.

"Don't feel bad, kid. You did exactly the right thing." He smiled at Chris.

Chris looked up and smiled back. "Thanks."

"So things that move fast, like baseballs... and... bullets... it doesn't make any difference. They're all the same to you, aren't they?"

"Yes."

"Dude," James said. "If that," he said, pointing to where Chris stood, "is what I have to compete against, I think I have to forget about sports and concentrate on academics."

"Don't worry, James. You won't have to compete against me. Nobody will. I just wanted you all to understand, that's all." And Chris knew the truth of the matter. "Competing in sports is not in my future."

"You promise?" James asked, smiling.

"Yes, I promise. But that doesn't let you off the hook. Paying attention to your studies is still a good idea."

"Got any more hits in that bat?" Sam asked, sitting on a bench on the other side of the walkway from the backstop.

"Yeah, I could watch you all day," Carter said to Chris, sitting next to Sam.

J.J. and James joined them on the bench. "Definitely worth the price of admission," J.J. agreed.

Chris smiled at them. This was his team. He turned and dropped his last coin into the machine, set the pitch speed to 'professional' once again, and prepared to hit another round.

And, as he hit away, Chris knew he enjoyed an unfair advantage so that hitting a baseball was not the best use, or even an appropriate use, of his Savant talents. What he was doing now was cheating. It wasn't fair. Baseball was a game for humans, not Savants. He knew Fixer, one day, would not permit his friends and Lieutenant Carter to remember anything of the Savants, the portal, or of what they were now witnessing.

But, he also knew he could crush a baseball.

And it felt good.

It felt so good.

So, as another laser erupted from his bat, and screamed like a bullet pinging loudly off the steel pitching machine, Chris knew a couple of things for sure:

"Newman #1" was the greatest ever.

And no one on Earth could ever know it.

But he knew it, and that was enough.

THE END

SAVANT

Made in the USA
Middletown, DE
01 April 2019